Death, Sex and Kant

(A Critique of Living)

By: Dik Edwards

Dedication

To Tony, the demon barber

Acknowledgements

David Walford, the tutor who turned me on to Nietzsche and

RR Rockingham-Gill, who coached me in Wittgenstein

Thanks

Dik

Hail Petronius

Prologue

(Hail Marquez!)

In the second year of the plague and third month of lockdown, as she faced suicide, Rose recalled that day decades earlier when she first properly met Will Slade.

It was a hot afternoon in the almost empty grounds of the Uni. Empty, that is, save for the group Will was with, sitting on the grass. I was on a bench watching them. He looked like a poet. Romantic poet. His hair quite long to his shoulders. He had a sensitive, kind of aquiline nose, blue eyes just in the right place and a sort of questioning look. And there was a super-attractive scar about an inch long running from the outside corner of his left eyebrow. And I imagined a pleading cock sculpted to perfection by a Praxiteles. From somewhere, probably the kitchen of the refectory where lunch for the students attending Summer School was being prepared, drifted the smell of onion and garlic.

He was looking towards me. I never took my eyes off him, and whenever he'd look at me directly, I'd add a sparkle, and he would respond with an O so sweet swoon of colouring! I'd seen him in town and sometimes would pass him when I'd swing my shapely arse but didn't ever think he noticed me; far away I'd supposed, in pursuit of some poetic turn of phrase.

When he got up to go, I assumed, to the toilet, I knew this was my chance, the moment I would get him to notice me, for me to find out if he was the one. I followed him into the quiet 200-year-old vestibule with its oak panelling and the small chapel on the side that threatened hell and hellfire for what was on my mind. There was a silence like study hour. I coughed. He turned, smiled. We were at the toilets. As he got close to the gents, I suddenly grabbed his hand and with a wicked luring smile led him into the ladies. In a cubicle I said take your piss which I'd heard was not so easy from a hardening penis, but which he did and then I blessed it like a priest blessing young boys, took it in hand and mouth looking up at him and, if you can imagine, smiling mouth firmly planted upon his starlit golden bough. When he came, I swallowed his poetic outflow with its tang of urine, adding a note of terror. I was shocked by my audacity. Not so much for doing it – I had never done it and swallowed before (but what true lover has not drunk the soul of her mate?) - no, shocked for so challenging my natural politeness!

As for that note of terror, that was something new to me. Yet, terror in sex, thinking about it later, seemed the most obvious thing. The terror that comes with that hunger for experience; the terror is in the fear of it not being there; the fear of the death of philosophy; the fear of the unusable you. The terror in the need for a philosophy for life, and the demand from life that makes us drive too close to the edge for safety. If sex doesn't contain that imperative, then it's merely the icing on a cake that's nothing more than flour and water.

Before he got back to his group, I said: Isn't it great that we both like sex so much.

He said: I've been watching you for a long time. To me, you embody the passion of coming summer.

Even in the autumn?

Summer has to return.

Then after a few seconds, he said: in two days, I'm going to Cambridge to begin a post-graduate course. Would you want to, and would you be able to come?

And I said: I would love to come.

Cambridge!

Since my first sexual encounter in my early teens, I'd had this idea: to understand sex through knowledge and knowledge through sex: a synthesis between knowledge and sex. It had built in me and now burned through me with that flaming fire that often ignites with the first stirrings of self-awareness and its brooding power. My thoughts on the terror of his piss tempered cum together with the acknowledgement of Cambridge's place of learning confirmed me in this odyssey.

Table of Contents

Part One

The Rising Sun

1983

Chapter 1

Rose

(Hail David Jones!)

My name is Rose Angwen. Angwen is a Cornish name. I'm from Cornwall. I'm not thin or fat, but Rubens-rounded. Late teens, nearly twenty. My face is pale, almost white like a dove, contrasting with my deep black eyes and hair, black and long and luxurious, creating the effect of an aesthetic perfection.

Cambridge!

I'm well read. Very well read: Most of the Russians, the French from the Abbé Prevost, to Sartre, Camus *et al,* Hardy and Scott Fitzgerald! And, of course, Hemingway, whom I didn't really rate. And I have a precociously strong memory.

I'm with Will in a greasy spoon on Mill Street in Cambridge.

I'm eating the bones of a chicken carcass, breaking bits off and chewing hard all the time, looking at him with my magnificent eyes, uptilted, searching.

Will told me I reminded him of a fuller version of a Basque girl he'd met a few years before in Paris. The same kind of crazy energy. Though I was bigger. A bit. There was something solid, statuesque about me, he said, that in no way compromised the outstanding beauty of my face.

He said: you're eating the bones.

I said: I know. A cock's. Don't want to waste anything. No morsel of meat.

You're sure it's a cock?

A hen would be tough. A cock is just hard.

Can hard be satisfying?

That's what I've learned.

You're young enough to learn.

I like learning.

My lips glistened with the grease of the ravaged bird.

In a wild moment, I know his mind turned to running two fingers along my suddenly voluptuous lower lip, turning me over across his knee and pleasuring me with the cock's grease.

The wine he'd drunk now stimulated the meat of his own bird as my face suddenly came alive with the scarlet rose of venereal promise, and the want in my eyes became a command. This he told me later.

Let's go.

I wiped my mouth, swigged down my remaining wine and followed him out and into the street.

When looking at that beautiful head as we ate - his head and imagined brain – I knew I had to get a grip. To make this decision. Embark upon a great odyssey to bring together the deepest knowledge with the deepest sexual experience! And also get over that Plymouth Brethren shit I'd grown up with.

Later I came across Nietzsche's *Birth of Tragedy* in which he said, in simplest terms, that tragedy sprang from a fusion between the Dionysian and the Apollonian: Dionysian, wild, dancing, sexual abandon and the more ordered, structured beauty of Apollonian form – me, arguably, the wild Dionysian, him, perhaps, the more Apollonian and I wondered in an anxious moment whether this wasn't the path I'd set out on. Then I thought: Fuck it, there's too much at stake: I'd make a marriage of those two things and master the tragic and glory in the dodgy aesthetic! That's my answer to Nietzsche!

On *this* day, in Cambridge, I knew Will was the one, that special one to take with me to make success of this project a bit more certain.

I'd have to have many lovers and indulge in every sexual practice, even to the point of perversity! Something about Will told me that he would be up for it and at the same time feel free to have a go himself!

Chapter 2
Wild Imaginings

(Hail Dylan Thomas!)

My mother had often said I was getting fat, was almost fat. You'd think I was one of those women whose lower belly was so huge it formed a kind of enormous dewlap which hangs over her pubic area, creating the shape of some animal not recognisably woman! Sure, I was bigger than her, but she was anorexically thin made so by her obsession with the notion of an abstemious Christ. The worst you could say about me, I think, is, as I said, that I was Rubens plump, which is not a bad thing anyway!

One night I had this dream: down Mill Road in Cambridge in a cart filled with faggots and tied to a large wooden stake placed centrally, came Joan of Arc. The flames that burnt the saint and that would pursue womanhood down the centuries would be ignited here in Cambridge. I felt a deep anger to see how the people, so many of them women, cheered on the destruction of the sorrowful Joan. Then, a pregnant young woman whose head had been crushed beneath the wheel of a bus got up somehow and made a point of returning an eye to its socket, then walked on down the street. I thought she must have had something to do with Will, though I also thought it was me! A policeman came up and asked her if she wanted to be arrested. She/I said: No, of course not. Then he said: Then what are you doing with the eyes? Leave the eyes! Now it was eyes where I thought it had only been one! Then I fell to my knees and started to cry, blood gushing out of my eye sockets. The blood got everywhere, covered the pavement, then the street and became a flood. Already, Will and someone I didn't recognise were in a dinghy paddling on the river of my blood. Then the women in the street were throwing things at me, tied to the stake! I was naked. There were men shouting your arse is too big! Tears. Women were shouting: whore! *Putan*! Then we were on Jesus Green. An ugly man carrying an enormous knife jumped onto the cart. I was sure he was going to cut the ties that bound me. Then I thought perhaps he was going to stab me so that I wouldn't have to suffer the pain of burning. Instead, he used the knife to light the fire! Nooooooooooo!

Chapter 3

Cambridge

Will's college was a post-graduate institution centred on a grand, Victorian building inaugurated at the end of the nineteenth century.

Will had embarked on his academic career when he was 24 as an independent mature student.

His lodgings were on the second floor of a terraced house built in the 1930s.

The landlord, a retired librarian, a thin, mild-mannered man who looked mid-sixties but could have been younger, thin oiled-back hair and rimless glasses, felt comfortable renting the room out, I'm sure, because it was to a Cambridge student. The best families. A rule of the house was no women overnight, which, naturally, one almost needn't point out. Daytime never came up because it was assumed Cambridge students used the day for studying. Afternoons, Mr. Sternbend took his wife out for lunch and very often a ride across the fens, sometimes stopping at Ely Cathedral, which would always overwhelm them and in a mysterious way, lift their small lives. I learned all this in due course. And more.

It was the afternoon when Will took me to see his room on Chesterton Road. He'd been to see the digs in the morning, leaving me in the car and met Sternbend, who'd laid out the rules and quirks of the Sternbend life. As we went into the Sternbend-free house, I was struck by the smell of resignation and a vulgar talc. There was a letter on the hall desk addressed to Will Slade from Broadmoor, the hospital.

Will was still young enough to explode in sex but too young to have developed a finessed foreplay. It didn't matter much when I was in this mood because I was ready to go, especially after a few glasses over lunch. And I loved getting immediately naked. Freedom! And in a house empty of the judgemental, I could yell as much as I wanted, like screaming in a silent library.

After, I was curled up on the bed in the narrow room like a hairless cat while he, also naked astride a wicker chair so that his unprepossessing penis hung like a curious, flaccid tap, opened the letter from Dewey Ronson of Broadmoor.

He said he's losing it. He read: *It's hell on earth. This morning, I had breakfast with Frankie Frazer, the gangland murderer. Worked for The Richardsons. I couldn't eat.*

I said: Jesus! Why is he in there?

For attacking a police dog. An Alsatian.

Attacking a dog?

Police dog.

What happened?

He came home one night, high as a kite. He'd taken a cocktail of the most serious drugs and, in a fit of laughter, thought it would be fun to set fire to the dog.

The dog!

Sorry, no, this was his dog. The family dog. It was a replacement for his dog, which had died, so maybe he hated it for not being the original.

Jesus.

It was his father who called the police. Since he was adopted, he'd been spoiled.

He was adopted?

Yes. From a single girl two streets away. His father, adoptive father, had allowed him to do whatever he wanted, but that night was too much. The cops came to the house, but Dewey got past them and ran up and down the streets of the estate laughing like a madman with a squadron of officers chasing him! They cornered him in a neighbour's front porch where he was collapsed still pissing himself! Then they set the dog on him, and the animal got Dewey's arm in its jaw. Dewey jumped up with the dog hanging on. This huge Alsatian. Dewey swung his arm around and smashed the dog's head on the house wall, knocking it out.

My God!

Then they arrested him and he's still pissing himself. There was no trial. Two doctors said that only someone mad could be so strong and sectioned him, and when he complained about the lizard they'd served him for breakfast, there was no question. Broadmoor.

Broadmoor. That's heavy shit, isn't it?

Oh, yes.

Do people get out?

Well, I suppose so. If all you've done is knock a dog out. Anyway, he wants me to visit him.

What do you think?

I don't have to enrol here until the day after tomorrow.

Chapter 4

To Broadmoor

On the way to Broadmoor, I asked Will how he got his scar. He told me it was during a week in Paris.

I said: is that it?

Yep.

That doesn't tell me how you got it!

It's too long. I'll tell you another time.

I teased him: what are you trying to hide?

I got smacked in the head over two lesbians!

Oh well. Now I really need to know!

Later!

Then he asked me to perform an act of fellatio on him just to take the edge off things. I said: What's in it for me? As it was, I was suddenly sexed up with the thought of the lesbians. He said: Well, I'm driving, so, unless I stop, you'll have to pleasure yourself. I said that sounded cool; I hadn't done the two together before, and it carried with it the wicked pleasure of knowing that some dirty old bastard truck driver could get his own rocks off with a view from the commanding seat of his pantechnicon. As Will came, I came and I understood for the first time the aesthetic experienced in a sex act, that that spurt was the slash of colour on a throated canvas and my release was the ecstasy of sharing an artwork with its creator.

The visit wasn't easy. You knew Dewey wanted us to take him out of there. You could tell he was sane as hell. Read loads of books and spoke with a professorial authority about everything. This wasn't a villain; this was someone with tremendous will turned on that night into a wayward energy lost in the bewilderment of many conflicting drugs. His eyes were tired from carrying the weight of an unrelenting sorrow. In here, even the air was hopeless.

As we left, I looked back and did not see a dog swinger: I saw someone trapped behind the clamp of dead eyes and stateless shoulders. I felt deeply sad.

He said that he was hoping to get out of there soon, but you never knew.

Chapter 5

Olsen

(Hail Modiano!)

On the afternoon the two were driving back from Broadmoor, at 3.07, Sten Olsen, Swede, stopped at The Hungry Heart, a roadside cafe on the A4074. Next to the cafe done out recently as a colourful mock American diner and already in need of a paint job, was a shed of a garage with a range of vintage wrecks on the front yard and around the side and inside a dungareed 60-year-old with a burnt tonsure and round red face working on a depredated 56 Austin Healey 3000.

Sten Olsen stepped out of his car, took a stroll to the dark mouth of the shed, and called to the toiling man:

Hallo.

Dungarees answered:

Go in!

Olsen was tall with blonde hair as you'd expect and blue eyes: every feature of the finely proportioned face broadcast a restless sexuality. He walked to the cafe door. Inside, the place seemed empty. He sat at the far end of the cafe facing the door.

Springsteen's Thunder Road was playing. In fact, the only tracks ever played at The Hungry Heart were Springsteen songs.

Inside, alone at a table sat Rose Angwen.

Will Slade and Rose Angwen had pulled up in their Renault 5, got out, and Slade had said: you go in. I want to check out these old motors.

What do you want?

I don't know. A burger? And a strong tea.

Will was drawn to a light blue Mark One Vauxhall Victor.

Inside, the smell of aged fried onions ironically suppressed the hunger. The place had a damp chill. Rose sat facing the back of the cafe. When Olsen came in, she looked at him, and he looked at her. She got up, walked to the counter, said hello!, shrugged, walked to the door, looked out where she saw Will talking to a man in working clothes, walked towards the sign that said *toilets* and as she passed the Swede, smiled at him and made a gesture which caused him to get up and follow her. Inside the toilet, after his initial tentative proposal, she wasted no time in removing her jeans and knickers, getting his dick out, pushing him down on the toilet seat and sitting on that crazy Scandinavian stalk. This was something she had to do. Something she had to initiate. And she knew consciously for the first time, the power of the clitoris to determine action; the power of the demanding clitoris; that a woman can weaponize herself through her clitoris.

When she came back into the cafe from the rear rooms, Will was sitting where she had sat earlier. She was flushed. On her pale face, the flush was unmistakable. Bright red like a pre-ripe plum.

She sat and said:

There's no one serving.

Will said: it's the guy in the shed. He'll be in now. You hot?

Not really.

She moved onto the seat next to the wall.

Actually, the place could do with a bit of heat.

Yeh, he said. Must have changed the name recently. *Hungry Heart.* Get the punters in. Looks like it didn't work.

Just then, Olsen came in from the back.

Olsen was the kind of man who made a hole in the air. Place deferred to him.

Will looked at him. He felt uneasy as if....but hell, he supposed he just looked like any other blond and blue-eyed Nordic type, which is maybe, thought Will, what he was. Will watched him move to his table.

Will said: I wonder where he came from.

Toilet?

Were you with that guy?

Rose turned around to look. Then turned back.

Would you hit me if I said yes?

Hit you? Why would I hit you? We're not married.

Wow. And if we were?

No. I'm not a hitter.

Why would you think I was with him?

I just asked. You were flushed.

It's true. I'm sorry, Will. I couldn't help it. I get this, like, incredible itch. Clitoral itch. And sucking you off on the way over wound me up. And then the forlorn Dewey.

You screwed?

I'm sorry. I don't know what came over me.

I'd say he did.

Rose, without thinking, hastily wiped around her mouth and neck.

Where's he from?

He's Swedish, I think. We didn't talk much.

The shed man appeared behind the counter.

He said:

What can I do you for?

Will said:

Two burgers and two teas. Can I have one strong and sweet?

Cheese?

Will said to Rose: Cheese?

Ok.

Onions?

Please.

Chilli sauce?

Can you bring the bottle? And have you got English mustard?

Ok.

Then the Swede said to the counter guy:

Black coffee? Strong. Thank you.

Will looked at the tomato ketchup bottle and the hard deposit of centuries old sauce at the screw top and felt a moment's despair. Didn't understand why he didn't just walk out and leave her to the Viking.

Good fuck?

Throughout their eating, neither the Swede nor Will looked at each other as if both were afraid of making a discovery that would leave no room for compromise.

That night, back in Will's room, as we did it, I suddenly became aware of him sobbing. Despite his moving on me and into me, I summoned the strength to ask him why he was crying.

He said: I'm not crying.

I said: of course you are. My face is getting wet.

Ok, I'll stop.

Incredibly, he did stop and then came. And then, rolling off me, he began to cry again like a child.

I said: is it because of today?

Today?

You know, the Swede. I let my hand glide over his face. I felt remorseful, which was unlike me; perhaps I'd hurt him.

Oh no, not that. Well, not...not obviously. Maybe Dewey. But not even that. Not exactly. I feel done in.

I said: you're beautiful.

I pitied him, which was another revelation: the pity of sex. I know from the reading I'd done that Nietzsche hated pity: a slave emotion, and, as far as I could work out, he hated sex. Was that a slave indulgence for him? Crazily, a slave may not own his own body, but he/she owns their sex – that can't be bought or sold by anyone but the owning slave, and if they did sell it, that would be a demonstration of their incontestable freedom. It's as if the pity in prostitution, *oh, what a pity she has to do that,* is an emotion that protects the rights of sex, wrapping round it like a steel glove.

Chapter 6

Helix

(Hail Crick and Watson!)

It was obvious I wasn't going to be able to live here with him. Sternbend notwithstanding. I needed to get a job if I wanted to stay around while he studied. And find a room. I'd pose as a Cambridge student. Tighten up my vowels.

Next morning, he went to enrol and I went to look for a pub and found The Eagle in Bene't Street off King's Parade.

They gave me a job as a barmaid.

The Eagle is famous. It's where, one lunchtime in 1953, Crick and Watson announced that they had discovered the secret of life: the DNA double-helix.

And in that very seat, which is more like an open booth, I sat with Quaid Laurel, the head barman, before the small plaque as he went over the ropes with me. In fact, it was he who pointed out the plaque and explained to me about Crick and Watson. Quaid was a lean man in his late twenties with black swept-back hair and a configuration of a bold nose and dark eyes that asserted his intelligence. And just the trace of something feminine, which I found endearing. He wasn't particularly handsome but solid: someone you felt you could trust. Quaid had himself graduated as a science honours student and was pursuing a post-grad degree. He also told me about the pub – how it was more than 300 years old. I like all that stuff. I have to admit, I like knowledge; I'm reluctant to let anything of interest pass me by without investigating it. My view, as I've said, is that there is a relationship between my love of sex and my love of knowledge. I need to know the ins and outs of both. I remember seeing one dude – or maybe I read it–saying how no man who ever made it didn't have a strong libido. You hardly ever hear about women's libidos!

I have to say here: I'm a bit of a depressive. It began with anxiety when I was a kid, probably because of all that brethren crap. It led to my passion for sex. Reduced the anxiety and kept me away from that dark place where I'm trapped in a dark room, stalked by grotesque spiders.

For example, after listening to Quaid for over an hour, who was flirting with me the whole time, and taking everything in so that I could have just sprung up there and then and started serving like an old pro, in a minor lull, I could see he had a hard-on. It was unusual for an arousal to produce such an obvious and exaggerated expression of approval in someone, to my knowledge anyway, so I had to assume that, as in my own case, his fever for knowledge was reflected in a sexual feverishness. And after all, this was Cambridge, the apogee of epistemological enquiry! As for sex I'd never heard that Cambridge was a particularly horny place though I do think that there's a link between people who study at the highest level and sexual promiscuity.

I wanted so badly to touch him but didn't feel sure enough of myself to approach him directly about it, so I fashioned this dodge: I'd get up to go to the toilet and slip and fall back and, attempting to steady myself, let my hand come to rest there. It worked, and I immediately sprang back full of the most effusive apologies, and he said:

It's alright. It was nice. We exchanged meaningful glances, and I excused myself.

When I returned, he said:

So much of my life takes place in my head. That can give you a headache!

I should think so.

That headwork is conscious, something that's forced on me by myself. In life, there is no meaning to any point without counterpoint, like there is no meaning to good without bad. Light without shade. Sex is the counterpoint of thought because it's instinctual. In order for thought to be meaningful, we need its counterpoint, sex. Sex is the only way I can restore the balance that gets rid of the headaches. I work here to make myself available to the counterpoint of sex while never losing the point, which I find here in Crick and Watson's seat. Let's fuck. We can go to my place during my break.

Wow! Didn't he finally get to the point? I said, ok, but his erudite echoing of my own beliefs shocked me.

At five we went to his place and I soon realised that this guy would get first class honours in fucking which seemed to further give credibility to my theory about the relationship between knowledge and sex; I could write an authoritative paper on it.

After, he said:

I'm excited you're starting tomorrow.

I said: I was worried you might find me fat. Once undressed. I'm bigger than most girls.

You're not fat. Anyway, it's nice. It's soft.

Chapter 7

PhD

(Hail Flaubert!)

When Rose Angwen arrived at the house in Paradise Street where Will Slade had his flat, she could make out through the opaque glass of the front door the shape of two men in earnest conversation. She tapped the window, and the door was opened by Sternbend. He said: Hello.

She said:

Um.... Mr. Slade?

Slade came to the door.

Slade said:

Oh, hi. This is a colleague, Mr. Sternbend. A fellow student. She wants me to go over the calculus we looked at today.

Will's presence anywhere was immediate. He was a star. But he was also a fine representation of the illusion/reality dichotomy. Meeting him, one was immediately impressed by his apparent confidence. This is why he never had to chase sex. It would come to him.

In his room, Rose could see he was shaking badly. She was about to say something when he lunged at her and began to feverishly kiss her.

Why are you shaking? Are you ok?

I'm sorry. I've been thinking about you all day.

During your calculus session?

I wasn't doing calculus. That was the first thing that came to mind.

He had begun to undo her jeans.

What about Sternbend?

What about him?

I can imagine him listening at the door.

Slade's mind was an earthquake. Nothing was stable. His raging desire shaking his reasoned certainties.

He got her onto the bed, and it was all over within half a minute.

If, sex is spliced with knowledge and in their conjunction is an argument for meaning, then in young men the build to sex comes as an encyclopaedic tornado driving for the heart where meaning is glorified, which quickly collapses in a change of weather: its arrival meaningless which is why, in the immediate aftermath of sex, men are so often so utterly bereft of drive.

Now Rose herself felt confused. The purely instinctual joy of sex that Quaid had talked about and which seemed to make so much sense had been disturbed by this exhibition of something close to illness, which made her think about what they'd done. She and Will. Brought thought into sex. And now she thought about the night before when he almost collapsed in a flood of tears!

He said:

I'm sorry about that.

It's ok. You needed it.

She got off the bed and picked up her jeans.

She said: I've got a place.

Where?

The people in the pub arranged it. It's alongside Midsummer Common. Parsonage Street. Number 8. I've got the key.

She put her jeans back on and fished out the key to show him.

He said: you were quick.

She wanted to make a crack about his recent performance, but left it.

I couldn't stay here. Sneaking out this morning totally freaked me out. I need to pick up my bag with my clothes. You should be able to stay over with me now and again.

Are you rushing off now?

No.

Do you want to stay here tonight?

I'll sleep much easier in my own place knowing that there's no Sternbend snooping.

Ok. Do you want a drink? I need one.

Have you had a hard day?

Not really. I've got Mateus rose. Is that, ok?

Fine. As he went for the bottle, she said: You've never really told me what you're studying.

He opened the bottle. I'm doing a PhD on the poet Thomas Chatterton.

I've never heard of him.

He poured two glasses.

He was an eighteenth-century poet, born into poverty, raised in poverty, he killed himself because his writing would never, he thought, make him enough money to keep himself. He drank arsenic in an attic. He was seventeen.

Oh, my God! That's so sad! Arsenic. That's how Emma Bovary killed herself. It's terrible. The worst!

Yes. My working title is *Premonitions of Early Death by Suicide in the Works of Thomas Chatterton*. I don't know if it'll work. You have to do something original, and I don't think anyone's tried anything like that. He was a great influence on the Romantic poets like Shelley, who came a bit later. So if my idea won't run, I should be able to find something in that area.

They relaxed.

Then she said: finish the story about Paris. About your scar.

He paused. Then said: ok.

You got banged on the head over two lesbians?

Yeah. So what happened? I was with Albine, who I told you about. We'd spent the afternoon in my *pension*.

What's that?

A *pension*?

Yeah.

A *pension* is a cheap hotel in France.

Oh, right! Was Albine the Basque girl?

Yes. I met her on a street called the Rue de l' Huchette. It's quite famous – one of the oldest in Paris. It's in the Latin Quarter where the students and artists hang out.

Was she a student?

I don't know. She was about seventeen? Very Spanish! I told you, you remind me of her. Facewise.. She was pretty reckless. She wore a summer skirt and no knickers.

Here we go!

We had a wild afternoon! You can do that, can't you? When you're eighteen. You can drink all you want and just carry on! Then she left just as it was getting dark, and I drank some wine and went out. A really warm June evening. Young people everywhere. It was like these were *their* streets. Their Left Bank. Paris in the late sixties! I went into Shakespeare and Co and Shakespeare and Co.

It's a famous bookshop. Anyway, in the shop I saw this other girl, Yvonne, whom I'd met that morning. She was there among the book stacks. She remembered me, and I asked her if she wanted to go for a drink. She said, ok. After I've found the book., It turned out it was a translation of Schopenhauer, which was weird because he was an infamous misogynist.

She probably wanted to swot up on the opposition!

Yeh. Anyway, I took her to George's, a café, and got two glasses of wine. *Deux verres du vin,* then she says: I am a lesbian. I was speechless! I am a lesbian! I think I suddenly wanted to be a woman!

Rose laughed. are you bisexual?

Those things are complicated. Anyway, she says: you are very sweet, Will. Perhaps I could with you. I don't know. I love vaginas. You have secret vagina? What a thing to say! I said I'll see if I can pick one up on the street!

Ha-ha!

She went, and I had a few more drinks and just mooched around the boulevards and the back streets looking for Albine. I wandered some of the back alleyways for a while, hoping my luck would change and then in a dark street - Place Saint-Michel, I think - I see her! A woman leaning with her back resting against a wall, her lower body thrust out in a sexy arc, in a state of ecstasy with another woman going down on her! She was wearing no knickers, as far as I could see. It's Albine! She's groaning with joy and the other woman it turns out is Yvonne attacking Albine's cunt like a hungry dog! Like something slurping up oysters! I could do nothing else but watch.

Jesus Christ, Will. Sounds like Anais Nin!

You've read Anais Nin?

As if it's the most obvious thing: yeah!

Ok. Then this huge guy turns up! One side of his face is tattooed. He pulls Yvonne off Albine and wallops the Basque across the face. Then I jump onto the gorilla's back. And that is the beginning of my first death!

A bit extreme, Will!

Someone took me to the hospital, where they treated me for a concussion. And I had broken ribs, a broken jaw and a broken arm. And my face!

Sounds like you went through a war!

That hospital was a really freaky place. To fix the jaw, they put me in a ward with people in the worst states you could imagine. One old guy had skin cancer.

Sounds awful.

They'd cut away a lot of his face below his eyes and he wore a mask to hide it. One morning, I walked into the bathroom; I didn't know he was in there. He had the mask off and was throwing water into the cavity where his face once was.

My God!

Yeah. You know: I'm vain. I feel like I'm getting old and look in shop windows hoping to see the golden boy of my youth and look for the angle that will encourage me to think that I haven't lost it all. Something residual. Something to hang onto. Something reassuring. But he had lost his face! No possibility of the residual. No reassuring.

They drank, and Rose put her arms around him.

In Rose's own words:

The talk of the lesbians made me horny and, I guess, him too and we really went to town on one another and I left with the intriguing thought that Will had more or less said he was bisexual. It seemed to me that the more one rejected the restraints of circumspection, the more doors into palaces of wonder presented themselves.

But before she left, he said:

You're not fat. Besides, you've got the prettiest face.

This knocked her sideways. You'd think he'd overheard her conversation with Quaid Laurel. So, she thought, he thinks I am big! Otherwise, why would he say *Besides,* you've got the prettiest face.

And then, she thought: I think I almost know Will. And know that he's a poet and his poetry is fed by the brassy bell-ring of abandon: the real world the poet authorises behind the realistic.

Chapter 8

Chatterton

(Hail Shelley)

In early October, Rose visited the library of King's College. She snuck in behind a bear of a man in his early twenties with a scramble of black hair and florid complexion who was clearly well known for his loudness and affability and always likely to cause a distraction, which would allow someone of Rose's stature (5ft 5ins) to gain unsanctioned entry.

She looked in the catalogue for Thomas Chatterton, but not before taking a panoptical sweep of the interior of the building and subjecting herself to the heartbreaking scents of ancient endeavours captured in these books.

The feeling of overwhelming and welcome belonging she experienced let her believe that her hunger for knowledge had now matriculated into an inarguable empiricism defined by an age-old rubric.

She found a book on Chatterton and took it to a desk, where she first went to the photographic plates, pausing at the reproduction of an image of the dead poet painted by Henry Wallis. Pre Raphaelite and late Romantic in the extreme but moving too, the brilliant young thing beneath an attic window, his body draped upon a lonely sofa or *chaise longue* with the arm that lifted the poison now hanging useless to the floor, a bit like Marat in David's painting.

I wandered about the part of town his house was in: mid-18th-century Holborn and in particular Brook Street. August 1770, I found myself on this very street on a balmy evening in August where couples promenade, the men with canes, the women with parasols and rococo dresses and coming towards me, head lowered in deep thought, a thin, pale young man a little over five foot seven with glorious, flowing auburn locks wearing a white linen shirt and pale blue breeches and white stockings. And aqua-marine eyes, the bluest I'd ever seen. As I got near to him, he suddenly stumbled and all but fell onto me before reaching out and laying hands on my shoulders.

Oh, forgive me, forgive me please!

It's alright. I'm fine.

I'm afraid I'm a little preoccupied.

He spoke in a distracted, almost feverish way. Blue eyes like a troubled sea.

I could feel myself wetting. How could those glands that so studiously celebrate life to lubricate the passage of continuing reality so take possession of unreality? Was this a metaphysics for ecstasy: proof of the abandonment of self in sexual pleasure that becomes new knowledge for life?

He said:

Two days ago, I was walking with a friend in St Pancras Churchyard and fell into a freshly dug grave – because of my preoccupation! And now I'm preoccupied with thoughts about that! What did it mean? I'm afraid I've been at war with the grave for some time now. I'm sorry. My name is Tom. Well, I would prefer Thomas. Chatterton.

My name is Rose. Angwen.

Angwen. That's Cornish. I know the West Country. I'm from Bristol.

Well, I'm pleased to meet you, Mr. Thomas. I offered my hand and he shook it vigorously. My hand was nervously shaking anyway!

My rooms are just along here. Would you like to come in for a drink? I'm afraid I can offer only water.

I'd like that very much.

Was I going to experience the ultimate incursion into the deepest secrets of intellectual fucking: sex with the historically dead?

We entered the house and began to walk up the stairs. Three flights. At the top, we came to his small attic room.

Not really rooms at all! This is where I live.

On a small round table were books and pamphlets open to learned papers on syphilis.

I asked him if he was a medical student.

Oh, no. I want to find out whether I have syphilis.

Why do you think you have syphilis? Do you have the symptoms?

I don't know what they are.

Then why?.......

He poured drinks and said: it is my pride, my damned native, unconquerable pride: it plunges me into distraction.

He sat on the *chaise longue* and invited me to join him.

You do know how syphilis is caught?

Yes, of course, but it's nothing to do with that. I let myself down with a young woman who threw herself at me, and I have to pay for that.

But it doesn't make sense!

Oh, I know! Happy is the man who, not by priest but by reason, rules his span. I, so often, am in the mood the self to scath. I do know that the cure for syphilis is arsenic.

I was alarmed: arsenic!

Yes. Here it is.

He held up a small bottle containing a liquid.

Will you sit with me while I take it?

No! Of course not!

Listen. The happy life, the life in which the pleasuring of the senses can mean something, is delusional. We must live for the imagination, and the imagination is a hard master. I must be a slave and find majesty in that. I have fallen, and the only cure is arsenic.

Can I ask you: when did you last eat?

I don't know. Three days ago?

Please, let me get you something.

I'm not hungry.

Please.

I got up and left the distracted young man, making sure to leave the door ajar. But I waited at the room door and watched through the crack.

Holding the bottle up, Chatterton said:

You refuse to pay me for my work, perhaps a penny here and there; you refuse to take me seriously and in a distracted moment, I subject myself to this affliction. But you will not conquer me.

Then, before I could get to him, the poet swallowed the arsenic as a draft from the street rose. He got up and closed the door and closed me out. I heard him as he returned to the *chaise longue* where he would die, begin to sob.

Soon he was groaning and I realised there was nothing I could do. I had no power over history.

Chapter 9

Parfitt

One day, the philosophy student, Parfitt, said: I'd like to take you to meet Goldstein. He's one of the richest men in Cambridge and lives on De Freville Avenue. He's a fanatical Marxist. Will said: Is that philosophically sound? Parfitt said: That's the point. Let me know what you think after our visit.

Parfitt had been at University in L. a couple of years before Will. Will had got to know about him from the philosophy lecturer Rockingham-Gill, who Will knew from the poker nights they attended. When Rockingham-Gill had found out that Will was heading for Cambridge, he'd told Parfitt to look him up.

At L. Parfitt had been the darling of the philosophy department. He would be seen around campus, lean, about 5ft 9ins, always suited with an almost priggish, studious air. He was not known but rather pedalled a reputation which was bolstered in that second-rate institution by a posturing accompanied by Kantian refrains.

Today, Will and Parfitt were playing snooker in the students' union, and Parfitt was about to take a shot with the curtailed cue. The snooker table had been positioned between the street wall and a ceiling supporting pillar which prevented the use of a full-length cue and so the curtailed cue had been fashioned from a regular cue by removing a substantial portion of the butt.

At first, Will had been in awe of Parfitt, but here not so; it was as if being here alone at this table with the legend had stripped the latter of all pretentious advantages.

Parfitt's speciality was Wittgenstein. This was Will Slade's first ever game with him, and he said about the situation of the table and the culled cue:

Don't you think this is absurd?

Parfitt had replied: you may if you look for meaning in the meta-world like one of the French thinkers but if you apply Wittgenstein you can find resignation to the reality and just get on with the game: the limits of language are the limits of our world; the limits of the cue are the limits of the game. The end. And he'd taken his shot and almost torn the baize.

Of course, he said, as with language's limitations, you have to get used to it.

Strange to say, Will thought, Parfitt actually looked like the great British/Austrian thinker with the same set of face haunted by enquiry, which in Parfitt's case was reflected in his posture with its tortuous angularity. And Parfitt had even mastered the intense piercing stare of the European thinker.

Will said: are you yourself a Marxist?

O, yes!

But the Wittgenstein?

No conflict.

What about dialectical materialism?

It's quite straightforward. Wittgenstein said that when we speak, the only things we can say that hold any truth are tautologies: a triangle is a figure with three sides. The notion of a figure with three sides is contained in the word triangle. He took his shot and potted a red into the top right corner. Will was impressed. Parfitt had managed to come back nicely for the blue, which he would be able to despatch with the complete cue. As he moved around the table, he continued: you cannot make moral judgements that hold any truth, and so, as Witters said, whereof one cannot speak, one should remain silent. For Marx, the proletarian is a wage slave. True and a tautology. Morality is determined by the way we act. After Wittgenstein had finished the Tractatus, his early great work....Parfitt walloped the cue ball, sunk the blue and screwed back for the red on the bottom cushion..... he believed he'd finished off philosophy, gave away all his money to his siblings and went to work as a primary school teacher in a mountain school in Austria: that's socialist morality! For Marx, socialist morality is found in the revolution, which is determined by the scientific dialectic of materialism. He went for the black, hit a red and snookered the cue ball behind the black.

Is it true he didn't get on with Russell?

Russell was a sentimentalist. Read his autobiography. All that stuff about never masturbating. Expecting an emotional response from us. Cheap. Sentimentality is the exploitation of emotion for effect rather than enlightenment.

Looking closely at the balls, Will said: I don't think I can get out of that.

Parfitt said: you don't have to. I made a foul shot. You get a free ball. Knock the black out of the way. Don't you know the rules?

I've mostly played pool.

Ah, well, you see? This is Cambridge. A higher class of balls.

Will took the curtailed cue and pushed the cue ball and cleared the black.

Foul.

What?

It's a push stroke. You pushed the cue ball with the cue. You didn't make a proper shot.

What's a proper shot?

When you pull back the cue and stab the cue ball.

How can I pull back the cue? There's a fucking brick pillar in the way!

We are all at the same disadvantage. It's precisely what the shortened cue is for.

So what happens now?

Penalty. And my shot.

Parfitt looked closely at the layout of the balls and said: I don't want it. You go again.

I can't do it!

Parfitt said: ok. A further penalty.

I do know one thing Wittgenstein said. I checked him out after our last meeting: philosophy is the struggle against the bewitchment of language. You're bewitching me with language to win, and it's just not philosophical and therefore I can't carry on! I give in! And he threw the curtailed cue onto the table.

Parfitt laughed and said: got me there, Slade!

On their way to Goldstein's, Will said to Parfitt:

So what do you believe? What's your philosophy? Your own original philosophy?

The supremacy of absence.

What's that?

The absence of proof; certainty, ultimately, the world.

That doesn't make sense. We're in it! Will gestured with his arms to suggest he was holding the world.

In order to believe in anything, you have to believe it's not there.

Are you sure you've fully worked this out?

In his first philosophy, the Tractatus, Wittenstein said that there are some things you can't speak about, like morality. I've already told you this. You should just keep quiet. He also said that our world is limited by our language, in which case, our world doesn't contain morality. You see? Absence. In his last work. In the Investigations, he said that language can't contain absolute meaning. Language is relative. Words convey a sense of where they're spoken – the context. Words build up a picture. That's all. Absence of meaning. Absence of morality and absence of meaning amounts to the absence of the world: the world as you know it.

So what about Marx?

Easy. Revolution demands the absence of ruling-class authority. That's the only way society will work. That demand for absence determines that the ruling class is there and is pernicious.

They got to Goldstein's, which was a huge six-bedroom Georgian house, and Parfitt rang the bell.

The door was opened by a very smart, handsome woman in her forties who wore her hair a` la français. Seeing Parfitt, her face lit up with a beaming smile, a smile that could crush granite and from her eyes a look that would only ever search for love and happiness burning through the evening air. Will was transfixed by her grace.

Anthony! Leonard said you may be coming.

Hello Carla. This is Will.

Come in, both of you come in! Then she shouted to the interior: Leonard! Anthony's here.

After a moment, a short, white haired, well-fed man in his 70s with a permanent smile came out from the back. Will was struck by the wisdom and delight in his eyes. It was as if he'd just heard a good joke that had revealed the truth about something that, for now, he was keeping to himself.

Shalom, Anthony, *ma nishma*.

Parfitt said: Shalom, Leonard.

Do you remember what I told you, *ma nishma* means?

Well, what am I up to?

With a chuckle, Goldstein said: that's fine!

Parfitt said: this is my friend Will. He's a PhD student at Hughes Hall.

Goldstein held out his hand: another philosopher?

Will shook his hand and said: no, English. Actually, Thomas Chatterton.

Ah, yes! The poor English poet! Come in.

Carla said: I studied Chatterton in my first year at Trinity.

Will said, demurely: maybe we could have a chat about him sometime.

Carla carried about her the ambivalence of the émigré even though she'd spent most of her life in Britain, as if she'd never forget her first visit to the circus. She was an adult overcome with shock and excitement. Curiously, she had the tight-muscled, balletic walk of a trapeze artist. And the refined mien of the traveller.

In the living room, on a small occasional table, sat a chessboard on which a game was already in progress.

Goldstein said to Parfitt:

Make your move. We have been playing this game for some months. Every time Anthony arrives, we each make a move, and then it's left until the next time. And then he said with a laugh: Does that sound Jewish?

Will said: it sounds like it could be a game for life.

Yes! A game for life. That's excellent.

Parfitt made his move.

Goldstein said: ah! Very good. You anticipated my bishop!

Will couldn't imagine this squat fellow pumping away at the divine Mrs. Goldstein, who was watching the masters with, it seemed to Will, that Goldstein's smile.

You're looking at my wife. I know. It doesn't seem reasonable – a little old Jew like me with such a beauty, but you see, I believe always that one should defy expectation. For example, when one thinks of the Jew, one pictures an optimist with a worried face. Jewish history with the persecution and all the driving out makes Jews pessimistic, but Judaism is optimistic. This conflict is where our humour comes from. But I am always smiling. Yes? I am a pessimist with an optimistic face! I don't believe you can ever dehitlerise the souls of some, but you can at least smile while organising the revolution! Shall we have drinks? And Carla, darling, could you arrange for some nibbles? I've got a very argumentative Chateau Haut-Brion! Please, find a comfortable seat, but not this!

He indicated the voluminous port coloured armchair in which he was sitting. A worn velveteen.

I've had this for twenty years. It was given to me by John Cairncross, the great Cambridge communist. He was left it by his close friend Guy Burgess before the latter popped off to share his life with the Soviets.

Will and Parfitt settled themselves into a pair of much newer and slightly more austere armchairs with a red leather finish.

Will said: Guy Burgess, the spy?

As characterised by The Daily Mail, but what would they have said if he'd gone to hobnob with Hitler in the 30s? Let me show you this: he lifted himself and took from under his seat cushion a photograph. It showed a distinguished-looking gentleman with a white moustache standing next to a business-suited Hitler, looking like a stern headmaster.

That's Rothermere, owner of The Daily Mail, just after congratulating the great dictator on his annexation of Czechoslovakia. That was put under the cushion by Cairncross so that in my refined years I could sit on them and fart.

As they settled in with their large glasses of wine, Carla Goldstein arrived with the nibbles. Will now felt bold enough, without reserve, to enjoy the smell of her and the little smile she sneaked to him as she placed the small occasional table onto which she would rest the canapés.

After some talk of the Queen's Gambit and Sicilian defence and a couple of glasses, Will asked Goldstein:

Were you ever encouraged to spy?

Parfitt objected, saying:

Now look here, Slade, what kind of question is that?

It's ok said the benign Jew, he would never understand the answer to his question.

What do you mean, said Will.

Goldstein replied: the MOD placed Cairncross at Bletchley, where they were decoding German messages, knowing he was a Soviet double agent.

I've never heard of Bletchley.

Exactly!

And a little later, Will, in the presence of the ever-lovelier Mrs. Carla Goldstein, said to the old man: I really admire your optimism; it must be so difficult to smile after the holocaust.

As they left, Mrs Goldstein gave Will an understanding look and a smile and touched his arm in a way that sent an electric shock through him.

In the street, Parfitt raged:

What the fuck was that Slade?

What?

It must be so difficult to smile after the holocauste lost family in the camps! How could you say something like that?

I was trying to congratulate him on his...you know....mien. Optimism.

Mien! You were talking to him like a cheap quiz show host. What you probably don't understand about Jews is that they are a very philosophical people and that nothing, nothing they ever do or think is without purpose: they live teleological lives! Marx's philosophy owes much to teleology, particularly in its Hegelian account of history, whose purpose is to give us the dictatorship of the proletariat, which is why Marxism is attractive to Jews, in particular this Jew! And, of course, Marx himself was a Jew.

Ok, Parfitt, so are you saying that the purpose of Jewism is the holocaust?

You're drunk! Of course not! The Final Solution was not final! In fact, Judaism thrives and the world benefits. The purpose of the Jews is to educate us and civilise us: Dylan, Cohen, Salinger, Roth, Pinter, Koestler!

I'm lost.

You need to read more widely!

No, I'm lost geographically!

Down here, turn left: that's Chesterton Road. And before you go to sleep tonight, think of the corpses of Auschwitz.

They walked in silence, Parifitt mimicking the indifference of a deep in thought Wittgenstein, until they parted to follow their own particular road home, at which point Will said: The man never stopped smiling! Throughout!

Will walked on, refusing to let the bombast Parfitt qualify his merriness. One had to understand and sympathise with someone like Parfitt, Will reasoned, most likely born with a poker up his arse and then attended a public school where the older lags would avail themselves of the subjucative orifice. He breathed deep the chill air and smiled smugly: he was in Cambridge mixing with toffs like Parfitt and millionaire Marxists and holding his own and carrying past the great houses with their turrets and own lumiere the trophy of the smile from the divine Mrs. Goldstein. What he would think about before sleeping, what he would imagine, would be the breathing, living corpse of Carla Goldstein in his room.

Chapter 10
Bubovsky

In the toilet of the diner, The Hungry Heart, pulling up his pants, Sten had said to me: Where are you from?

I'd said: at the moment, I'm living in Cambridge with my boyfriend.

Your boyfriend?

Yes. He's out there.

Holy shit.

It's ok, he was talking with the car guy in the shed.

What if he's come in?

He'll think I've gone to the toilet, which I have. I'll go out first. Just be natural.

Do you have an address?

Where are you from?

Sweden.

I thought: good English.

I said: good English.

Most Swedes speak it.

No address. I'm staying with Will.

That's your boyfriend?

Uhu.

And if I'm ever in Cambridge?

You'll find me in the university sector.

But where?

I then made my way out of the toilet, my face flushed.

So I wasn't surprised to see one day in my second week in the Eagle, Sten standing at the bar.

I'd been musing on Will's anecdote about his Paris experience and it had given me a vicarious pleasure, particularly the image of Yvonne dining on Albine, precisely because it allowed my imagination freedom; allowed me to wander in some garden of forbidden fruit and gorge and full-mouthed have the juice cascade over my chin. The anecdote is almost nothing without that moment, and I learned this lesson: that sexual desire can be experienced and enjoyed by indulgence in any dimension.

At first, Sten didn't acknowledge me and, to be honest, in the murk of the evening bar, I had some difficulty recognising him. But I was aware of him watching me, and after a while, as I moved down the bar towards him, he said:

Hello.

I said:

Oh, hi! And then that cliché: what are you doing here? Which sounded a bit dismissive, I realised. What I was feeling was how things may develop with him into an anecdote of my own.

Oh, I have business in Cambridge. But what are you doing here? Working in a bar.

Working in a bar!

Yes. Of course! Ha, ha. Do you have a break for lunch?

I said yes at one.

One o'clock? Can I take you for something to eat? There is a Greek restaurant across the road.

The Green Olive, I know it. I've eaten there a few times. A drink while you wait?

Give me a pint of this ale. I like ale.

I drew him a pint of Adnams. He remained at the bar.

I moved up and down the bar, returning when required to Sten, who was sitting at the Adnams pump.

On one occasion, he said:

Are you a student?

Not in the university. But I've developed an interest in Thomas Chatterton, the poet. Do you know him? Well, of course, ha! I don't *know* him; he's been dead 200 years. Have you heard the name?

Oh, yes.

As I pulled a pint, I said: good, we'll have something to talk about over lunch.

He watched me occasionally drinking from his pint as I worked up and down the bar, and then he said:

I am moved by the innocent but expert way you measure out a wine glass, pull at the beer pump and punch in the charge on the till. And I am enchanted by the way you tie your hair and pin it back like a roll of silk.

Wow!

As we crossed the road to the restaurant, he said: I have a confession to make: I have come to Cambridge to meet, I hope, the Soviet dissident Vladimir Bubovsky. I know that he eats at The Green Olive.

I said I think I've seen him. I've seen on a couple of occasions this man in his thirties who sits at the back of the cafe, always alone. One time, I was sitting facing him, about ten tables away, and I think he smiled at me and smiled again as he passed me to leave. Yes. He did look Russian! What are you going to do? Interview him?

Oh, no! I wish! No, I just want to *see* him. Sitting in the West. And, maybe, if I'm lucky, to say hello. I think it would be easier if you were with me.

That's why you invited me to lunch?

No! I would have asked you anyway!

In The Green Olive, I immediately looked to the rear to where I said I'd seen the Russian. Sitting at the table he may have occupied were a couple. Bubovsky was not in the restaurant.

We sat and looked at the menu. And the scents everywhere: Lemon, oregano, garlic and olive oil. Sten told me about how Bubovsky had been a dissident and had been locked up for years in a psychiatric institution – for the Soviets, if you were a dissident, you were mad. Finally, they kicked him out of the country, and he came to Cambridge.

At the table, I was facing the door, and Sten the back wall. We were about halfway along a row of ten tables. I said: I love these aromas.

Yes. They transport you.

As did the plaintive, plucked music of the bouzouki gently falling from speakers above us.

Then he said: I can't believe what we did in that diner. It was not surprising that it was called the Hungry Heart. You were very hungry.

The door opened. An elderly couple came in. But then they paused at the open door, talking with someone. Then they came in while the one they were talking to left, and the young couple from the Russian's seat got up to leave. As they passed my table, I suddenly realised that the young man was Will. He was with a young woman. I didn't call out to him, but a shot of, I suppose, jealousy stung me. The old couple took a table on the other side of the aisle from me, which left Bubovsky's table unoccupied.

Sten said: what do you want?

Just a plate of meaty *dolmades*.

Hungry again?

So, so.

As I looked up from the menu, I saw Bubovsky walking up the aisle. He was looking at me with an enigmatic smile. I coloured up and returned the flicker of an uncertain smile! Sten picked up on this and began to turn his head just as the famous Russian passed and took his seat.

While the dissident, I suppose, studied the menu, I could see Sten studying his face, probably overwhelmed to be sitting here so near to this man who'd caused a sensation in the West. Been over all the front pages.

I wondered what was going on between Will and the girl.

Then Sten said, he's looking over here occasionally. I think he wished he was looking at you.

I said, he smiled at me when he came in.

You see? Why don't you go over there and introduce yourself?

On what grounds?

What do you mean?

Well, I need a reason.

You've got a reason: he smiled at you.

Ok.

And then, you can call me over, but I will only say hello. I am not prepared for more.

I just got up and boldly went to him. I offered my hand.

Hi. I'm Rose. You're Mr. Bubovsky. I know about you. My friend – I gestured towards Sten – has told me the complete story.

He shook my hand, half standing and said I am pleased to meet you. I have seen you in here on some occasions.

Yes. Can I call my friend over? He's Swedish and would love to meet you.

Yes, but first – let me.....you know, so many people welcome me and everyone is so kind, but in here – he indicated his heart – I am alone and I think it would help if you could, perhaps, do something for me.

Of course.

Would you have dinner with me in the evening? One evening.

Yes, yes. But I work most evenings in The Eagle – you know it?

Yes.

Sunday is the one that I don't work.

Sunday then. Let me tell you: all my years of incarceration have made intimacy in me an abstraction. Do you understand?

Yes, I think so.

I need help to make the abstraction something real. Someone to remove the ice from my soul. Do you think you can help?

Yes, I do.

Then he smiled almost tragically as though the smile was something he had rescued from a violation. A wounded thing.

Then he said: let us meet here at 8 o'clock on Sunday.

Yes.

You are a Renoir painting: sharp black eyes beneath heavenly, misty lids.

Oo! Thank you!

And then I called Sten over.

The men shook hands, and Bubovsky invited us to sit and join him.

Sten said:

Oh, no. Thank you very much, but we have to be somewhere.

He promptly turned and returned to our table. I realised Sten was overcome with embarrassment. Before I left the Russian's table, he took my hand and said:

A dimanche!

In the street, Sten said:

How much longer have you got?

What did you have in mind?

Well, I'm staying at the Regent Hotel. It's just around the corner.

I've got about twenty minutes.

Wine at lunchtime always gets me going, and Sten, too, it seemed. He was like a crazed dog. We did it all around the room, upside down, sideways, even had me standing on my head propped against the bed while his one leg was on the floor and the other kneeling on the bed! If you get the picture. At one point, while I was in this posture which he seemed to read as an invitation he popped his dick into my rectum, which was not something I was entirely unfamiliar with but it did take me somewhat by surprise. And all in just over half an hour! He was one of those guys for whom orgasm was not a handicap. He could have one after the other and just plough on! When, later, I reflected more on the afternoon, I recalled that his body was completely nude of hair – everything but his head shaved and I thought: porn actors remove all their hair. I knew that from looking into a school friend, Mary's, hardcore magazines. And it occurred to me that, today, sex had been a pleasant distraction – like climbing a mountain; you know that thing about Mallory and Everest: when asked why he wanted to climb it, he answered – because it's there.

Afterwards, I said goodbye to Sten and I wasn't sure if I'd ever see him again but what was more important was me getting enough of a walk back to The Eagle so that I could calm down, during which I turned my thoughts to Will and determined that I would go round and see him this evening and find out about the girl I saw him with.

When I got back to work, I was well and truly – forgive the colloquialism – fucked. Quaid was at work, so I was very pleased that it was busy. Did not want the attention of Mr Laurel this evening.

Chapter 11

Tarita

(Hail Brando!)

Will met Tarita Begrum on a bus. It was a single-decker at lunchtime and was pretty full, so he took the first seat he found. That seat was next to Tarita. He was immediately overwhelmed by her aura of scents: a fusion he figured of lavender, jasmine, geranium and angel trumpets! He learned about perfumes from his older sister, who was a beautician. That was in the days before she hated him.

He found himself unable to resist saying.

I love your smell!

After leaving Parfitt to his blue anger and absurd assessment of his perhaps careless words, Will thought: it's Cambridge, you're with the sons and daughters of the aristocracy, legitimate children of an unjust society and Lord's bastards; you don't belong here so to counter their arrogance you have to assert yourself as you had to in Grammar school where you also didn't belong. It was, perhaps, this reasoning that drove him to address the girl as he did.

She said a little nervously:

Thank you.

I'm sorry, that was a bit rude.

No, it's ok.

She liked his face. Benign.

Do you work in town?

No. I work in a hotel in Cherry Hinton. I'm on an errand to buy cheese.

Cheese?

Yes. A variety of cheeses. There's a shop near Trinity. In All Saints Passage. The Cambridge Cheese Company.

Will said: I've always wanted to eat cheese with the writers and philosophers at Les Deux Magots!

What's that?

It's a famous restaurant in Paris. I would taste all the cheeses, all the commanding existential cheeses: the soupy eblochon and gamey Epoisses; Brie slavering over the edge of the marble slab; innumerable varieties of radical cheese: goat cheeses blue with hard crusts or crowned with fresh herbs; absurdist cheese: tiny pyramids of sharp flavoured logs of creaminess rich with the democratic vice of complacency! (This was a routine he'd researched and put together for a poem he'd been working on.)

Tarita laughed and said: are you a student? A writer?

Both. What's your name?

Tarita.

Tarita? That's unusual. Exotic.

I was named after the actress who was in that film with Marlon Brando, Mutiny On The Bounty. My mother loved that film.

I know. I've seen it. I was a kid. I loved it too. Marlon Brando was a god.

Yes. I think my stop's coming up.

I'll get off with you!

They got off in Sidney Street.

Will said: ok, if I accompany you to the shop? (She loved the slightly formal tone!) I'd love to see the cheeses.

Yes, ok.

The shop, as you might expect, smelled of cheese, all the sweet and sour of it: all the complex milkiness. All the musty sadness.

Tarita handed the girl behind the counter a list, and the girl began to put the cheeses together.

Will said: listen, do you have to go straight back?

Why?

There's a little Greek Restaurant near here. I thought you might like coffee and maybe baklava.

Baklava?

It's a kind of cake.

I've never even heard of it!

Now's your chance! It's beautiful, sweet with honey! And truth!

Ok.

In the Greek restaurant, they found a table at the rear of the room, and Tarita sat with her back to the wall. Will ordered coffee and baklava.

Now he saw her face in full Ultra Panavision 70 widescreen, and his heart sank a little as the honest light revealed that one side of her face had once suffered a beating. His sorrow was not for the way her beauty was compromised because she was beautiful, but for his sadness for what must have happened.

Tarita said:

Where are you from?

Wales.

What, all of it?

Mostly. What about you?

Hastings.

Isn't that on the south coast? On The Channel?

Yes.

And you didn't want to be by the sea?

I had to get away from someone.

Her eyes were pinned on his eyes, looking at her old scar.

His name is Rolcord. He's been in gaol. They're letting him out soon.

What was he in there for?

For beating me up.

Is that what he did? Will indicates the scar.

Yes. He used to beat me around the room. Kick me till my belly bled. When I first met him, he was an angel. Afterwards, he'd apologise. Those moments were like a remission from cancer. You'd live for them and put up with the shit. Because if you left, you wouldn't get those moments – see in his eyes the fear of your judgement. That's when he would concede to you the seat of power. At that moment, you were stronger than all women. It was a clever game. It meant that in the moment of his deepest humiliation and regret, he was, in fact, in charge! It took me a long time to see that, and when I did, I left. Obviously, he found me one time and almost killed me, so I knew I'd have to go somewhere where he wouldn't find me.

Jesus. That's awful! I don't know what to say.

It's ok. Tell me about yourself.

Will was overwhelmed by what she'd said. She seemed so frail. Smaller than Rose, as slight as Rose was, full. He couldn't understand how she hadn't been broken. Physically and mentally.

The coffee and baklava arrived.

When Tarita took the baklava from the waitress, Will got a good look at her hands; saw the breezy leaf quiver, the chewed quarry face of her nails, the flawed lift.

She said: It smells nice.

I think you'll like it.

He suddenly felt as if he wanted to nurse her. As if she'd come to him in bits and he had to put her back together. Stitch her, bandage her, cradle her like a baby, feed her vitamin-rich soups. She had become incomparable.

She said:

It smells... well, it smells... like love.

And he couldn't believe she'd just said that.

Will said: what were you before you knew? What was it: Roll....

Rolcord.

What were you before you knew him? I mean, what did you want to be? What were your ambitions? Did you read books?

I was a teacher. Primary school. I had to give it up. Too often, I'd need time off after he beat me; time to let the bruises die. And I miss my little children.

You've got children?

No, the ones I taught. They're like little birds struggling to get out of the shell, always bewildered with wonderment as learning displaces instinct. This is so sweet, so delicately honeyed.

I could say the same about you.

I don't want to be sweet. Don't want to be a honey.

Sorry.

It's ok.

Finishing their coffee and baklava, they sat in silence for a moment.

Do you have to go back to work?

Yes.

Where do you work?

The White Hart Country Inn. It's near Cherry Hinton.

Oh yes. You said. Cherry Hinton. Do you have a room there?

No. I live in a bedsit in Walpole Road. That's also in Cherry Hinton.

Though she stirred miraculous, original feelings in him, Will knew his motives behind the questioning weren't designed to achieve some sexual positioning: she was too uncomplicated and complex for that. And she knew that he felt that way; that he wasn't predatory.

She said: it's number 32A.

Is there a phone?

817602. I'll have to go. I need to collect my cheeses! Thank you for the coffee and sweet.

Baklava.

Yes. Baklava.

Will had been so involved in the conversation with Tarita that he'd been unaware of the arrival of Rose and the Swede, nor, as he left, did he register her presence as he passed her table.

Chapter 12

Dewey

After work, I went straight round to Will's. I wasn't sure whether I was feeling jealousy, which was not really my thing, or anger, which I had no right to after my earlier session with the raging, priapic Swede.

Will was there and he let me in and I was surprised to find him in an almost contemplative mood by contrast with his usual cunt hunger. And perhaps because of my own subdued mood, I became aware of just how small his room was: bed along left-hand wall as you entered barely eight feet from an incongruous, space-stealing fireplace in the opposite wall, a small table in the corner piled high with books and above the bed a window no more than two feet by four. A gaol cell. Debussy was playing low on a turntable. I knew it was Debussy because he'd played it for me before. The spirit of the moment convinced me of what I'd suspected: that he'd fallen in love with the girl. So I was surprised when he said:

I've had a letter from Dewey. They're letting him out.

Really?

Yes. And he wants to come here. I think he wants to shack up with me. But obviously, he can't. On the other hand, I can't reject him; he's going to need all the support he can get. I can't let him stay here. Not for even one night.

When's he arriving?

Sunday. Sunday evening.

I knew what was coming next, and my first thought was not: he could stay at my place, but how would I know how to deal with this damaged boy, but I'm meeting my Russian! And who knows how that evening will develop? So, before we got onto that, I made a quick side-step and said:

I was in The Green Olive at lunchtime. I saw you.

What were you doing there?

I was about to meet a very famous Russian.

Bubovsky.

You know?

Everybody knows he eats there.

Yes, well. I saw you there with a young woman. You were so distracted by her you didn't see me. Who is she?

Her name is Tarita. She's hiding in Cambridge from an abusing husband. I met her on a bus and took her for a coffee. I felt sorry for her.

Are you seeing her again?

I don't think so.

Bubovsky has asked me to see him again. Insisted. On Sunday. Said he needed someone like me to unburden himself to.

Is that what he said?

Yes.

Not to fuck you.

He's a damaged man. I don't think he's thinking of that. But it means I can't help with your damaged man, Dewey, on Sunday. When he gets here.

But later?

How do I know?

You won't be talking all night?

How do I know?

What will I do?

I wanted to tell Will that he could have my key and that Dewey could let himself in. But how do I know what condition he'd be in? Maybe he will have hit the dope as soon as he's released. But I could see Will was in a real agony of moral wrangling – that Dewey was coming to him because he had no one else, which meant Will was morally bound to help him. And no point asking Sternbend.

Then Will said: can't you leave your key?

I said: that's a big ask, Will. Not only that, but how do I know how things will develop with the enemy of the politburo?

I'll stay with Dewey till you get back!

There was a silence for a moment. Then he said:

Have you lost your feelings for me? Your heart hasn't gone to the Russian's?

Listen, Will, two things motivate me – knowledge and sex. Knowledge first, then, as if it were a dissertation, a reflection on the knowledge: sex. Of course, I haven't lost my feelings for you. I went to the library and studied Chatterton for a morning.

When?

I don't know. A week or so ago. Then I met him somewhere in a world of infinite possibility. He had syphilis, which, I suppose, he didn't want to give to me and which he was about to treat. And he said: We have this rite of passage into adulthood, and the most significant thing about it is acquiring complete knowledge of sex. Sex is our road to freedom. Society deplores sex because of its power to free us. He said he'd betrayed himself and misunderstood this power and caught syphilis. I don't think he's right about that. I think he was just unlucky. That was nearly 200 years ago, and even today, we're afraid of that complete and frank knowledge of sex and too readily settle for innuendo.

And then, as though overlooking my creative century hopping, he said: nice discursion, but I don't think he ever said anything about that. Are you saying that if your Russian indicates that the only way for you to get inside his head is for him to put his slavic cock in you, you'd let him?

Why are you getting nasty? You, above all, should know that the demands of knowledge determine that everything, including morality and ethical codes, is subordinate to it.

So, where does this leave us with the key?

Where it leaves us is, if I give you the key, I may have to go with Vladimir back to his place to discover his interior rather than bring him back to mine.

Where he would discover yours.

Don't be so childish, Will. As I was coming over here, I was asking myself why. Why was I coming to see you? Was I jealous? And I immediately dismissed the thought because I would never allow myself to be compromised by such a base emotion. What you should be primarily concerned with is getting Dewey a bed for the night and then figuring how to deal with him thereafter.

Then he said: I'm sorry, Rose, I'm stressed. And then he put his arms around me and began to kiss me, and I felt him harden: he made sure I felt him harden, and then I thought: hey, ho! Be interesting to know how this works out: what kind of energy will drive him spurred on by his jealousy and his relation to my little essay on knowledge and sex.

You would think, after the tempest that was the Swede, that I'd be looking for calmer waters, but that, frankly, would be a little bourgeois. There are simply things I need to know that marginalise all other considerations. And to encourage enlightenment, I imagined this: that I could see inside my uterus in the instant that he and I both came in order to understand the physical reaction inside me that would then light the path to the deepest psychological insight. But what really knocked me sideward was the bomb going off in that instant, shattering all thought and reason and sending me spinning off into the clouds beyond clouds.

Chapter 13
The Boy Will (In Stockholm)

When Will was sixteen, he left school. He had won a scholarship to attend a prestigious grammar school and hated the authority: the superior, upper-class masters and rich-kid prefects who, with quotidian regularity, would taunt him about his lowly birth. And they had a point: growing up in a house too small for books or any musical instrument—or any music—until, when he was fourteen, his parents splashed out on a new stereogram which took up half the living space in the front room. It came with a recording of Tchaikovsky's *1812*, complete with clarion bells from a monstrous Mormon cathedral and real cannon, and an EP containing excerpts from *Carmen*, *Il Trovatore* (*The Anvil Chorus*), Wagner's *Tannhäuser* Overture, and an aria from Bellini's *Norma*. They squeezed it into the corner, and he would use it whenever they were both out. For them, it was merely a piece of furniture. As for the classical pieces, they became his bluff, convincing his music class of a classical music education he didn't have.

This philistine world he matured in ensured that he had no stomach for study in school, and a feature of that reality was his repeated scrapping with the prefects.

He spent the summer of his eighteenth year waiting tables in Quay West, and later that year, while still seventeen, he hit the road. After a week of travelling north through Europe in late September, he found himself in Stockholm, almost penniless, heading for a club called Radical Wave. He'd been told about it by a kid called Ball down on the coast, who had some connection with people in Boden in the north of Sweden. In the Radical Wave they played the latest hits through the night and would pay you to do the cleaning up the next morning.

He remembered nothing of the night except for occasionally coming round from a dope-happy mist and hearing *Good Vibrations* by The Beach Boys or *Sunshine Superman* by Donovan. In the morning, he did the cleaning and picked up 5 kronor.

It was there that he met Stig Engström. He'd picked up his gear—rucksack and rolled-up sleeping bag—put on his parka and was about to walk off into the cold Stockholm afternoon when Stig said in perfect English:

Where you headed for?

Uppsala. I know someone at the university there.

Not much traffic heading north. And how far do you think you'll get before it's dark?

There was something about Stig that was attractive and, with his long blond hair, something androgynous. And with his own long hair, they looked almost like a pair of girls. It discomforted Will and made his pulse quicken. He guessed Stig was homosexual and that he'd make a pass at some point. Will felt uncomfortable because he wasn't sure how he felt about this. Truth be told, Will had had a lot of thoughts in that direction—particularly one night, just turned seventeen, in his flat on Beda Road in Cardiff, after sharing a spliff with a boy who had simply turned up.

But he liked girls! And he could never do it fully with a bloke on his home turf. But this was Sweden. So he didn't know. If Stig did make a pass and Will didn't want to know, Stig looked like the kind of guy who wouldn't push it. And there was this: that with his long hair, the Swede was actually very attractive—he guessed mid-twenties—and had about him this air of authority. Will knew a moment was coming when he either walked away from the Swede or he stayed, which meant that whatever followed, followed: that he would have no more decisions to make. No question of rejecting the Swede, no matter what he proposed.

Stig went on: You'll find it getting dark about two in the afternoon. About three hours from now. Have you eaten?

I had a piece of that sweet bread....

Kavring. Rye bread.

Yes.

That's not enough for the road. How much money have you got?

About ten kronor.

Phhht. Come with me and I'll buy you breakfast and we can discuss what you'll do.

Will was feeling more at ease. In those days, there were many young travellers on the roads of Europe: from Europe itself – mostly

Western – and from Canada, the States, and Australia and there seemed to be an unwritten code among the young of the countries they travelled in that they all shared a common purpose, as if in celebration of the youth revolution that was taking place.

So Will went for breakfast with Stig—for an open sandwich, which Stig called *smörgås*: cheese and ham and cod roe on crisp rye and, unusually, Will thought, tomatoes and cucumber. And after, a warming sweet coffee. Will ate hungrily.

Over coffee Stig said: I am a photographer. That's my profession. Can I tell you, you have a very beautiful face? How much did you earn in the Radical Wave. For the cleaning?

Five kroner.

How would you like to earn 100 kroner for a couple of hours' work?

Will guessed Stig was making his move. Whatever Will answered now would determine what would happen over the next few hours.

Will hesitated, then said yes.

Good! You'll come with me to my place.

As they walked, Will was surprised to see that he was actually a little taller than Stig—maybe an inch or so. And then he thought: maybe it's a psychological thing – earlier he had felt a little inferior to the Swede. Now he didn't.

On the way to Stig's flat, interestingly, they travelled down Sveavägen. Many years later, as he faced his own demise in 2000, Stig

Engström would weep recalling that February night more than twenty years from now, in 1986, on Sveavägen in Stockholm, when Prime Minister Olof Palme was shot dead.

Stig said: I hope you'll like my pad and feel comfortable there. I am only interested in helping you. Will thought this was a strange thing to say – the Swede *was* helping him.

Will said: I'm feeling a lot happier than I was.

That's good. Do you smoke weed?

Will said enthusiastically: yes!

Good. I've got some mind-blowing stuff. They said it's laced with opium.

Opium!

Don't worry. You won't get addicted.

Stig's apartment was spacious. Benign and welcoming. A large mattress on the floor which was obviously where his host slept. In a corner was Stig's photographic equipment with a tripod. Everywhere were Oriental drapes. And Oriental perfume like a balm.

What music do you like?

Will said: most good stuff. Beatles, Stones, of course.

Beach Boys. Dylan.

O, yeh. Dylan, man. I've got some really cool sounds. Take your stuff off and make yourself at home.

Within a short while they were drawing deeply on the spliff Stig had made, and Will felt as relaxed as he'd ever felt. In fact, he'd never had stuff like this, which gave him such a feeling of being safe and embraced by kindness. He felt good about Stig.

Finishing the joint, they lay back on the mattress.

The album *A Kind of Blue* was playing.

Will spoke out of a scented bubble and said: this music's far out. What is it?

Stig said: it's Miles Davis, man! Ha, ha. Miles Davis. You haven't heard it before! Then they both began to giggle, and it was soon uncontrollable.

As they subsided, Stig said: how old are you?

Nearly 18.

That's cool. Are you a virgin?

Will said: no! And laughed. And they both laughed as if it was the craziest thing anyone had ever asked anyone else.

Stig said: girls?

Ye-e-eh.

No, it's just that in Sweden, boys love girls but also boys. All boys in Sweden are bisexual. Like Lord Byron and Shelley – you know, your poets. Even little Tommy Chatterton. In Sweden, everyone is more relaxed about these things.

Will thought: this is it. But OK.

Will lay looking up at the ceiling, and Stig's face suddenly appeared above him.

Will wasn't exactly new to all this: there'd been that kid in Beda Road.

Stig said: Will, let me kiss you. Just gentle. It will be good for you. Liberating. You will see the world open.

After a pause, Will said: OK.

Now, it's always been my belief that literature about someone who's out of their mind in some way is a waste of time; it's not going anywhere because the character can't develop. In a sense, he can't think - if we assume that useful thought in a literary context needs to be rational: that literature ought to be an account of how characters change as a result of what the story is putting them through.

What's offered here are things the writer can't comment on; they are little more than speculation. So when Will said: ok to the kiss, he was so out of his mind with the opium-laced resin that one could say he said it as a slave to his impulses, not, as philosophers have argued, as a free man if freedom is predicated on clear, rational thought.

Though when the gentle kiss developed into a full-throated, tongue-pounding assault from each, he did remember how he sucked hard on the tongue filling his mouth. But that was followed by a further, bigger joint, which sent Will even further out – too far to rationalise - followed by the call a little later from Stig, which caused

Will, giggling, to make his way to the bathroom where he saw a naked Stig masturbating and only thought that Stig had a great body.

And when he began to turn back and Stig said: wait and saw Stig come into the toilet bowl and began to get hard and when Stig told him to take his clothes off and Will did and Stig said: look, you're hard and Stig was himself, miraculously still hard and giving Will a pill saying this will relax you before kneeling and putting Will's penis into his mouth, manipulating it with his tongue in such a way that made Will soar and come which Stig was happy to swallow—

Nor when they returned to the mattress (though not before Stig sprayed himself and Will with a wildly fragrant deodorant), and Stig explained to the utterly relaxed Will who was unexpectedly aroused and hard again that he wanted to film them having sex and Will feeling too unperturbed to even begin to argue with himself over whether this was a good idea or not, allowed Stig to shave him and giving him an enema so they could "keep things clean" and then giving himself one and then, back on the mattress...

None of this is of any consequence in a literary sense to our understanding of Will as a thinking character in a developing story because Will was responding with all he was left with in this miasma of confused consciousness: his impulse.

And we can only speculate on whether Will, as a consequence of these events, asserted to himself that he was bisexual and enjoyed the sex with Stig as much as he would later with Rose and many other girls. We would have to wait for him to tell us. Or get to see the film.

Before they slept, Stig gave him a jar of cream which he said would soon get rid of any soreness he might feel in the morning.

The next morning, Will got up early while Stig snored loudly, picked up the 100 krone Stig had left on a small coffee table, and, leaving a note which said simply: *Dear Stig, thank you for a most enjoyable and revelatory evening,* left to walk through the city and find the road north and give himself the opportunity to collect his wide-cast thoughts and try to draw a conclusion from what had happened.

The streets of Stockholm, which were still quiet and lamplit, played like a fantasy in his as yet uncollected mind. But as he began to return to the corporeal world, he discovered that he felt a little excited; wicked; free – he'd *done* that! Felt fine, with no soreness he was aware of – that Stig! – and had a pocketful of kronor! And no harm done.

But he did wonder: had the night opened the door to some deep secrets? Or not?

Chapter 14

Parfitt Again

One morning in early summer, a rumour surfaced in one of the smaller colleges and began to make its way across the university community: that Parfitt was a thief. That he'd stolen a dissertation from a quiet second-year genius called Buckland and presented it as his own work. Buckland had shown the paper to one of the Dons who hated the haughty Parfitt.

The allegation against Parfitt centred on this paper that appeared in an issue of *Philosophy*, concerning the Jewish philosopher Hannah Arendt's famous assertion of the *banality of evil* in the case of the Nazi Eichmann, whose trial in Jerusalem she'd reported on for *The New Yorker*. Eichmann had claimed that he had simply followed orders, but more importantly, that he had, at all times, followed Kant's categorical imperative and so was beyond moral reproach.

Trying to understand how a mediocrity like Eichmann could be responsible for such enormous crimes, Arendt reasoned that, in relying on Kant, Eichmann had abandoned the need for his own thinking and had become a non-thinking thing. And, as according to Arendt it's thinking that makes us human (an idea she'd got from her mentor Heidegger), Eichmann had become a non-human. (Ironically, given how the Nazis felt about Jews.) Philosophically, then at least, he couldn't be held responsible for the deaths of those he sent to the camps from his office.

Eichmann had said at his trial that, as a bureaucrat committed to serving the state, he had been unlucky because the state, his state was Hitler, but he was nevertheless bound by duty. In a matter like this, the question was: to whom or what does one owe responsibility for one's actions? Bureaucracy (as immanent!), a philosophical abstract like Kant's categorical imperative (which Wittgenstein would have dismissed as meaningless), or, for a Marxist, the utilitarian concept of maximising happiness which, Buckland argued, for the Marxist would mean, in an ethical state, the proletariat.

And as Eichmann destroyed many among the Jewish proletariat, even if, as Arendt had at one point claimed, he was not an anti-Semite, he was still guilty as hell.

Of course, this kind of stuff would have been right up Parfitt's street, which made the accusation against him all the more plausible.

But all this was neither here nor there, because Parfitt hadn't stolen the paper, nor knew anything about it. Someone else had stolen Buckland's work and submitted it in Parfitt's name.

Or had Buckland himself done it?

Chapter 15
Buckland Himself

(Hail B Traven!)

Very few knew Buckland, though they had heard of him, and not even the Don—too self-important to remember the face of a second-year—could identify him. Buckland was the B. Traven of Cambridge (the man who wrote *The Treasure of the Sierra Madre*, the book made into the great film with Humphrey Bogart). Only Will, for certain, could identify him. Will and Buckland had studied together at the university in L. Buckland had arrived in Cambridge a year before Will, so it was fair to say that for an entire year, he had lived in the shadows. After registering, he vanished. He never attended lectures or seminars, yet would, at intervals, submit these mind-blowing papers on arcane areas of philosophy.

Even Will hadn't seen Buckland since arriving in Cambridge. But he had told Rose about Buckland and his genius for original thought, which clearly had its origins in an astonishing breadth of knowledge. This immediately excited Rose, who then became determined to find Buckland, though the search was on hold while she dealt with Bubovsky.

There was no doubt that the Arendt paper was his. The question was, how had it appeared under Parfitt's name?

Parfitt first became aware of the piece and of his supposed authorship when browsing through the journal sometime after it had been published. He read it with interest and was very impressed with the quality of the writing and the arguments. He didn't immediately contact the editors, though it did occur to him that there might be a connection between the paper and the hostility he'd recently encountered from fellow students in common rooms and elsewhere. Instead, he decided to speak with Goldstein, the millionaire Jew.

Parfitt explained the situation over glasses of deep red wine, and the millionaire said:

Write a response explaining that you didn't write the original piece and that someone was being scurrilous. Say that had you written it, you would have included a reference to the fact that when Arendt was hired by *The New Yorker*, it was to write a report, not a philosophical essay. Her purely cerebral approach to the trial overlooked the emotional weight of it. It was all emotion. Everyone knew what he'd done the only question was whether to execute him or lock him up for life. Arendt's arguments were an insult to the temple of sorrows the Holocaust had built. And her talk about the collaboration of leading Jews with the Nazis was for another time.

Parfitt told him about his own thoughts and analysis, including the Marxist interpretation that had appeared in Buckland's overarching work. Goldstein farted into his velvet cushion, yelled Mazel tov! drained his glass, and threw it into the faux fireplace where it shattered inviting Parfitt to do the same. Parfitt did then Goldstein called out to Carla:

Can you bring us glasses, *ahuvi?* (My love). Then to Parfitt: You must find this Buckland. Perhaps he stole his ideas from you! Ha, ha!

Chapter 16
Return To The Green Olive

(Hail Greene!)

Bubovsky was there in his usual seat, waiting for her. There was something almost feverish in his anticipation, his eyes a little deliquescent, a predisposition encouraged by years spent staring at the forlorn bars of a lunatic asylum from his immuring bed. Tiny beads of sweat clung to his nose and upper lip.

As I walked into the restaurant, he was the first person I saw. Somehow majestic at the back, he seemed to tower above all the other patrons, though he wasn't a big man at all. His face, with its strangely attractive, slightly overhanging upper lip, broadcast a benign welcome.

As I sat down, I said, am I late?

No, you are not late. How could you be late? Perhaps you are even early.

I'm trying to give you a flavour of what his speech was like in the 'structure': In English. You'll have to imagine those rolling Russian r's and the particular fricative 'sounds': And the don't use articles.

I said: hmmm. That's intriguing.

For years, time was silent for me. But perhaps things would always be late. I became unaware of time. Good things, I would think, would be early. Only once was a thing early – when they came to tell me I would be free. Except, I was not free until much later.

We both laughed. Politely.

Let me get you drink.

I looked at his glass.

Is that ouzo?

Yes.

I'll have one of those.

And what will you eat? Do you eat meat?

O yes. I'm afraid I'm a ruthless meat eater.

He laughed: ha, ha! Ruthless. Yes, this is good. So, shall we have the lamb kleftiko. It is like stew, with much garlic and olive oil, and perhaps, I think, paprika.

Alright. Yes, please.

He called the waitress over and ordered.

Then he said:

Can I ask how old you are? I know it is impolite, so please, don't answer if it is too scurrilous.

Scurrilous? Ooo!

It is wrong?

No. What could be wrong? I'm 19.

Yes, I knew. Do you know the work *Crime and Punishment*, by my great hero Dostoevsky?

Yes. I set myself the task of reading all his books when I was 17.

And you know the sorrowful Sonya who Raskolnikov falls for? She too is nineteen and, like you, like a bird. Perhaps frail. For him, she is all humanity suffering. You are her.

Wasn't she a prostitute?

But she was forced into it, to feed her family because her father is a drunk. Which ennobled her. But I wasn't thinking of that. I was thinking of simple, pure, sorrowful joy of Raskolnikov – saint who had killed – and Sonya. What they shared in a time when all the world seemed hopeless.

Does the world seem hopeless to you? Now.

No. That is point. They transcended pain. And you cause me transcending.

The drinks arrived. He knocked back the one he already had, and I quickly attacked mine. I needed the unspringing.

That's good, I said. I'm glad.

I'll get you another drink.

Thank you.

I have been in Cambridge for perhaps three, four years: this beautiful city, where the physical hardness of world becomes a cerebral glow. But this is first time I have felt like dancing.

I remembered something you said when I first met you: that because of your years of incarceration, intimacy had become an abstraction.

O yes. You have already begun to warm that corpse!

We laughed and the food came. And it smelled divine: the garlic, oregano, the lemon.

As I prepared to eat, Vladimir said, quite craftily I thought: when we have eaten, I would like to show you my apartment. I let myself hesitate for a moment, then said: of course. What else?

Chapter 17
Dewey arrives

(Hail Pinter!)

At five-thirty, on the same day as Rose's soirée with Bubovsky, the Sunday, Dewey had knocked on Will's door. Will had been expecting him at around three and had hoped he would arrive before the Sternbends returned from their Sunday afternoon jaunt. He was dismayed when he heard them come in shortly after four, their voices breaking through the silence of the house.

When he finally heard Dewey's knock, he flew down the stairs, almost flooring old Mr Sternbend, who was crossing the hall towards the door.

Sorry, Mr Sternbend, I believe it's a colleague of mine. He's very shy, and if anyone but me were to open the door, I think he would run away.

O, alright Mr Slade, I understand. As a young man, I was chronically shy even in my years as a librarian. But in that occupation, one could exploit the silence and remain shadowy. Of course, now, in retirement, I only need to present myself to my wife. And, of course, the occasional student who will always, I believe, because of their breeding, be sensitive to my frailty.

Dewey knocked again, and Will worried he might leave. Fortunately, Sternbend retreated. As Will turned the Yale lock, he was suddenly anxious. What would the open door reveal? It was one thing seeing Dewey in Broadmoor quite another to have someone who'd been in Broadmoor standing on his doorstep.

He opened the door on a clean-shaven but wet-faced Dewey. His friend had clearly been crying. Will was relieved that Sternbend hadn't seen him or he might have baulked at letting him in.

Dewey saw Will's surprise and said, with sweet, sad innocence

I've been crying for joy!

As they climbed the stairs, Will said: how did you get here?

I hitched.

From the gates of Broadmoor?

Dewey gave a little laugh, no, I walked to Frimley

When you wrote, I imagined you were going to use public transport. Now I understand why you're two hours later than you said. Here's my room. I imagine the first thing you'll see is how small it is

Will looked at Dewey's suddenly ragged face and said: what is it.

It's too small

Listen, Dewey, you wouldn't be able to stay anyway. But it's OK. Do you remember Rose, who came with me when we visited? She's got a place across town. It's much bigger. She said you can stay there until you're settled. I'll take you there.

Why aren't you living with her?

I don't know. It just worked out this way. I'd already rented this room before I came to Cambridge.

How far is it? Is it far to Rose's place

No, it's over by Jesus Green.

I like that. Do we go anywhere near King's Chapel?

Could do. Why?

I really want to see it. I got a book from Broadmoor library about Cambridge and decided I really want to see King's Chapel.

Ok, let's go, then.

Out on the street, Will said: you seem different.

Like I've seen the light?

Well. Then he paused.

Have you?

Dewey said: You remember when we were kids, how we cried together?

Did we?

Yes! I think we'd found my cat that was all ripped up by that Captain Ingram's Alsatian. I never got it at the time. You crying for my cat. Now I think I do.

Will said: I don't think of you as ever being a crier.

When I was a kid, I was spoiled, so the sensitive side in me was hardly ever came out. Until, for example, my cat. When I discovered hash, the real me ascended.

That's true.

Then I discovered all the other narcotics and fucked up.

So are you clean of all that now?

I think so. When I was in Broadmoor, one of the nurses gave me a book called *The Little Book of Inner Peace*. It's the Dalai Lama on Buddhism. I think I'd like to be a Buddhist. He said that the mental poisons like hatred and ignorance are not inherent, because they're distinct from primordial consciousness, and we can simply eradicate them. Through this action we can find enlightenment, because we've proved we understand the true nature of the mind.

Will said: I don't get it. How is hatred distinct from primordial consciousness?

Well, because if it wasn't then our hatreds would dissolve when our consciousness dissolves. But they don't. Get our consciousness back, and hatred's still there unless we eradicate it. In other words, that old lazy excuse for all the negative stuff we do, that it's human nature, is manure. If I thought it would help, I'd kick the hatred out of every shitty bastard and bring them to enlightenment that way!

Will laughed heartily.

They came to the great perpendicular structure – perhaps one of the finest examples of that architectural style anywhere – and entered to the ecstatic sound of a practising choir. Henry VI was a poet and aesthete who lost France, but thanks to him, England gained King's and Eton College, which was intended for the poor. Later, the aristocracy gained Eton and King's; later still, the gauche, reviled nouveau riche gained Eton and King's and Britain gained generations of sub-intellectual Prime Ministers and high office disorderlies.

The choir was rehearsing Tallis's *Suscipe quaeso Domine*. The notes, like soaring medieval tears, at first confused Dewey: did he belong sufficiently to the great human soul from which such beauty was born; the eternal aesthetic which can never die, though every last idea of reason die infinitely? Or was the idea of ultimate immanence it suggested blind to matters of qualification?

At first there was six-foot Dewey, grass-eater, built of horse muscle, an imponderable strength, anachronistic knight, one of Becket's slayers before jumping the centuries into the arms of the hippy dharma and lap of the Buddha.

Chapter 18

At Bubovsky's

(Hail Richard Ford!)

By the time we left The Green Olive, I had legs like palm fronds and was carried on the Russian's breath to Parker's Piece. His flat was somewhere nearby, just off Gonville Place. The streetlights sparkled as he tickled me with his light, tripping talk, and in a dark place on the grassy park he laid down his overcoat and invited me to lie on it, which I did. Then he got down too and removed my knickers. I was wearing a dress and, though it was late autumn, I didn't feel the cold.

He put his head between my legs and, like a man who hadn't eaten for days, devoured my yielding pussy. With his tongue showed the strength and determination of a burrowing prairie dog, driving me wild. His mouth was warm beneath the late November sky.

When I came, he drank me , then raised his head and said, like a resurrected kingly boyar, aperitif! Come!

Afterwards, at his place, he made love as if on behalf of every sorrowful dissident who had ever dreamt of that vital human contact they were denied. It sobered me up. I asked him a question that, I think, angered him.

I said: I've been reading about you, and how you were released in exchange for an imprisoned Chilean communist leader. I was wondering: how did you feel about this man? You'd both been imprisoned for your beliefs. Do you think your differing ideologies made you different, even though your circumstances were the same?

He suddenly seemed embarrassed. Sitting up at the edge of the bed, he pulled at the blanket I was lying on. I lifted myself so that he could release it and wrap it around himself.

He said, a little impatiently, I thought:

That man was wedded to ideology that jailed me. He would have jailed me. I would never have jailed him.

Are you annoyed?

I became a little concerned, but also a little angry, when he said intemperately:

We came for love! I do not want to justify my life!

I'm sorry, but for me I can't just experience the body. That would be like being insulted by an artwork that had no depth. I need to understand

No, I am sorry. But there is not much to understand: I believe in freedom!

I put my arms around him and said:

O but I think there's so much more to you than that.

What is more than freedom? He said it with a smile that half cracked my resolve.

I flopped back onto the bed: ok, but I don't know what freedom is.

He turned to me, his face bearing down on mine.

He said: freedom is knowledge of who we are: oneself, within oneself. Utterly and completely. Knowing why we do what we do. Utterly and completely. Freedom is deepest understanding of our motives. Isn't it clear? Once we are told by state or anyone else what to do, we are no longer free, because we have no authority over our motives. You can only be responsible for own actions, for own morality. Once state takes on responsibility for morality, there is no freedom. And you are only free when you respect everyone's freedom.

Was I confused? This was my goal, wasn't it? To know utterly and profoundly who I am, so that I am strong and fully knowledgeable in everything I do.

I said: that's me!

Then he sat astride me and let the blanket fall, his body excited again.

I said: do you think that greed is, or can be, an emotion?

Chapter 19

Deeper into Parfitt's Mystery

(Hail Maugham!)

Parfitt set out to find Buckland.

He had seen posters advertising an ecumenical meeting of all the colleges' second-year philosophy students, to be held at The Eagle pub on Ben'et Street. A symposium, he supposed. He would go along but watch from the sidelines. He would look out for Buckland and hope to identify him somehow. Of course, he was sure Will would be able to identify him, but part of Parfitt was curious about the meeting anyway.

Rose came to him at the bar and he ordered a beer.

He said: the philosophy meeting?

She said: through there – the RAF bar and indicated the room with its own bar.

Parfitt went through, paid for his pint, and watched as the students arrived, bought drinks, and took their seats at tables that had been arranged to suit a meeting of this kind. After about ten minutes it was clear that most of the attendees had already arrived, including Farquhar-Groyne (the don to whom Buckland had shown his paper) and Sten. They all seemed to be waiting for someone else – a speaker, perhaps.

Then Parfitt noticed a sheet of paper pinned to the wooden wall near the bar. He stepped closer to read it:

Freedom and the Individual

Vladimir Bubovsky

Parfitt immediately thought: *Right-wing poppycock* and returned to the bar. He was taking a drink when Bubovsky arrived. The Russian barely exchanged glances with Rose, who had come to work the bar, and she didn't appear keen to acknowledge him either. Yet, when he entered the room, a cheer went up. Rose felt curiously proprietorial. Curious, because they had parted on that Sunday in psychological disarray: in cerebral and corporeal pain.

After a brief introduction from an undergraduate, delivered from behind the chair that had been placed for him, Bubovsky remained standing and began:

Throughout childhood and most of youth, I, like all citizens of Soviet Union, did what Soviet authority told us to do. This as part of collective, but also as individual. An action of which the agent does not know why he performs it cannot be free

This opening made Parfitt bristle.

If collective cannot offer freedom, then individual, through introspective observation, must become conscious of his or her motives for acting. The sole possibility of human freedom must be sought in awareness of motives of our actions. As individuals! Consciousness is thinking. Thinking in service of knowledge. But we

97

must, as individuals, know we are thinking. We cannot think unless we know we are thinking. And we can only know we are thinking if we are free to think. In collective, we are not free to think. Thinking is unobserved element in our ordinary mental and spiritual life. Politburo forbids thought!

Parfitt suddenly felt compelled to speak.

Are you saying the Soviet citizen can't think? Are they cattle?!

Gasps of impatience rose from the room.

Bubovsky replied, no, they are not but they are a new 20th-century species, bred to be ignorant of their individual power.

And you think the Soviet citizen may not want to embrace the collective?

Some may be fooled into thinking they want to!

Parfitt: Rubbish! Man is born free, yet everywhere he is in chains! Man can only be free in society by giving up freedoms!

Now the call went up: who is that?

What's this Rousseaunian claptrap?

Bubovsky replied angrily: I know Russian soul! You do not!

Soul! Where will you find that – next to the kidneys?!

Someone shouted, Shut up!

Someone else (probably Farquhar-Groyne):

That's Parfitt. The plagiarist! Parfitt, who stole the work of the genius Buckland!

Parfitt shouted back angrily, as in all things, you are ignorant of the facts! I didn't write that piece and have never claimed to. It was submitted without my knowledge.

Liar! Let's ask Buckland. Is he here? Who is he?

No one knows! He's a mystery.

At this point, Will, Dewey, and the young woman Tarita came into the pub.

During the commotion, Rose managed to say to Parfitt: Excuse me, aren't you Parfitt, Will Slade's friend?

Parfitt said yes, then to the student audience: "You don't even know if Buckland exists!

Rose: Please, you'll have to stop this shouting; you're disturbing the other customers.

Then Will came to the bar. Hi Rose. Hi Parfitt.

Parfitt said: Slade.

From the assembled students, a quiet voice asked, Can I speak, please?

Who is it? Stand up!

Then Bubovsky said: I would like to continue.

Parfitt shouted,: haven't you said enough?

Two large students – rugby players, no doubt – approached Parfitt and began to manhandle him. Will moved to defend him but was pushed away. Dewey arrived in the middle of the melee and looked ready to take a swing, but Quaid Laurel held him back by the arm.

Bubovsky tried to regain control.

Please! Please, gentlemen!

And Rose, suddenly shouted in support of the Russian:

Quiet or you'll have to leave!

The room fell silent. The two rugby players backed off.

Bubovsky said: Please, let us hear the gentleman.

The quiet, mild-mannered man stood and said:

I suppose it's a point of order. When is plagiarism plagiarism? For example, our distinguished speaker has just plagiarised the German philosopher Rudolf Steiner.

Several voices:

What?! Who's Steiner

You're insulting a man who's suffered! And: whose talking about plagiarism?

The mild young man answered: Steiner was a German philosopher who specialised in the analysis of freedom. His thoughts on thinking anticipated Heidegger!

Bubovsky intervened:

May I continue?

Parfitt, without shouting, pointed at Bubovsky and said, this is the real plagiarist in the room!

The mild-mannered young man said: I just want to say, in your defence, Mr Bubovsky – and in defence of every thinker who ever borrowed an idea, doesn't the re-interpretation of the same idea preclude it from charges of plagiarism!

Will said to Parfitt, that sounds like Neil!

Parfitt said: who?

Buckland!

Bubovsky continued:

Thinking must never be regarded as merely subjective activity. Thinking lies beyond subject and object. It produces these two concepts just as it produces all others. When, therefore, I, as thinking subject, refer concept to object, we must not regard this reference as something purely subjective. It is not subject that makes the reference but thinking. Subject does not think because it is subject; rather, it appears to itself as subject because it can think. The activity exercised by thinking beings is thus not merely subjective. Rather, is something neither subjective nor objective that transcends both these concepts. I ought never to say that my individual subject thinks, but much more that my individual subject lives by grace of thinking.

Someone called out:

What does this mean?

Another: you've lost me now!

The mild-mannered young man suddenly shouted excitedly, that is plagiarism! That's a direct quote from Steiner without citation!

Someone: what?

Someone else: who are you?

Then Farquhar-Groyne shouted:

That's Buckland!

Will shouted towards the mild young man: Neil!

Neil looked at him and waved demurely.

He's a fraud! someone yelled, referring to Bubovsky.

Another: shut up!

Bubovsky tried to continue, raising his voice to be heard above the growing noise:

But freedom is not defined by being subjective! You must be free to think, and to think is to be objective. Soviet citizen cannot be objective because state controls objectivity!

Someone got up and moved aggressively towards Bubovsky, shouting:

Throw him out!

Another cried:

Fifth columnist!

One of the rugby players stepped in to protect Bubovsky just as Parfitt shouted: Buckland!

A voice called out:

Where?

Parfitt pointed at Neil.

That's Buckland.

Farquhar-Groyne echoed:

That's him! That's Buckland. And that's Parfitt!

Suddenly, uproar as the fifth columnist landed a firm blow on the rugby player's chin. A couple of students pulled Bubovsky away from the anarchy and led him out the back way while Will and Dewey went to Buckland, who was attracting the wrong kind of attention, and guided him to the bar.

Farquhar-Groyne slipped out with the group around Bubovsky.

Outside, Farquhar-Groyne pulled Bubovsky to one side.

I'm Farquhar-Groyne, a Don at Jesus. I need to speak with you.

Not now, please. I am feeling ill.

Another time?

In The Green Olive, any lunchtime, Bubovsky muttered, and pulled away.

Back inside, Rose and Quaid Laurel had cleared the room. When everyone had gathered themselves, Will said to Buckland, you stirred the hornets' nest there, Neil. He now noticed that Buckland was standing beside Parfitt.

Have you two met yet? Parfitt responded to Will but directed his words to Buckland. No, but I do have a lot I'd like to talk about. He held out his hand.

Buckland shook it. I'm sorry about the confusion over my Hannah Arendt piece.

Parfitt said: yes, absolutely. Perhaps we can meet at some point. He took out his wallet, extracted a card, and handed it to Buckland. Here's my card. There's a telephone number there.

Thank you.

Sten slipped out unnoticed.

Rose, clearly keen to be introduced to Buckland, gave Will a look. Will obliged.

Rose: this is Neil Buckland. I've told you about him.

Hello, Neil.

Hello.

Will said: we studied together at L. Neil got a first and came to Cambridge. I went to Cardiff for a year to do an MA.

Rose studied Buckland. He was young, perhaps only a year older than she was about five foot six, almost thin, with black hair combed to one side and parted on the left. His face was pale, and his eyes hung tiredly beneath self-effacing lids.

Quaid was now firmly attached to the group. Rose said to Will and the others:

This is Quaid Laurel. He works here – bar manager. He's studying for a PhD. Then, turning specifically to Will, and indicating Tarita, she asked, who's this?

Oh, I'm sorry, this is Tarita.

Parfitt said to Quaid, what's your research?

Graphene.

I'm sorry?

Graphene.

O, right.

Rose said: hello, Tarita. Are you a student?

Will said: no. She's a civvy! So, Neil – what made you put your head above the barricade?

Neil said, glancing at Dewey: Slade, you haven't introduced your friend here.

Sorry again. This is Dewey. Dewey Ronson.

Pleased to meet you, Mr Ronson. Thanks for helping during that fracas.

It's alright. I'm a bandit.

Rose laughed:

Oh yes! That's true!

Parfitt said: Buckland. My friend: the article. Some are saying you submitted it yourself and used my name. But why would you do that?

I didn't. I showed it to a don – Piers Farquhar-Groyne.

Parfitt: Farquhar-Groyne! That toerag! Your paper on Hannah Arendt's assertion of the banality of evil, is not something I've much interest in. Certainly not something I would've written a paper on! Isn't Farquhar-Groyne at Jesus?

Yes.

Do you think he submitted it?

Probably.

Then I must confront him!

Rose said to Will: I'm finishing now. Why don't you all come back to my place?

Buckland said: I'm sorry, I can't. In fact, I need to go. Goodbye. And then he left.

Will said, Okay. I'll bring Tarita.

Quaid Laurel said: am I included?

Rose gave Will a sly look and said, of course.

Laurel said:

Do you mind if we go by my place. I want to pick up my guitar. It's across the river.

Rose smiled.

That'd be great. The others agreed.

Parfitt said, thank you very much for the invitation, but I'm afraid I'm a little too preoccupied with Farquhar-Groyne to be at all sociable. Then, turning to Will: Will, we must meet. Snooker, perhaps?

Fine.

And then left.

Chapter 20

Journey To The End Of Night

(Hail Celine!)

On his way from The Eagle, Buckland had to cross the Cam on Silver Street. Having met Parfitt, he found oddly that he couldn't get him out of his head. Much as he'd felt about Farquhar-Groyne when he'd first seen him: the six-foot blonde who could have passed for a young Michael Heseltine, had they been young together.

And then, of course, he'd taken him his paper to read.

Like the politician's Farquhar-Groyne's hair was swept back in two luxuriant waves on either side of a mid-skull parting, that screamed self-confidence and the joy of self-indulgence. When Buckland had first arrived at Jesus College, one of the earliest impressions he registered was of Farquhar-Groyne striding across the quad. Buckland knew instantly that he would need to make himself known to the gymnasial Spartan. Upon learning that Farquhar-Groyne was an old Etonian, the feeling only solidified.

As he made his way home from the symposium, Buckland walked slowly, sometimes sitting on a low wall, especially when the Arendt paper came to mind. The connection with Farquhar-Groyne disturbed him. He had heard rumours: that Farquhar-Groyne had a following among rough local youths – known admiringly as Farquhar's Fearless and, to detractors, as Farquhar's fuckers. They were reputedly anti-

Semitic, something Buckland doubted Farquhar-Groyne would admit to openly. Still, it helped explain the theft of his paper – how the don had taken it, submitted it under Parfitt's name, then quietly spread word that it was Buckland's work and that Parfitt had plagiarised it.

It was a strangely balmy evening on the cusp of winter, the avenues of well-off Cambridge seemed scented by the late evening arboreal life singing: a murmuring and the air like the soft lifted and lowered fan of a lover in a warm night. His mood grew almost complacent. He took pleasure in the shameless opulence of some of the houses with their cared-for complex architecture that seemed only to want to be left alone and so, posed no threat to him.

Eventually, he came to rest on the bridge over the Cam and was leaning over the cast-iron railings looking into the bleak swell beneath lit by the street lighting on the bridge.

This river!

He recalled reading about Paris on the night of 17 October 1961 – an episode he'd stumbled upon during one of his many forays into French history, a subject that had always fascinated him.

In his mind's eye, he was looking now into the Seine and seeing in the half dark moving slowly with the river a construct that seems at first like the product of some daring *avant garde* artist – a dreamer's scow made of cotton and corduroy, wool and worsted and in the diminishing light struts and ribs of pale Parisian plaster. And he recalled learning about how downstream the next day and for many days, bodies that were the material of the extraordinary barge began washing up on innocent beaches: the *numbreux Algeriens* who had marched peacefully past the 8.30 curfew against all Muslims imposed by the police chief Maurice Papon a man profoundly deaf to the streets and the post-war sweep of nations across Europe, a man who from the dark back yards of Parisian cafes had murdered the War's French Jews with the stroke of a nib. It was difficult to reconcile Paris with a place of night and bleak violence. But for that time, Paris was Papon. Papon the killer.

His thoughts were interrupted by a burnt voice which said:

It's not a fucking wishing well, but I bet you wish – get it, *wish?* – it was.

Buckland turned his head and was met by the terrifying face of a young man with a broken nose and several scars – an ugly and terrifying face and around him three other faces, one of which said: he's a Commie!

Broken nose said: are you? He's a student, you can tell. Smells like shit. Students never clean their shit up. Isn't that right? Undo your trousers.

B-but...

Don't fuckin but me!

Broken nose thumped him in the stomach and Buckland let out a terrifying squeal.

Listen to that! He squeals like a pig! Turn him round – let's get his trousers off!

They turned Buckland around and began to pull his trousers down. Just then, a head came from beyond the circle of friends and crashed into the scarman smashing his already damaged nose into a hissing pulp. And almost immediately the injured man was hoisted and hurled into the river.

The attacker – his rage not yet spent – swung at the other three, who were already running and shouted: better fish your friend out before his whimpering drowns him!

The man turned to Buckland, and Buckland saw that it was Dewey Ronson.

Chapter 21

Tarita At Rose's

(Hail Virginia Wolf!)

At my place, after the riot in The Eagle and the incident on the bridge which the few of us left had been unable to think clearly about, we smoked some dope and listened to Neil Young.

It was late. Quaid hadn't come after all; he said he needed to rest and get the shock of what happened on the bridge out of his system. Will and Dewey had crashed, so it was just me and the pretty Tarita. Pretty, notwithstanding the scar from some injury she'd sustained. In fact, if anything, the scar enhanced her beauty.

We were sitting on my sofa. I looked at her profile – the unsullied side: Natashia Philipovna as I would imagine her in Dostoevsky's *The Idiot*.

She looked back at me. Her eyes yearned for peace.

She said: Will is beautiful. Do you love him? Are you... you know.

I said: we're friends who sometimes sleep together. I've got a bottle of rosé. Would you like some?

Okay.

I went to the cupboard above the sink. This large room served as kitchen, dining room, lounge, living room, and drawing room all in one. Off it were my bedroom, a smaller room, and a toilet with a shower.

I took the bottle from the cupboard and pulled the cork with an almost acrobatic lack of dexterity which caused Tarita to smile and say: you're very strong.

I poured two glasses of the Mateus.

Returning to the sofa, I handed her one, sat down again and said: here and we drank. Then I said: do you love him? We both quickly emptied our glasses.

Well, we haven't made love, but I love that he cares.

Will is one of those rare men who never chases sex. He doesn't need to. Sooner or later, it'll come to him. Though it doesn't always work out the way he might've expected.

I understand that.

Listen, if you want to sleep with him, I won't mind.

She didn't reply.

I'm sure that was inappropriate. Who am I to give permission?

We sipped.

Will's told me you've had a bad time. Your husband?

Yes.

He's in prison?

Yes. He tried to kill me.

God, that's terrible.

They're releasing him soon.

Are you worried about that? Worried that he might come looking for you?

But why would he come to Cambridge?

O, no. I didn't mean that. It's probably the last place he'd think of. Did you know he was violent before you married him?

I didn't think he was. No more than any other man.

I went to get the bottle from the draining board and returned to refill our glasses.

I said: what happened? Why did he start abusing you?

She was silent for a moment, then took a drink. Then said:

It was after I had the coil fitted. The fitting really hurt and I couldn't let him do it for a few days. That made him very angry. He said I was putting it on because I didn't want him. So I let him do it but I suppose they hadn't fitted it correctly and there were wires coming out of the coil that shouldn't have been there and they cut him. And cut me too when he did it.

Cut his... cock?

Yes.

O God!

That drove him crazy, so he hit me. Then he decided that because, as far as he was concerned, we could never make love again, he'd hit me instead. He began to drink more and hit me more. He'd have other women, which made him even madder. I didn't understand any of it. There were times when he was really nice, promising he'd never hit me again. I had the coil removed and would wait for him to come home those nights he went out and try and be seductive. But then he accused me of taking it out so that I could have other men. Then he started controlling everything. I wasn't allowed out; had no money; lost all my friends and when he was being nice, he'd say that his control over my life was for my own good. But then my helplessness and weakness made him even madder. And he hit me more. And more. Until he tried to kill me.

Maybe it was the Neil Young song Natural Beauty, but her natural beauty suddenly shone above the almost imperceptible bubbles of the wine and I wanted to kiss her. Her heart-shaped, sad mouth moved me. I wanted to lift her. Unburden herself to my uncoded care. Just to say: we are connected beyond pain, like flesh on loving flesh.

I said: I would like to touch your lips with my lips.

Kiss?

No. Just the touch of my mouth on yours and the whisper of your escaping breath on mine."

She looked at me unflinchingly with apprehension, and with wonder.

I said: it's alright. Whatever you want.

Chapter 22

Porth Meur

(Hail Malcolm Lowry!)

Sometime in late autumn, I phoned my mum.

She was almost beside herself with, I suppose you could say, outrage. For me, parents are what you have when you're a kid: to feed you and protect you and give you a grounding in how to live your life. But given the kind of life I'd chosen for myself – this quest into the relationship of sex with meaning, I just couldn't bear the weight of their ethic crushing me by having too much contact with them. They were Plymouth Brethren, and that's really heavy shit.

She said: do you know how long it is since you've been in touch? Months! I tried to reach you in L. and managed to speak to Sandra, but she didn't know where you were – you weren't there! Where are you? Are you putting on weight? Your father's dying!

What's wrong with him?

Prostate cancer. It's metastasised.

What's that?

It's spread.

Shit.

Rose!

Sorry.

Sandra said you went off with some chap.

Yes. Will. Will Slade.

So where are you?

Cambridge.

Cambridge?!

He's doing postgraduate work there.

O. Well, I suppose that's something. So. Will you come home? Your father misses you. He needs you.

I could hear tears in her voice. And then I felt myself welling up. Poor Dad.

Of course. Can I bring Will?

Are you sleeping together?

I don't live with him.

You know you couldn't sleep with him here. It would hurt your father.

Is he there?

No.

Where is he?

In a hospice.

I'll come tomorrow.

Dad sold cars at a small garage in St Austell. In fact, they got mixed up with the brethren after Dad sold a car to a pastor, which is what he called himself though there is no actual ordination of the pastor in that church because they believe that everyone's a pastor. Belonging to the priesthood of all believers. Maybe it was that quirk that got them. I would have nothing to do with it which is where the real difficulties between us began.

We were lower middle class, though I always thought of myself as working class. Dad was a worker, and so was my mum – she delivered the post on a bicycle. They'd inherited their house from my father's mother, who was married for a second time to Frank Worrel who had a petrol station. It was probably that connection that got Dad into selling cars. My father's father had died of cancer in his thirties – you'd think that might have been a warning. Dad who was himself pretty young – in his forties. And even his mother, who my mum didn't like, died of cancer. She died and left the house to a woman – my mother – who I didn't think would ever be grateful.

Whenever I started to get sentimental about her, my mother, I would think of that meanness and sidestep those self-conscious emotions. My feelings of antipathy towards her had matured, I'm now sorry to say. After I left school at seventeen and her saying: what *do you think you're going to do, loaf around here all day*, she'd got me a job at a local clothing factory, working eight hours a day at a sewing machine for not much more than pin money. I fled after a couple of months to L. in Wales with Roger, who was going to study there who was too scared of sex holes to want to do anything but study.

Porth Meur is the Cornish name for Charlestown, where I grew up and where my parents still live. The Cornish language is mostly dormant. Governments don't want to promote it because they're afraid the Cornish will get ahead of themselves. My feeling is this: if the Cornish used only their own language during seduction, foreplay, and fucking, it would soon become vibrant and before long, you'd have the independent nation of Kernow. *Fucking for Kernow!*

And here's a thing: it seems that if a man has at least a couple of orgasms a week, he can reduce his risk of developing prostate cancer. Even if it means masturbating because the wife is non-compliant for whatever screwed up brethrenic reason. But you can be sure that, to those low church crazies, masturbation itself would be out of bounds. The evils of the righteous!

These were the sorts of things I was thinking in quiet moments on the journey down. And I was thinking about the first time I had sex with a boy. It was the night the circus came to St Austell.

Oh, that circus night; the hurdy-gurdy smell inside the hot dog halo, and the aromas of what may come tonight! His name was Joseph Perkins, known as Dolphin Joe, because he was reputed to have ridden a dolphin one time on a holiday in Cardigan Bay in Wales. I met him on the harbour wall in Charlestown. I was fifteen. He was older. And I looked and acted older. He'd just moved into the village. We flirted and I saw him a couple of times, and then he told me the circus was coming to St Austell.

I didn't know, of course, that we'd sneak out during the trapeze act and slip around the back of the marquee, and that he would, with astonishing speed, almost without me being able to take in what was happening, do it. It was like needing an operation which you would ordinarily fret about to the point of sickness, only for it to be decided, suddenly, that your case was urgent and you'd be taken straight in – before you could deliver yourself of those obscene terrors.

But that wasn't my first experience with sex. That was with a girl called Angie. I was fourteen, she was a bit older, maybe sixteen. She was quite skinny like I was then with small tits like me. But I liked that. Her hair was cut to shoulder length and bounced in blond waves. A beautiful full mouth with lips that seemed inflamed and maybe were when she kissed me. And her eyes! One had the slightest cast which made them seem challenging and testing and even a little sorrowful. And unbearably attractive! I can remember how I shook with anticipation.

At first we only kissed and felt each other's bud-like breasts. I went further alone in my bed on the first night, feeling my wettening self.

And then, in Hammet's hay loft we stripped and laying on our sides enjoyed our first *soixante neuf*! I knew how she would taste: sweet like musky pineapple. And with Sappho's crowns of violets and roses. That was the thing: I found out about Sappho because of Angie and my knowledge of poetry was expanded because I'd had sex with her. We decided we would pull the vaginal lips of the other apart and look for each other's hymen. Looking in there into that sweet architecture was as empowering as embracing the secrets of Christendom's holiest place.

And Sappho said:

May I write words more naked than flesh.

What I learned from this experience was never let gender get in the way of sexual exploration; gender plays no part in sex. Sex is about the physical world; gender the metaphysical. That the other body either engenders a sense of warmth and security and beauty or it doesn't. I never enjoyed sex that was not embraced by love irrespective of gender.

After having sex with Dolphin Joe, which happened because my evenings with Angie had emboldened me, I wanted boys. What had worried me was being penetrated which was different from being fingered by Sappho. But I needn't have worried because after Dolphin Joe, what I wanted was cocks. Boys with big cocks. My feelings for girls remained a fall-back, an option for the hard times.

I turned up on their doorstep with Will leaving Dewey alone in my flat back in Cambridge. I knew I could trust him. It was there in the eyes; but not superficially as in an aesthetically pleasing but random positioning of eye parts, but deeper from behind the iris, a light of truth as though reflected like that from the tapetums of some animals.

I'd first seen it on the night I returned to my flat after spending the evening with Bubovsky. I was still a bit shell shocked. After our conversation about freedom which I told you about and me asking him if he thought greed could be an emotion, I was expecting us to do it again: he was so poised. Instead, his face suddenly contorted, he slapped me across mine and screamed: You are whore! Grushenka! Overweight like whore! Brute beast not Sonya! You want to empty me of virtue! Greedy for my pain. Want to dine on the terror of my isolation! He even had his hands around my throat and I thought he would strangle me, but I heaved and pushed him off and he collapsed to the floor weeping terribly. I left as quickly as I could.

By the time I'd got back to my flat, Will, who'd been with Dewey, had gone to an urgent meeting (with Tarita I guessed) and so Dewey was alone. I suppose he could see I'd had a rough time and straightaway said: Are you alright? I said I was and he asked if I wanted to talk about it. I said: I don't think so, do you want a drink? I've got a bottle of cheap French white – supermarket stuff. He said: no thanks. If it's ok with you I'd like to get my head down. That was when he looked at me and I saw that light. Again. And I saw uncertainty and fragility and fear and hope. He laid on the sofa and pulled a coat over him. I said he didn't need to use that and got him a blanket. During the night, after Bubovsky's aggression, I half expected Dewey to force his way into bed with me, but I was wrong. He left me to find some peace in the detritus of my dreams.

I said I turned up on "their" doorstep. I should have said "her" because he, my dad, as she'd said, was in a hospice on a stay from which he would never return. And you could tell he was no longer at home because the living room no longer had the scent of a new car but now the feel of an empty salesroom.

On the doorstep she said: hello Rose and to Will: you must be Will.

She looked older but self-concern can be aging and she would obviously have been thinking about what she would do after he was gone.

Over food which was a bland vegetable stew with pitta bread – which was, I suppose, the closest she could get to unleavened bread she told us about the day on which he got his diagnosis.

Chapter 23

The Dead

(Hail Joyce again!)

They kept him in a corner room. That's how you would describe it. Like a utility room where they put brushes and pans and cleaning materials. The corridor to the room was painted in a sorrowful, dirty cream gloss, and in the low lighting you could imagine the dead as spectres beseeching you with outstretched arms, trying to reach you to pinch off a pick of life; to escape from this mortuary of the soon-dead, where, with your squeezed breath, you live your own wake. The smell was of disinfected dying.

The door was a hepatitis yellow, and inside the windowless room in the corner there were, indeed, brushes and pans and even one of those suckers on a stick for unblocking toilets. And Dad was lying with eyes closed on a cot, like a twigman. Like ET. Cheated of feature by dissembling time. Impatient to sound the ring of death, the bells of forever black.

I'd left Will in my mum's car, which we'd borrowed. I didn't want him to confront what he couldn't expect.

There was a single chair, which I pulled up beside the bed. I wasn't sure if he was sleeping. Wasn't even sure if he was alive, so I put my ear close to his face and felt the softest movement of air, like a passing damselfly. I began to cry, pulled back not to wake him, and suddenly felt all my teenage certainties dissolve and my journey into the deepest, most mysterious caverns of sex confronted with this reality: my dad's own sex was killing him. That thing that had produced the dancing frog that sprung upon my mother's sleeping fertility was an assassin. And now I suddenly felt sick. Stuck in a morbid stasis. My life's search took me into the place of ex-stasis. *Ex-stasis. Ecstasy!*

I wished I could have put my mouth over his nose and mouth and stopped the moving in and out of the small air, but I couldn't. I only thought: no one should come to this. He had worked and bred, brought home the bacon, been my friend behind my mother's back, and, in some desperate subplot of life, had looked for something that would give meaning, that would lift the spirits above the low plateau of his experience. And now not even the consequent brethren could help him, nor give him, I dare say, final, limping succour.

I left him asleep. For ever.

In the car Will said: you've been crying.

Tears of love and fear.

Fear?

I love sex. This you know. And in him the earth source of what makes him sexual is devouring his life from within.

It's not the gland that's killing him; it's the cancer.

It's a terrible, savage thing. I had an uncle who had it and didn't know. One night, after he'd been out and got pissed, he came home and couldn't pee. He was dying to go. In desperation, he began to thread a knitting needle up it.

Up what?

His penis

O Christ, Rose! That's unthinkable

Will, if I get cancer and you're with me, still with me, kill me if I can't kill myself. Promise me.

You're experiencing a surfeit of rarely used emotion. You're overwhelmed. It'll pass.

Rarely used? Will!

You're young. You embrace the moment. You live for fucking! Death does not figure.

I can't believe that was my dad.

Will put his arm around my neck and pulled my head to his.

Holding my head back on taut neck, I said:

What about Tarita? Your girl.

She's not my girl.

How can I believe that?

What if she were? Would it matter?

No. Anyway, she told me.

Told you what.

That she hasn't fucked you.

She told you that?

Yes.

When?

At my place. The night of the riot. You were crashed. She told me loads. I probably know more about her than you do.

We began to kiss. Then we stopped and I said:

Much more.

Then I thrust my exceptionally long tongue deep into his mouth, and he sucked on it like it was a different thrusting thing.

Chapter 24

Return From The Dead

(Hail Gide!)

Dewey was in when I got back. I was feeling too down to get into anything with Will, though we had done it in my mother's kitchen after she'd gone to bed. In the morning, over breakfast, Mum got a call telling her to go in, as Dad was on the last leg.

She said: will you come, Rose?

I said: Mom! What good....

He'll want to see you!

But I don't want to be there when he goes.

Please, Rose.

Do you want us to take you there? No one knows how long he's got. We don't have much time. How will you get back? We have to hit the road.

After a sorrowful pause, she said:

Don't worry. The brethren will help.

We took her, and this time Dad was awake, but I can't even talk about it. I'm choking. There must be a better way of doing these things than putting people through such trauma.

Dewey was reading. He was in my armchair and got up as soon as I came into the room, then sat on the cane chair I'd bought in an antique shop just for him.

I said:

Sorry if I'm a bit late, Dewey. He'd been eating chips from the chip shop. The place smelt of rancid fat and vinegar.

I said: had chips for tea?

Sorry, does the place stink?

No! It's alright. It'll go. I'm going to have a glass. Want one?

No, thanks. I'm on the wagon.

Why? You couldn't have been drinking much.

No. I'm not touching anything. I've had one joint since they let me go and I realised I can't go back into all that.

I poured a glass from the Mateus bottle, which needed to be drunk because that little sparkle the wine has had gone. I sat in my armchair.

Then I said: Dewey's an unusual name. Sounds American.

People think that. A lot of Americans are called Dewey, but it's Welsh.

Welsh?

My mother – who's not my mother, which, when I found out, was one of the two things that freaked me out and made me lose it – the woman who was always my mother when I was a kid, told me, after I'd found out about my real mother, that when it came to naming me, they thought of me as a poor, lost boy who, in a sad way, didn't belong. So they thought Dewey would be a good name because it's not sure whether it's Welsh or American. Kind of mid-Atlantic. But it *is* Welsh.

I took a drink. Then I said: what was the other thing?

What?

You said two things freaked you out. Your mother and something else.

Over the next few minutes, as Dewey spoke, any doubt about the positive feelings I had for him, which were many, after the incident at the river, left.

He said: when I was seventeen, I joined the fire service. I was going out with a girl called Judy. We'd been together for a couple of years. If you can love someone at fifteen, then we were in love. Even used to talk about getting married sometime. She lived in a posh part of town, so I imagine her parents would make it difficult for us to ever realise that goal. I loved her house. Five bedrooms; double fronted with those stucco bits that make you think of cathedrals and velvet. All of them detached and in their own grounds, built by people who didn't mind how much they spent on them. I loved the way the streets bred confidence, reassured you, cleared your head of the riot of your own streets. I think she was proud of me when I became a fireman.

One night in December we were called out to a bad smash outside The Pilot in the dockland area of the city. The worst kind of night. Wet and cold. The main street through the docks, north to south, is straight.

You can get up to speed on it. Tiger Bay. Most people stayed away from that area. Let them get on with it. Some kids had stolen a seven-tonner and, travelling south to north with the foot flat down, lost control and hit a small Ford coming the other way. Driving south into the Bay.

We got the call: someone needed to be cut out of the car. The truck had almost flattened it.

Just going down that street into the heart of the black city filled you with excitement. And for me, on that night, trepidation. We could see the blue lights way down the street and I was getting very anxious. This was my first serious car crash and I didn't know if I was ready for what we'd find.

You know you get those times when it's as if you're standing outside yourself; watching yourself; watching what's going on in your life: safely cold-hearted and emotionless. Or maybe you don't know. And the one who's beside you isn't able to make decisions about how to react to things, and you're not free because you've given up your rights to the other. You're trapped and unfree. That's what happened to me.

Then he was silent.

Then he said: ok if we call it a day?

Ok. But.......

I finished my wine and put the glass in the sink. I began to go towards my room when he said:

It was Judy.

O God, Dewey. That's so awful. You poor....

But he was already on his mattress and covered with a blanket.

A day later he told me how he'd wanted to be able to ask the rhetorical question, *what was she doing in a car travelling into Tiger Bay?* But the driver who was crushed with her was a young black kid, and that made all questioning redundant.

And he said: that other, the one standing beside me, the cold-hearted, emotionless one? I realise now that's who I became. I began to drink – pissed all the time then I got into drugs and began dealing; made a pile of money. I'd drive down St Mary's Street throwing fivers out of the window just to see the people grovel for it.

Then there was the night I was arrested. I'm trying to get rid of the other; re-establish myself.

What about the night on the bridge when you threw that bloke in the river?

I just hated the bullying. I became the other for a moment and was happy to.

I was worried that you may get into more trouble.

But do you think I should just let them hurt Buckland?

Will said you were into Buddhism.

Yes.

How does that fit?

Buddhism says we have to turn our minds into an effective weapon to cut the root of suffering, so it becomes sharp as the blade of a sword. You could say I interpreted that literally.

Ok.

Then he said: Rose, I went with Will to King's Chapel. Have you been there?

No.

You must go. All England's poor, betrayed by the nation's elite, haunt the air about the clerestory. Will you come with me?

Sure.

Chapter 25

At Jesus

(Hail Coleridge!)

In Xanadu did Farquhar-Groyne a pleasure dome decree.

Except not Xanadu but a room in Jesus.

And here, among the smouldering essential oils and the scents of vased flowers – the freesias and gypsophila, scented double lilies, roses, and the azalea (pink) in jute pot Sten had arrived.

The day before, Sten had attended a talk given by Farquhar-Groyne on Crick and Watson and was amused at how Farquhar-Groyne rather audaciously managed to turn his observations on Crick and Watson into a right-wing tirade.

After the talk, Sten approached Farquhar-Groyne to tell him how impressed he was with the talk and how he agreed with a lot of what he'd said. Farquhar Groyne invited Sten to his room; to attend the following afternoon.

Overnight, Sten had dreamed up his own contribution to the Crick–Watson homage: he would suggest a physical representation of the double helix using their two naked bodies, which he hoped he could talk Farquhar-Groyne into allowing him to film. Sten had arrived prepared for an (un)dress rehearsal! (He knew how enthusiastic for buggery F-G was)

It had become clear to Sten that sex was a double helix with some additional acrobatics.

They set about it, limbs entwined and erect penises buried in fundaments, to achieve the coming together.

During the lulls in the afternoon, F-G elaborated on his hatred of Jews, and in particular Goldstein and his associates, Parfitt and Will. In the course of things, Sten mentioned Will's refugee, Tarita, and her ex, who was about to be released from prison. He told Groyne they were from Hastings, and the latter quickly came up with a scheme that would allow them to put the cat among the pigeons: making a trip to Hastings, finding Rolcord Wyre, telling him she's in Cambridge and working in Cherry Hinton.

He persuaded Sten to agree to a trip to the coast, which he – Farquhar-Groyne would pay for. And not only that, but Piers F-G promised Sten a re-run of the human helix, which he would allow Sten to film.

Chapter 26

Tarita's Nemesis

(Hail Hemingway!)

Rolcord Wyre, Tarita Wyre's husband, was a five-foot-eight, fourteen-stone, fatless thug built like a brick shithouse. One might wonder why such a delicate child as Tarita would choose to spend her life with this paleskinned gorilla. But it happens. Look around you. And one never knows how powerful, languorous, and deceptive the overtures of such men can be. Yet, his facial features carried a certain charisma.

Anyway, for the past twenty months she hadn't. He'd been locked up for battering her and had had it made clear to him that if he ever got near her again, he'd be going down for a lot longer. Of course, once he'd breathed deep of freedom's streets, he was king anew; master of all he could subjugate. So fuck their imperatives.

As soon as he'd settled back into his nuptial home, his mate Fordham Creek turned up.

Fordham said: Hey, Roly!

Rolcord said at the opened door: Alright, cunt?

Yeah. When'd you get out?

Today.

Pint?

I was just about to have a wank. Welcome myself home.

Be my guest. I'll wait.

Fordham left Rolcord to do what he had to do and sat in the living room. All was quiet, and his eyes were drawn toward the large, framed photograph of Joe Frazier that hung over the fireplace. Joe Frazier had beaten Ali in 1971 and had lost to him 75 in the *Thrilla in Manilla*. Rolcord hated Ali, who, he thought, had too much mouth for a black cunt.

When you're a young man in your late teens or twenties or even thirties and forties and, who knows, fifties and beyond, the likelihood is that when you masturbate, you achieve a kind of celestial freedom, an absolute release from the chains of the moment, a sexual liberation that comes without the complexities of mire and blood, without the emotional tangle masquerading as a superficial meeting of flesh on flesh.

For Rolcord, masturbating was an expression of his power his granite force, the domination of the moment through the exercise of the fundamental drives of male existence.

After a few minutes, Fordham heard Rolcord come. Rolcord Wyre had the habit of howling when he 'came' as if he'd just killed a feather-crowned Indian. Fordham got up and made his way to the outside porch to await the returned hero and take him to Ye Olde Pumphouse. Rolcord liked the name of the pub – it made him think of what he used to do with Tarita and what he would continue to do once he found the bitch.

In The Pumphouse were a couple of regulars. They grunted at Rolcord as he came in.

He said:

Before you say anything, I was stitched up!

A fat boy in the corner said back:

Had to be, mate. My old girl tried to lay that one on me. They're all at it. Cunts, every one of them.

Rolcord said: yeh, that's true. The trouble is, they're the ones who've got them: the cunts!

The few boys present laughed outrageously.

Fordham ordered pints and they pulled up bar stools.

Rolcord said: you seen her round?

Fordham said: who?

Who the fuck d'you think! Tara!

I dunno. I thought you might've had another bint on the go.

Where the fuck d'you think I've been? Magafuckinglouf?

Fordham laughed: yeh, no, I knew you weren't there! Fucking Magalouf! Ha ha!

So. Have you seen her?

Christ, no. She's gone, mate.

Ok. Gone where?

I don't know. Then he called to the fat boy in the corner: Hey Slim, know where Roly's bird went?

Rolcord said: wife.

Slim said: I think Loamy Balls was talking to someone.

Rolcord said: Balls! What would that cunt know?

I don't know. I think there was someone in here looking for you.

Looking for me?

Yeh, I don't know much about it.

Someone from the slammer?

I don't know. Just heard the rumour.

Fordham said: is he coming in, do you know?

Should do.

Rolcord said: what time?

Usually about 12.30.

Rolcord said to Fordham: we'll wait.

At about 2.30, Loamy Balls swaggered into the bar. A beer large man in his early forties with *fuck you* tattooed across his brow which he'd have to wear a hat to hide in polite company, but not today. He'd obviously already had a few.

Loamy said: Look here! Ulysses come back from Troy! See who's been fucking his misses!

Rolcord said: I'll fuck you in a minute, yu cunt.

O yeh? You and whose cock?

Listen, fuck that. They said someone was here looking for me.

Looking for you?

Yeh.

Get me a pint, Slim.

The fat boy got up from the corner and ordered a pint as he walked to the bar.

Loamy said: looking for you.

Rolcord said, impatiently: yes! About my misses.

O yeh. Some foreign cunt.

What d'you mean, foreign?

Like, from another country.

Loamy sat at fat Slim's table in the corner.

Rolcord said: I know that! Like, *what* was he? Kraut? Frog? Some kind of wog?

Scandinavian.

Scandinavian?

Yeh. Swedish, I think.

I don't know any Swedish cunts!

Yeh, well he seemed to know you.

What d'he say.

He said: 'Do you know someone called Rolcord Wyre?'

What'd you say?

Yeh.

How'd he know to come here?

Went to the Albion. They sent him to the Horse and Groom. They sent him to the Brass Monkey. They sent him to the Jenny Lind, they sent him to The Stag, and they sent him here.

So what'd he say?

Said he wanted to tell you where your misses was.

Yeh. So where?

Didn't say. You weren't here.

For fuck's sake! Where was he from?

I told you. Scandinavia.

Not *there*, you tattooed cunt!

Well, maybe she's in Sweden!

Slim put pints on the table.

A thin man on the other side of the bar said: Cambridge.

Rolcord said: how d'you know that?

I asked him where he was from, cos he was foreign. He said Cambridge. But originally Stockholm.

Fuck me! Cambridge? What the fuck's she doing in Cambridge?

Fordham said, Maybe she's gone to do some learning.

Learning? What the fuck would she want to learn?

I don't know. You hear about it. People who were always thick as shit going to college later in life.

That'd be your local poofter shop, not fucking Cambridge fucking University! She hasn't gone there to learn. She's gone there to fuck someone! Hang on. Hey Loamy, you mean *Cambridge* Cambridge?

There's no other Cambridge?

Not as far as I know. Anyone heard of another Cambridge?

Negative grunts from several sources. Then a voice said:

There's one in the States.

Rolcord said: who said that?

Someone else said: Dickhead.

So, OK, Dickhead. What states?

Dickhead said: The United. It's the equivalent of this Cambridge. Where Yale is. Or Harvard. One of those.

What you on about, cunt? Is that where they make locks or what?

No. Universities.

Fuck me. Back to that again. So you saying she's in the States

The thin man said not in the States, she's in England

Thank fuck for that

Rolcord said to Fordham: ok, I want you to get up to Cambridge and do some snooping for me.

Me? Why can't you go?

I can't go, Fordy! The cops probably know she's in Cambridge, and if they find me heading up there or snooping round there, they'll lock me up again! I want *you* to find her, get back here, and tell me exactly where she is so I can make a direct hit. Efficient. Slice through the night like an arrow, straight for the bull.

How'll I get there?

I dunno. Get a train! Or borrow a car. Borrow that old van of your brother's.

And where'm I gonna look?

Start in the pubs! Start where all the students are, probably in the centre then work out. You know: outward.

Got any money for me?

Course I have! Have you got a suit

Have I fuck

Hey Loamy, give me a pony

I haven't got a pony. Nowhere to keep one

Not a fucking horse! Twenty-five quid

Loamy said to Slim: Give me a tenner, you tight cunt.

He did then Loamy gave Wyre the twenty-five, which he passed on to Fordham.

Get one. And get your hair cut. You look like a fucking hippy You need to look important. Nobody's going to talk to a rough looking cunt.

This is fucking getting me down, Roly.

I get it. I've just done half my life in nick for a crime I didn't do, and my best mate is too far up his own arse to want to help me get justice.

I'm your best mate?

Course you are! Who the fuck else?

Ok. I'll have to tell my mum I'm going.

Rolcord gave Fordham a look of utter incredulity.

Chapter 27
In King's Chapel

(Hail Golding!)

Dewey asked me to hold his hand as we entered the building. I could feel a slight tremor. I'm not a great assessor of the psychology of others, but I'd say Dewey was conflicted. He told me there were significant tracts in his life when he could remember nothing. He knew he'd done some bad things – setting fire to his dog, and the hurt he'd caused the Alsatian, obviously, but there were other things, things he'd done to people, that may not have been criminal but could still have hurt. And I think he wondered whether he was sufficiently without significant sin to have license to be here.

King's Chapel can certainly put you in your place. I wonder why it hadn't had a humbling effect on the thirteen Prime Ministers, from Walpole on who studied at Cambridge but rather may well have increased their insufferable sense of superiority. And therein lay the key to the British political system: the rulers are trained to see King's Chapel as an ally in the domination of their class: ordained to bring to sufficient numbers of the people their godly need for humility, and to vote for what will reify that humiliation.

Dewey, pointing upwards, said: that is the world's largest fan vault. And this whole building is the greatest example of the permanence that testifies to the impermanence of man.

Wow. I might quote that!

I don't think I ever met anyone, speaking now, years later, who could search so deeply into things and at the same time throw young men off bridges.

He said: I was sure that when I came here, it would release me from the vanity of wanting to understand everything. And it's done that.

I wasn't sure about that. I wanted knowledge and understanding. Wanted to know how the tendrils of intellect wrapped themselves around the secret places of my humming sex.

Dewey said: let's sit.

There was no choir practice today, though someone was practising on the organ. In between snatches of Widor, Bach, and even a brief foray into Jimmy Smith, there was less a silence than a pause—where you felt that every murmur decorated a moment of huge significance. Nothing in this place could ever suggest pettiness.

Then Dewey said: when we were young, I fished Will out of a dirty canal. He was about six.

Right! So you saved his life.

He did go under three times.

No wonder he feels he owes you.

Look down there. Straight down the nave. That, going across the nave, is the rood screen. It was put there by Henry the Eighth to celebrate his marriage to Anne Boleyn. It's different from the Gothic perpendicular architecture of the chapel: it's Italian Renaissance. That fuck screen.

I was surprised to hear Dewey speak like that. It's weird how, when someone reveals themselves in the spirit in the way he had, they seem to surround themselves with an aura of saintliness. As if the godly never fuck. And he seemed to have just ruptured that aura.

I said: why do you say that?

Because that's what it represented. She wouldn't let him near her until they got married. Once they were married, he could possess her. And once he could possess her, he got bored. The rood screen is a whim: Anne Boleyn's hymen broken through to the altar on which he could consecrate his lust. Of course, for her that breakthrough had happened long before. You know, I brought you here to show off. So I could impress you with what I know about this place. I'm always having to convince myself that I'm worth something. It makes me seem pretentious. And then he said: sex is the exploding cannonball of betrayal.

And why did you say that?

Because ultimately, you humble yourself before it and it delights in your humiliation.

This was surely about Judy, the girlfriend who'd been crushed in that car, whose tragedy, incidentally, had nothing to do with any sex Judy and Dewey had shared.

I said: I've always found that any humbling brings a rebalancing humility. Have you had another woman since Judy?

You see how you say "had" as if lovers have each other like a meal. Except they do eat each other.

I'm sorry. I wasn't meaning to convey that. He'd side-stepped my question neatly.

It's OK. I'm glad you came today. So grateful.

I'm afraid I see sex differently from the way you do. I see myself on a riverboat sailing into the mysteries of the endless Amazon.

You know, Christians argue for life after death. Buddhists believe in the pre-existing mind. Death is part of *samsara:* the cycle of existence: birth, life, death, rebirth but not a resurrection of the individual who is reborn in heaven—more a new revolution in the eternal turning of the same wheel. There was a row of candles as we came in. If I snuff the end one out, that's a death but then we light a new candle at the beginning: a birth. Part of the eternal continuum. The row of candles is always burning, always alive. Christianity is so afraid of death, its own Godman wasn't allowed to die but had to be reborn in the flesh and then ascend to heaven as if of his own free will. As if not dead. Most of the men I knew in hospital—the murderers—killed because they were afraid of death. The exercise of murder demonstrated their power over death.

After a pause he said:

What did the bra say to the hat?

I don't know. What a weird thing to say.

It's a joke.

O.

You go on ahead, I'll give these two a lift.

I laughed very loudly, as if released from a tense preoccupation, and had to check myself. It tickled me.

I was told that one evening over rice pudding by Peter Sutcliffe. The Yorkshire Ripper. When he told it, he laughed like someone released from the clutches of an appalling terror.

Chapter 28

Parfitt And Goldstein

(Hail Ché)

Some days after the symposium, maybe as long as a week, Parfitt went to see Goldstein.

Goldstein was sitting in his fart chair, smoking a cigar. A Havana, in honour of Castro and Che, mountain men whose comradeship had enabled them to defeat the sophisticated weaponry of the American-backed Batista.

Farquhar-Groyne? Oh yes, I know Mr Fuck-you-Groan. His father was an associate of Mosley in the thirties. The father once stole my girl, who came back to me once she found he was dickless.

Parfitt laughed.

Carla said: Leonard!

The cigar rested between Goldstein's teeth until he began to extemporise, at which point he'd hold it in his right hand and tap the ash into a tray that stood on a stilt beside his chair.

Goldstein said: He was, of course, mostly queer and played around with Guy Burgess and others. He was on the Left for a while with the Apostles. All queer. Parfitt felt a little uneasy. Their view was that since society didn't accept their homosexuality, they wouldn't accept society and its creed. That's why Burgess and others became spies for the

Russians. Then Farquhar-Groyne joined Mosley because, it's said, he became infatuated with the uniform. And anyway, he'd argue: like Hitler, they were socialists. So what about your Farquhar-Groyne?

Well, he's the one who put it around that I'd stolen the work of the young genius Buckland on Hannah Arendt and had it published as my own. But in fact, it was Groyne who stole it from Buckland and then presented it as mine. What I can't understand is what would have been in it for him?

Carla, darling, could you bring us the bruschetta and the Vernaccia di San Gimignano I put out?

She said: of course. Where is that friend of yours, Anthony?

I think he's entertaining his guest.

O. O well.

She went to the kitchen to collect *il chibo*.

Carla had married Goldstein sixteen years earlier, when she was twenty-five and he was in his fifties. Of course, she'd married him for his money - a mercenary motive - but that wasn't the whole of it: she was enchanted by his politics and his erudition. And she wanted to be free from any squalid preoccupation with making money herself that might compromise the purity of her own Marxism.

She never asked him where he got his money and the only time she ever got close to asking him, he'd fended her off with a twinkling eye and the pithy: I'm a Jew!

As for sex, Carla wasn't complaining. Leonard was her Methuselah and that old biblical boy was at it way into his seven hundreds. (One wouldn't have expected him to have peaked at nineteen, limped on into his seventies, and then endured eight hundred years without sex. (Bitter years, even for a prophet.)

She did like Will, and she wondered what Parfitt had meant by "guest". A curious ripple of disappointment surprised her. He had a handsome, endearing face - seemed to her, in fact, self-effacing. Quite lovely. A little like the poet he was studying Chatterton, as portrayed in that Pre-Raphaelite painting by Wallis. When she'd found out that the poet was Will's subject too, it suggested a kind of symbiosis she felt eager to investigate.

As a married woman, Carla had been a guest of the sixties and developed a liberal predisposition from observing the new modes of behaviour in the rooms of that decade, where the women came and went. Meeting Will made her wonder whether she wasn't getting too old to investigate what exactly those women had been up to and had better act soon or never. But these were thoughts as private as toilet habits.

She took the bruschetta and wine to the chess players. As she entered, Goldstein was saying to Parfitt: is this Buckland one of Farquhar-Groyne's playthings?

Not intentionally.

What does that mean?

Farquhar-Groyne may feel that, in the world he is master of, the ideals he posits are more substantial than realities.

And what about Will? Not a Marxist?

A socialist. I think he calls himself a libertarian socialist.

Ah, like my old friend Michael Foot! Listen, Farquhar-Groyne is a malicious type, like so many on the Right. Their purpose is to humiliate and they enjoy seeing their opponents humiliated, usually in the face of violence. It's the *blague*! That low humour that permeates fascism. The *blague*, the expression of a society brought low by the diseased, over-indulged, powerful. Your run-in with F-G is an example of the *blague*. A grotesque practical joke which rewards no one but liberates all the shittiest instincts. Fascism is *blague*. Fascism is a practical joke of the meanest kind. That's what your Fucker Groan gets out of it.

But he has followers among the student cohort! As well as amongst townies.

Cohort, *schmohort*! My dear boy, so many of Hitler's hierarchy were intellectuals and culturally accomplished. Men like Heydrich, narcissist extraordinaire, creator of the *Einsatzgruppen*, that band of murderers who followed the army and, in their wake, murdered whoever. They killed two million – including over a million Jews – mostly by mass shootings. They'd make them dig an enormous trench, get the Jews to kneel along the rim of the trench and shoot each one in the head. They'd fall into the trench and be buried. That was Heydrich's

Einsatzgruppen. In Babi Yar in Kyiv, Ukraine, they used a ravine. In the first two days, they put 33,000 Jews in there.

The front doorbell rang.

Carla went to answer it and opened the door on Will.

A surge of happiness rose in her.

Will!

Hello, Mrs Goldstein.

Carla, please!

Is Anthony here?

Yes. Come in! But you look a little... are you alright?

Yes, it's ok, and went into the drawing room.

Goldstein, with ubiquitous smile, said: Will!

Parfitt said: Slade.

Will stood for a moment, as if unable to speak, then said:

I think Buckland's dead.

Part Two

Bad Moon Rising

Intro

(Hail Epicurus)

I am become a column of air. I am my breath. The breathing of my heart while I suck cock or lick clit. This is the air I am. The fury and the mire.

There is a rumour going round that Buckland is dead. Is it true? Where's the body; where's the evidence? If it's true, it's so miserable. So awful when life intrudes into reality. I had been hoping to fuck him. Like fucking Einstein. To have received inside me the impulse that gave the world $E=MC^2$.

When you feel pain, you experience life; when you feel the pain of others, you experience its meaning.

Chapter 29

Rose and Fordham

(Hail Euripides!)

As we left King's Chapel, Dewey had said to me:

Sten sends his love.

I was shocked.

How do you know Sten?

I met him in Broadmoor. After that time, you and Will came to visit me. He was visiting an assassin.

An assassin?

Someone he'd known back in Sweden when he was a kid who'd become a Brit and one night, a little like me, had taken too many drugs and gone on a spree of cat assassinations, including the cat of a Chief Constable. Sten had come to me and asked who Will was.

Will?

Yes. As if he knew him.

I'm remembering this years later. And then I recall Sten's first meeting sometime later, with Will, in the Eagle. I was working there that day.

From here, in these dog days, locked down, looking out of the small back window of my terraced house in Cambridge at the small yard taking a beating from an unexpected July storm, that afternoon back then had seemed one of the most significant of those times.

Apart from a sprinkling of punters, The Eagle was empty – everyone had gone to London to watch the Varsity match at Twickenham. I was on duty with Quaid. The afternoon began when Bubovsky came in at about 12.30. He came in from the rain. He took his Mac off and shook it and hung it on one of the tree coat stands we had. He ordered a drink from me as though we'd never met and as he took it and turned to go to a table, he seemed about to say something, then didn't. He went and sat alone in the room of the front bar.

Sten turned up. He too came in from the rain. He was wearing an occasional plastic mac which he took off and rolled up. It was raining hard. With the rain outside and everyone gone to Twickenham one can feel in need of company so I was glad when Sten arrived. The presence of the silent Vladimir only pressed home the feeling. Also, I had something to ask Sten.

He said to me: it rains too much in England.

I said: it's a temperate climate.

I will have a pint of that ale. He was smiling. Kindly.

I said: you didn't tell me you knew Dewey. That you visited Broadmoor and asked about Will.

Yes, I know. I thought I knew Will. I didn't tell you about Broadmoor because I didn't want you to think I was following you when I met you by coincidence in that diner later that afternoon. And then, in the diner, I didn't think I knew Will. So, there was no point in telling you about meeting Ronson.

I supposed that seemed reasonable enough. I gave him his pint and said: Mr. Bubovsky's over there. Now's your chance.

O God, yes. Maybe I will.

I had watched my one-time Russian friend and he had seemed lonely, which made me a little sad, even though I should perhaps have hated him for the way he'd treated me. And I was surprised that he could just sit there in my near-empty pub and not convey any self-consciousness about acting as though he didn't know me. Took a particular kind of Russian stoicism. Or perhaps the stoicism one must learn, to live with the injustice of an unfair imprisoning. I did think he was much more complex than this: the lonely bird in a heartless winter, though it was now Spring. Perhaps more complex than even he had yet to understand about himself after the few short years of his freedom. When he had been nice to me, when he had seemed to love me as though I were an angel fallen into his darkness, he loved with an incomparable innocence; the sorrow in his eyes tempered with a balm of gratitude. My intrusion into the details of his release had been arrogant and stupid: who did I think I was to even imagine that I could know enough to read into the chapters of his abuse and be assured enough to make my observation about the Chilean?

I was pleased to see Vladimir respond to Sten's approach so positively and to invite him to sit down and it didn't take long for them to be talking quite freely. But I had no idea what they were talking about.

****

Sten said to Bubovsky: the admiration I have for your strength in the face of your suffering has been monumental.

Thank you. I am not that strong.

You single-handedly caused the Soviet Union to weaken.

No. I was helped. In fact, your Prime Minister, Palme, helped.

From her place behind the bar in the quiet of the afternoon pub, Rose strained to hear what the two men were talking about. Occasionally, someone came in and momentarily the sound of the rain intruded and she felt almost afraid. The rain can stretch your nerve strings to the highest G.

Sten said: do you really think so?

If by that do you mean, am I sincere? Of course, I am sincere. I cannot be otherwise. When politics has condemned you, you do not then play games with political truth.

And you don't think that Palme was perhaps doing just that?

He is social democrat; liberal. To some level, he believes in freedom. Freedom has no time for self-aggrandisement of individual.

Sten took a deep breath and said: even though the end he wants is just that? As though the end justifies any tactic?

159

You miss my point: ends are specific, in this case, freedom is everything; breath to resuscitated body; breath to body politic.

I'm sorry, I don't like Palme. *He* is insincere. He exploits democracy as so many like him do and compromises the very nature of freedom. He may well become Prime Minister again and I don't know what I will do.

You must find a calm in reason. You must do what you must do. I'm sorry, but I must leave now.

Bubovsky got up. He shook hands with the Swede, went to collect his mackintosh, seemed about to leave, paused and went to the bar.

He waited for Rose to finish serving a famous actress who had turned up with a few minor actors who were performing at the Cambridge Arts Theatre. A visiting honeyed queen with attendant sexed up drones. They had come in with a loud flapping of coats and overjackets and merry chatter, shaking off the belligerent rain and hanging up coats or throwing them onto available chairs.

Some minutes later, Rose went to the patient Russian.

She was silent.

He said:

I have been too ashamed. I thought I knew what it was to be a man. Better than anyone. I had learned to despise myself for how I had helped to bring about my own suffering and then learned that that suffering made me strong. Stronger than any man could ever be. That was what made me hurt you. I am sorry I called you whore. Sorry, I said you have overweight. I was bitter in that moment for all women made thin by prison.

Rose had walked to the far end of the bar, leaving Quaid to take care of the actress who Rose didn't want overhearing Vladimir. He'd followed her as he spoke.

Rose said: you're better than most men, or you couldn't say that.

So will we meet again? In Green Olive?

Yes, ok.

Indicating Sten, Bubovsky said: so he is not your boyfriend?

No.

Do you have a piece of paper and pen?

Rose took a piece of paper from a small pad on the shelf beneath the many optics, picked up a pen – a soused Bic – and gave both to the Russian.

He wrote saying: here is my phone number. Please ring me and tell me when we can meet. I am always in at five.

And with that, he left quickly.

Sten remained sitting at his table as if he were waiting for someone. The actress and her attendees were noisy as if fame conferred on them the right to draw attention to themselves. When Will entered, he seemed quite surprised as if coming into a party he hadn't expected.

Then one of the troupe, a slightly older man, seeing Will, said: ask him. Ask this handsome young man!

Will was embarrassed.

Another asked: do you know this woman? Who she is?

Will quickly made his way to Rose.

The actor said: do you know her?

Will said: well, I've seen her. She's famous.

Another shouted: Bravo! You see?

The actor held his hand out: Boldo Gribbs, pleased to meet you.

Will took his hand: Will Slade. Boldo Gribbs looked uncannily like Buckland.

The actor piped up: everyone! This is Will Slade.

The actress said on behalf of everyone:

Pleased to meet you, Will Slade!

Will said to Rose: a pint?

Boldo Gribbs asked: are you a student?

Will said, yes.

What's your subject?

Thomas Chatterton. I'm doing a PhD.

Sten came to the bar and stood at the opposite end of the group from Will.

The actress suddenly said:

Dan! Dan! Come here.

The one she'd called Dan made his way through the assembled as the actress said: Dan played Chatterton.

Rose thought that Dan was, indeed, a beautiful young man. Looked, in fact, a lot like the Chatterton she'd imagined. Who, in turn, she'd always thought, Will looked a bit like.

Will said: pleased to meet you. Excuse me.

He left to go to the toilet. Sten, watching him, followed him and sat in the famous Crick, Watson seat. Will would have to pass it on his way back.

Meanwhile, back at the bar, Rose said: you do look like the Wallis painting.

An actor said: O, ho! An intelligent, nay, intellectual barmaid! Ah, Cambridge!The actress said: perhaps she, too, is studying Chatterton!

No. I'm a close friend of Will's. I just became interested and read about him. But I am interested in the studies of all my friends and acquaintances here in Cambridge. How can you be in Cambridge and not learn? I have also learned about the philosophy of freedom from a friend.

The actress said, before taking a mouthful of white wine: I am impressed

Leaving the toilet, Will approached Sten.

Sten said:

It *is* you.

Will came to Sten and stood close to him. He said: if I did know you and denied it, it would be because however we knew each other would belong to a different time; a different era; a different place, different world - a place that was dead to me. But I don't know you.

It's ok. But I want to tell you, I've loved you since that time. I think only of you.

Will said nothing and returned to the bar.

Sten returned to his seat. He sat a little angrily.

Boldo Gribbs said to Will: besides Chatterton, do you have any other interests? Do you have a philosophy? It's Cambridge. Everyone has a philosophy. What is your philosophy?

Will drank a couple of large mouthfuls and said: The supremacy of absence.

My my, said Boldo. What is that?

The absence of proof; of certainty; ultimately, the world. That is what I believe.

Another voice said: Descartes? A bit of Barclay?

Ploughing into his recollections of what Parfitt had said, he extemporised: No. I believe that everything not subject to the attention of our will is not there. It doesn't matter what claims are made on your behalf.

Maybe Schopenhauer!

Boldo Gribbs said: but if you commit a crime, you commit a crime. There is no absence about your having to face that.

Then Will said: unless I kill myself, finished his drink and left, saying see you to Rose and then a more general goodbye: pleased to have met you.

Voices shouted after him: bravo Will!

The actress shouted: good luck, sweet Will! And then to Rose: such an intense young man!

Rose said: yes, he is.

Then the actress said: back to rehearsals, men!

There was laughter and they downed their drinks, filed out amid the clamour of retrieving coats but not before the actor Dan who'd played Chatterton had asked Rose if he could at some point have a chat with her about the poet which Rose had responded to with an ok, and as the last left Rose saw standing in the doorway a sad looking figure in an ill-fitting Burberry. It was Fordham Creek.

Chapter 30
Creek

The man I got to know as Fordham Creek shuffled uncertainly towards the bar. I thought he was surely a used car salesman. He ordered a small whisky, which I got for him.

He said: I had to wait while all those people left. He grinned, showing blackened teeth. I felt sorry for him. Didn't seem to belong in this pub in this town.

He said: never been to Cambridge before.

I said: why've you come today? I realised my tone was a little over-familiar, but Fordham's self-presentation seemed to provide justification for it.

I had to deliver a dinghy. I brought it up from the south coast to a garage in Cherry something.

Cherry Hinton.

That's it. And then my friend said he used to know someone in Cambridge. A Swedish person.

Then Quaid said: that man over there – he indicated Sten – is a Swede.

Fordham turned to look at Sten and looked back with mild excitement. He said:

Do you think I could say hello?

Quaid said: I can ask him. What's your name?

Fordham Creek.

I said: I'll do it.

I went to Sten. I said: what were you talking to Will about? It seemed important.

He thought I was someone he knew. But, you know, a Swede is a Swede.

I thought you went after him. You were visiting Broadmoor and thought you knew him there.

The Swede looked at me kind of relentlessly.

Ok. I lied. We Swedes have to be careful what we admit to. I did think I knew him but I didn't. He confirmed it.

There's a chap at the bar. He'd like to meet you. His name is Fordham. Fordham Creek.

Ok.

I waved Fordham over. When he came, I introduced each to the other and went back to the bar.

After about ten minutes of vigorous chat, Fordham got up suddenly and left.

I went to Sten

What did he want?

Wanted to know if I knew someone called Tarita. Tarita Wyre.

What did you say?

No.

Took you a long time to say no. We were silent for a moment. I said: are you lying again?

He was silent with a look that almost seemed like hatred.

Then he said:

Fuck you! Got up and left.

That was the last anyone saw of Sten Olsen, until years later.

Fordham had mentioned the south coast and I was sure Will had told me that Tarita was from that area.

After work, I made tracks for Will's. The last time I'd seen Tarita was the night at my place when she interpreted my approach to her as an advance of a sexual nature and rejected it. I hadn't minded because I had learned then that the complexities of sex are, in the end, little more than a mirage; an abstraction, it's only in its rejection that one feels the sting of life – rejection is the affirmation of existence. She's still working at her pub in Cherry Hinton and living over there, so I wonder if my move that night had influenced her.

By the time I got to Will's I was out of breath.

Will came to the door. I said: have you seen Tarita?

He said, no. Why?

I think she could be in trouble.

I guessed he didn't want to ask me in because of Sternbend.

What d'you mean?

There was a bloke from the south coast snooping round asking after her. I think Olsen told him.

Olsen? What the hell does he know?

I don't know. He seems to know everything!

You'd better come in.

I went into the hallway.

He said: Tarita's here.

I thought you said you hadn't seen her.

I didn't want to upset you.

Upset me? Why?

You know.

As we were about to go up the stairs, I said: Why you introducing this tone?

What tone?

Difficulties. The complexities of mire and blood!

Chapter 31

If The Lion Spoke

(Hail Blake!)

Will had left the morning soiree, gone into town and returned.

Goldstein said: So dear Will, did Buckland die? And, if so, how?

Will said: He's not dead.

Not? So why would anyone think he was dead? Was there a body?

Well, there was, but it was a case of mistaken identity. Seems to follow him around. A pedestrian. Run over.

Parfitt said: but Slade, you seemed so certain. Did you want to think he was dead?

What I said was, I *thought* Buckland was dead. Rose told me. That bloke she works with told her.

Parfitt said: what, that.....

Will said: Laurel.

Carla, still hovering at the doorway, suddenly said: now look here, you two chaps, stop badgering Will. Get him a drink. Can I get you a drink, Will?

O, please. Yes.

The red?

Yes.

Goldstein said: not badgering, love, we're intrigued! Anything else you can tell us?

Will said: the pedestrian was an actor. Called Boldo Gribbs; I met him in the Eagle. He came in with a troupe of theatre people. Thinking back, he did look a lot like Buckland.

Parfitt said: good God!

I'm reporting what I heard.

Carla, pouring, asked: that Rose? Your source?

Carla was surprised she cared a fig about *that* Rose.

Will said: well, she works in The Eagle and gets to know most things. To Parfitt: The actor Boldo Gribbs was run over by a motor vehicle and at first, people identified him as Buckland. This is what I was told this lunchtime. The latest news. I said the actor did look a little like Buckland. *Before that,* having heard that someone answering Buckland's description had died, someone somewhere had put forward the idea that Buckland was vulnerable because, I assume, people thought he was *you*! Like the incident on the bridge! So you need to ask yourself why, prior to the accident, was this idea even out there?

Goldstein said: wishful thinking by Groyne and his mob. Believing that Buckland is one of us.

Now with the drink, Carla said: O Leonard, that's terrible!

Well, you know, Carla, that they can't touch me, so they want to get at others associated with us. On the other hand, as I have explained:

beware of the *blague*! This may simply be a sick joke being put around by Farquhar-Groyne and his associates.

Will said: what's the *blague*?

Parfitt said: fascist humour.

O.

Carla gave Will the drink.

Goldstein said: Anthony tells me you're a libertarian socialist.

I suppose so.

Parfitt said: it's a difficult position to sustain in the building of a socialist society.

Will said: you think?

Yes. People are happy enough to be libertarian but not socialist. People need to be encouraged to be socialist.

Coerced?

If necessary.

I would prefer people come to socialism voluntarily. I hate all forms of authority.

Parfitt said dismissively: anarcho-syndicalism! A pipe dream. The idea that the workers will organise society. Not among the British! You need a revolutionary vanguard to do it – to create the framework.

Goldstein could sense that Will had lost his footing a little and said: but you are in good company, Will. Chomsky describes himself as an anarcho-syndicalist *and* libertarian socialist.

Will said: oh, right.

Carla, feeling sorry for Will, out of the blue said: Will, let me show you things I found about Chatterton.

Things?

I've got a rare biography. Notes of mine. Come.

O, good.

Will got up and they left the room.

Parfitt looked after Will and Goldstein watched Parfitt and as Parfitt's head returned to face Goldstein's, Goldstein smiled and raised his eyebrows.

Then Parfitt said: tell me, Leonard: Chomsky. I feel uneasy about him.

Interesting.

Yes, well, he would say that we would be able to understand a lion if he could speak, while Wittgenstein said, as you know, that even if a lion could speak, we wouldn't understand him and that's simply because a lion doesn't exist in our world. Knowing the words isn't enough to bridge the divide between different worlds.

That's very interesting and I'm sure you're right but do you think that Will has a soft spot for Carla?

Parfitt, taken aback, said: I don't know!

What do you think Wittgenstein might say? Might he say: you could find out if you could understand the speaking lion?

No. He would probably say that your world and Will's are different worlds and you couldn't possibly know how Will feels about Carla.

Goldstein laughed. Parfitt joined him politely.

And Goldstein said: and Chomsky might say that for Will to understand Carla is simply getting a lion to speak.

But they inhabit different contexts; men will never understand women, nor vice versa.

In the small study with Will, Carla said: thinking about you and Chatterton, I felt a pang of real nostalgia. Do you understand "real" nostalgia?

I'm not sure I do.

The longing for belonging.

I heard someone say that, it's the same as the Welsh word *hiraeth*.

I would say, an awakening in me of something I'm not simply whimsical about.

That's deep.

Do you think so?

Carla took from a bookcase a biography of Chatterton by John Dix. Will had seen it before, of course. It was the first ever published biography, but he pretended as if he hadn't and that she'd really opened a door for him into the poet's world.

It's great. Then he turned to Carla and said: I think there's been an awakening in me of something I'm not simply whimsical about.

What do you mean?

You.

There was a silence and a clanging of symbols as Carla's eyes grew dark.

What about Rose?

Rose? She's just a friend!

You haven't made love with her?

Well.....

And what about the other young woman?

Tarita?

Yes. I know about her.

I'm just helping her out. Giving her a kind of refuge.

Carla's eyes softened.

You're one of the most beautiful young men I've ever met. Because, as you know, it would be different from simply seeing you in the street. But for you, I'm just someone in the street and I'm flattered by what you say, but for you to take me into a doorway would be terribly whimsical.

They paused and looked at each other. Will could see in her eyes the look a woman gets when her soul and her vagina open. And he knew.

They re-entered the lounge. Goldstein looked at them and smiled with that raised eyebrow while Parfitt frowned.

Before he left, Will said: the transit that killed Gribbs was a university vehicle.

Leonard Goldstein said: why does "Gribbs" ring a bell?

Chapter 32

Chatterton (2)

(Hail Plath!)

An early shift. Rose, a little late, arrived behind the bar and found Chatterton sitting in the front room. The same clothes as the painting, almost the same boy she met in her meta world: that magical place where reality is raised to such an improbable level it becomes the only possibility.

I went to him. I said:

You're Thomas Chatterton.

Am I that convincing?

Why did you come?

My love is dead, deathbed beneath the willow tree.

That's what you came to tell me.

When I met you the other day with our famous actress, Judy, I felt you knew me. But only as Thomas. Not Dan. I knew that unless I could meet you again to restart my heart, it would remain forever dead beneath St Mary's soil. Me, like Mary, a virgin, but in the philosophy of love.

Later that evening, we were on Jesus Green. He showed me his cock. It was huge. But before he used it, he went down on me. He said I had the sweetest cunt he'd ever tasted. As he fucked me, I realised this was something new: the power of his acting the tragic poet scouring me, for he was wild to do it after two centuries dead. And in me, those Buddhist resonances I'd picked up from Dewey giving me a role in infinity. This was love making beyond the quotidian: so far out beyond June and moon, we were crossing galaxies. And I learned that the philosophical virgin – she who searches Kantian noumena for the ecstasy beyond the hymen - can never but always die.

I asked Dan (though he insisted I call him Thomas to stay in character): did he have a lover? Was there anyone in particular he'd formed a unity with about which one might, for example, write love songs? Or a poem?

He answered as Thomas: before I died, I knew I had not completed preparations for a full life. I had only had one girl: Dora in London. I believe she'd given me syphilis. In my despair, I missed my sister and mother and took the attic room where I died, to remind me of the attic room in my mother's house where I would study when I was young and where I would live the medieval life I craved.

I said: could you complete your life with me?

Then he placed his hand upon my Venus mound and the feel of his gentle skin on my skin made me sad. And all I felt was the tender throb of his living.

Chapter 33

The Little Kosher Place

(Hail Roth)

In Will's room, the evening I hurried from work to tell him about Fordham Creek, Tarita was sitting on his bed. I was sure they'd been making love, but I didn't know or want to know how far they'd gone. Will was not there. I had come to warn her. I believe Sten had told Fordham as much as he needed to know to go back to Hastings to tell Tarita's ex-husband, who, fitting the profile of the woman-hating male who simply couldn't live with the idea that the woman who was his had left him and gone, would come for her. And maybe kill her.

To be honest, the impish, malicious thought occurred to me, against my will, that maybe it would be best if I didn't warn her; that my opinion of her husband was simply exaggerated and that he'd just take her back.

I said: I've come to tell you that I believe your husband is going to come to Cambridge after you, that he knows where Will lives and probably knows about Cherry Hinton. I think you should stay with me because you clearly can't stay here.

Then she said magnificently: I know I will be safe with you because our last tango was not danced.

It was brilliant because it was so ambiguous! Was she saying that it wasn't danced because what she interpreted as my pass at her was rejected by her, or that we may yet dance it? One of those moments when you simply have to live with the ambiguity or risk humiliation.

I said: good. We must all be vigilant. No one knows how or where or when he'll arrive. Do you have a photo of him?

No. He is dead to me and I hate his memory. You will know him if you see him. He will look like someone just released from a sentence he'll feel he didn't deserve. His eyes will be full of hatred and resentment.

What's his name?

Wyre.

I said: strange name. So your married name is Mrs. Wyre?

Yes. But I don't recognise it.

Too right. Would you like to come now? I don't think we should waste any time.

I'll have to go to Walpole Road first.

Walpole Road?

My flat.

O yes. Listen Tarita: you'll have all the privacy you need with me. I won't bother you.

I know.

Dewey will be there. He is the sweetest, most caring man I know. He's a Buddhist. He won't bother you or get in your way. In fact, he'll always help you.

Ok. I have met him. But, do you have enough room?

O yes, I've got two bedrooms. You can have one and Dewey can sleep on the sofa bed in my living room. I have to go now.

Will should be back in a minute.

Can you ask him to take you to your flat?

Of course

I left, passing Sternbend in the hallway and I said hello and he said: how are your studies?

I said: good. Fine thanks.

He said: tell me, your parents. Are they in business?

I said, yes. My father owns a Rolls Royce franchise in the West Country. I said goodbye.

I suddenly felt the deepest blue. You know that when blues music developed in the Delta land, it was to sing away the blues, not reflect the blues. And for me, the best blues for chasing away the blues was Jewish. If you've ever heard Bruch's *Kol Nidre*, it's music in that kind of vein. I knew a little Jewish place beyond Jesus Green tucked in behind Christ's Pieces that not many non-Jews knew about. I'd met a Jew in the bar who'd taken me there once and heard the music as if in a trance of melting agony. I'd go there and let that music wring the sorrow out.

I turned off Victoria Avenue to take a path across Jesus Green and in the twilight imagined I heard that sorrowful music as if leading me in a rolling of refrains to a shelter from loneliness. There was just no sound save a muted evening chorus to challenge the *klezmer* in my mind; the pulsing of weeping boughs and falling leaves, the yearning chords to clean out the sorrow.

I got to the small kosher place somewhere near Christ's Pieces and sure enough, it was almost empty save for a single male I passed who was sitting close to the door as I went to a table near the counter. There was no music. A young waitress came to me. I said:

No music?

She said: I can put some on.

Could you? The sweetest and saddest.

She said: are you sad?

I am. And in the twilight, I'm even sadder. Twilight is the loneliest time of day. But I want the music to tell me it's with me; to lift the sadness.

Ok.

Could I have a coffee?

One coffee.

The man at the other table was listening to me. I turned quickly. He was blonde. He gave me a smile which, to be honest, seemed more a challenge than something friendly. I think I'd seen him in the pub.

I couldn't really mistake that winged hairstyle.

I turned back and then took time to look around the cafe. There was a glass-covered counter with an array of what I took to be kosher foods: kind of snacky fast foods and behind that, on a working area, what looked like an old samovar. More ornament than actual water boiler, I guessed. On the wall were pictures of great Israeli leaders like Ben Gurion and Gold Meir and above the working area behind the counter, a panorama of Jerusalem with the Wailing Wall at its centre.

As the waitress brought my coffee, someone came in and sat at a table behind me. It soon became clear that it was at the table where the lone man was sitting.

The waitress said: are you Jewish? It doesn't matter.

I said. It shouldn't matter. I'm not. I love your music.

Bevakashah.

I looked questioningly at her.

It means: you're welcome. It can also mean, thank you.

So I said: *bevakashah.*

The waitress left and I heard a familiar voice say: Piers.

The other man said: Laurel. How are you?

It was Quaid. What the hell was Quaid doing here, meeting undoubtedly a *shkotzim*? A *goy*? I'm sure a hostile goy.

Quaid looked deeply into Farquhar-Groyne's eyes for any movement of emotion.

Quaid said: why did you arrange to meet here? You don't like these people.

Rose struggled to hear what they were saying, catching only the occasional word and using her power of lateral thinking to hang some narrative and meaning on them.

Groyne said: "don't like" is a misrepresentation of my beliefs. My ideology.

Laurel looked with questioning brow.

Groyne said: A man is going mad. He doesn't know it. His depression deepens. He is beset by images which solidify and become ideas which horrify him: voices which seem to instruct him in what he must do with these images: ideas – alien to him and all decent men, they tell him to hurt those he loves. They propose terror and murder against all he loves. If he were ever sane again, he would ask himself: what was that? And I ask you, Quaid: what was it? It was the Jew! The Jew is a maddening set of malicious, terrifying images in the body politic, which undermines and threatens it: to make it mad so that it will ultimately destroy itself.

So why have you come here?

To confront it. Only by confronting the image can you destroy it: *Before me floats an image, man or shade/ shade more than man; more image than a shade.* To make it more man than shade, you must confront it. So I dine where he dines.

And his hospitality couldn't make you change your mind about him? That you might now see him as a simple man who wants you to be comfortable? Pleased and comfortable?

It is impossible for the Jew to be simple. He is always calculating. A predisposition that originates in usuary. What happened to the Swede?

He went. Gone. Back to Sweden.

But, do you know – did he go to Hastings?

I believe so. A friend of Wyre's came into the pub. From Hastings.

Why can't you be with us, Quaid?

Quaid felt that, ultimately, he couldn't take Groyne seriously. He went to him on the earlier afternoon because he'd been smoking dope all morning and, relaxed as he'd become stoned, felt that this was an opportunity to satisfy his curiosity. He knew from Groyne's reputation that he could be trusted to do things *professionally*.

I answered your invitation this afternoon because I admire your mind and your lecturing. But I'm not built like that.

Like what?

Able to be distracted by ideologies as an expression of meaning.

Ok. You work in The Eagle. Along with the girlfriend of Slade?

Yes.

He is a friend of Parfitt's who is a friend of the rich commie Jew Goldstein. He has also taken under his wing this…..

Yes,An abuser's wife.

Yes, who I understand is also a Jew. Look around you. Look at the photographs. This is a hotbed of Zionism. Quaid began to look around the room and saw the back of Rose.

Groyne took Quaid's hand and nodded towards Rose.

Quaid got up. He nodded: yes! Then said: I must go. And as he left said: I don't believe that Will's refugee is a Jew.

He went to Rose.

Hi Rose.

O, it is you.

I wouldn't have expected to see you here.

Nor I, you. I come for the music. You?

Research. I'll see you later.

Ok.

Laurel left and Farquhar-Groyne waved his hand to attract the waitress. She hadn't attended the table when Laurel had arrived because the waitress knew how finicky Groyne was about her not approaching him until he'd called.

Groyne said to the waitress: I'm hungry. Can I have some meat in a sauce and a couple of vegetables?

It's kosher.

Of course.

Rose put together the words she'd heard and felt sure she knew what they were talking about.

And she'd heard it said, she was sure, that Tarita was Jewish. Rose couldn't refute it. And Tarita certainly had the melancholy of that age-old culture of the sufferer.

Chapter 34

At the Cathedral

An early Spring morning.

Will was playing a tape of Delius's *First Cuckoo in Spring* on the portable player in his car.. Will wasn't an Anglophile, but he loved English music. And not just Elgar, Vaughan Williams and Delius. But he didn't have any Tallis or Byrd on cassette.

This morning, he wanted to try and capture Chatterton's journey into the medieval world of the poet's mind by making a journey accompanied by the echoic chords of Delius into the past; across the fens to the mighty eleventh-century cathedral at Ely.

Further into the fens, he turned the music off and drove his Renault 5 in silence, but with his window open in order to substitute for Delius' nature music from the fens. He felt that if Chatterton were alive now, he would be driving a Renault 5.

He drove past Romany camps and the occasional Fen skater and wildfowlers, men in flat caps lying on their bellies in cobs rowing like great submerged birds paddling with fat featherless wings before deploying the culling shot gun; through the villages of Twenty, Prickwillow and Queen Adelaide and past the home of the Harley Davidson family at Littleport into the future and into the past and finally to Ely.

His first sighting of the cathedral – the Ship of The Fens - and its Octagon Tower was from maybe ten miles away on the road, like a discarded ribbon winding through the flat lands. The building rose majestically from the land, one of Britain's greatest churches and in it rose a feeling of awe and wonder and the belief that he was feeling what Chatterton must have felt on visiting Wells's Cathedral, another of those great buildings of the medieval world.

He came in on narrow streets and found a car park, parked, paid and began walking towards the building. As he left the car parking area, he saw a car which, for a moment, he was sure was Sternbend's but decided it couldn't be. He'd heard Sternbend leave that morning after saying goodbye to Mrs. Sternbend. He couldn't be sure anyway because he didn't know Sternbend's license registration number.

And so he entered the cathedral through the Galilee Porch down the nave towards the octagon and imagined Chatterton walking ahead of him, breathing deep, head thrown back, hair aflow. Crossing the transept, he walked past the choir and the presbytery and in a corner beside St Etheldreda's chapel burned a brazier and Will stood by it to warm himself. And then, in the corner of his eye, he saw something he couldn't imagine he could be seeing: just inside the saint's chapel, Sternbend and Carla. Sternbend and Carla Goldstein! They were holding hands and for just a moment touched lips and Will turned away to hide in the dark of the corner. Sternbend and Carla!

Chapter 35
Conspiracist

(Hail Hank Jansen!)

Rose said: *Sternbend* and Carla!

Will was at the bar of The Eagle following his return from the cathedral with its shocking discovery, which put from his mind entirely all thoughts of Chatterton.

Rose said: Do you think they're having an affair?

They kissed! *Sternbend*!

What do you feel for Carla?

I don't know.

I think you do.

Ok. The other day. I made a kind of pass.

And she rejected you. Rose gave a little laugh. For Sternbend. No wonder you're so shocked. Anyway, Sten's gone. Back to Sweden.

His name's not Sten. It's Stig. Stig Angstrom.

How do you know?

He told me, while trying to convince me, that I knew him.

O well. Anyway, hey ho, she didn't reject you because of *you*!

Later, Will recalled that Parfitt had recommended Sternbend to Will and presumably Will to Sternbend and Parfitt knew Carla and Goldstein! Was there some kind of conspiratorial link?

Chapter 36

London

(Hail Isherwood!)

On the following Tuesday morning, Rose left Tarita in the flat and got the London train. She took a seat by the window in the heavily populated carriage. As it sped on, she felt anxiety and excitement, anticipating the great unknown city before her. She looked out at the flying fields, the heat tall as from Larkin's moving window; the weddings long gone and forgotten even in the ghost memory of that dead dreamer.

As she approached Euston, she thought of the East End, emblematic of that insufferable ritual of subservience women of the working class had lived where their sex was little more than aping a cup men wanked into. Rose's need in life was always to rise above that outcome for herself, not using privilege, but her body and her will and the joyful science that accompanied it.

At Euston, she caught a Northern line train for Embankment. A touristy hour: Houses of Parliament; Number 10; Westminster Abbey. In Downing Street, she wondered if she'd catch sight of the Witch of Finchley who'd just taken up residence. The thought that she may be there just beyond that house wall filled her with awe, though not enough to dispel the dislike she felt for the woman. From there she walked into Soho and in a sex shop she bought several toys. Just being in there made her feel horny, a condition she carried with her onto the empty carriage of the homeward train and some future religious wounding.

Before the train left, a rough-looking young man with short shaggy hair got on and sat across the aisle from her.

As the train left the station, this young man said:

Looks like it's just us two.

I just smiled. He was making an effort to talk posh. Probably to hide a common vernacular. Generally speaking, I thought he looked pretty interesting. Rough looking and a little heavily featured with a mysterious charisma, well built and lean. Quite attractive in a villainous way.

He said: my name's Roly and he held out his hand for me. I took it and said: Rose.

I brought some wine with me. Fancy sharing it?

Ok, I thought, what's this a prelude to?

I said: sure!

Where I was sitting had a small table and he came and joined me, sitting opposite.

Out of a rucksack, he produced a bottle of Chablis (expensive!) and two glasses. He looked as if he had come expecting to meet someone.

Then he said, as if reading my thoughts: don't get the wrong idea, this is how I always travel. He said with a note of indifference and a shrug: still a little chilled from the fridge he took it from.

As he poured, he said: where are you heading for?

I said: Cambridge.

Same here. Business or pleasure?

I live there.

O right!

You?

Business.

Love business?

Weird thing to ask! Yeh, I suppose so. Kind of.

We drank. Nice.

The glint in his eye told me I'd opened the door for him to start talking about sex.

The train had stopped, dropped a few and picked up a couple who sat at the other end from us.

What about you? You got any love thing going on?

You could say.

One bloke or more than one.

O, bloody hell. Hundreds! I was being both ironic and playful.

I drained my glass. He looked at me, surprised, then suddenly began to laugh. I laughed. We refilled glasses.

I was feeling quite lightheaded.

He said: what about me. Could I be one?

You seem quite civilised.

Yeh?

We laughed. We drank.

Then he said: want to try me?

I said: where?

He said: the toilet.

What about the toilet?

Do it there.

Bit of a squash? And a bit risqué.

You go, I'll follow.

Yes sir! We laughed.

We did it with me leaning against the sink and him taking me from behind. Afterwards, I reflected that this boy had really needed a good streetboy shag as if he hadn't had one for a long time. It made me wonder whether maybe he'd been in prison.

Back in our seats, he said: I'd like to see you again.

I said: uhu. Well, I'm not working this evening, so we could meet later. I work in a pub called The Eagle. It's right in the centre of the college district. We could meet there.

Ok.

Listen, I'd ask you to come round to my place, but I'm looking after someone.

That's ok. I've got some business and I'm booked into a hotel.

O right.

Maybe you can come and look at it after.

You mean maybe I can come around and look at your room after we've had a drink?

Yes.

Ok.

Good.

Then, after a pause, he said: do you know how I can get to Cherry Hinton?

Is that where your business is?

Yes. I know someone with whom I was in the Navy there.

The train was now approaching the station. I had a nervous feeling that this wasn't a simple parting: a "see you". A bientot. Cherry Hinton seemed to ring a warning bell. A sense of falling. An arrow shower. Becoming rain over Cherry Hinton.

I said: you were in the Navy?

Not for long. Merchant, not royal. I spent a year on Norwegian Lines.

Maybe it was a shake in the wake of our fuck. I said: And your friend?

I heard his wife had died. Bad. She fell in front of a forty-tonner.
Got her head crushed.

O God.

I know.

Well, you should be able to get a bus out of the station.

Ok. Stepping off the train before her, he turned and said: Thanks.
See you later.

The Eagle.

Yep.

He didn't give me a kiss.

Chapter 37

Lowest Order

Fordham Creek had got from Sten that Tarita worked in Cherry Hinton at The White Hart hotel and he'd told Rolcord. So Rolcord got a bus for Cherry Hinton and soon found the hotel.

In the hotel, he asked for Tarita Wyre and they said they didn't know anyone by that name.

Ok, he said, Begrum – that's her maiden name.

The woman he was talking to said that she hadn't been in for a few days, maybe a couple of weeks.

Then he asked them for her address and they said: who are you? We can't give her address to just anyone.

I'm her husband. Rolcord Wyre.

How is it you don't know her address?

With a shrug, he said: you know.

It's somewhere over by Jesus Green.

Where the fuck's that?

Don't get angry with me!

Fuck you.

Rolcord left the hotel.

Rolcord found a phone and called Ye Old Pumphouse.

Hey Slim, is that fuck Fordham in?

Rolcord! Yeh, I'll get him now.

Fordham came to the phone.

Hey, Roly, how's it going?

It's not, you cunt. Listen, that Swede you talked to in Cambridge. Did he say anything more? Something you could have forgotten to tell me?

No. O, he gave me a name which I wrote down and then forgot.

Jesus, fuck! What is it?

Hang on, I'll get it out. He took a piece of paper out of his pocket. Here it is. I don't know if I can say it: Farquhar (Far – qu –har) Groyne.

What the?... Spell it!

F –a – r –q – u- h – a- r – hyphen – G – r –o – y –n – e.

Ok. I'll have to remember it: got no fucking paper. He said it a couple of times and then said it phonetically. And then put the phone down. And then looked in the telephone directory.

He found a number for Groyne and dialled.

A voice that wasn't naturally plumby answered:

Good evening, Jesus College.

Wyre said as poshly as possible: I've got this number for a Mr. Farquhar-Groyne.

Just a minute, sir, I'll see if he's in. Then, after a moment: I'll put you through. Can I ask who's calling?

Rolcord Wyre.

O, one of the Dorset Wyres.

Then he put Rolcord through.

Chapter 38

A reckoning

As she walked through the balmy evening, her feeling of anxiety grew: probably the wine wearing off. That had been a crazy thing to do. On reflection, she felt that he looked like the kind of man who could easily have a venereal disease. Why did she arrange to meet him in her place of work?! A place where Will drinks and her dear friend Quaid Laurel works. How would she be able to shake him off if she needed to? But there was something else deepening her anxiety: Cherry Hinton.

When she got back to her place, she was met by Tarita.

Her first words were: I need a drink and Tarita giggled at Rose's faux desperation.

She poured a glass of rosé for herself as she flopped down on the bed.

She lifted herself a little as Tarita handed her the glass and said: thanks, babe. As she took the glass, Tarita noticed that Rose's hand was shaking.

Tarita said: are you ok?

Rose was silent for a moment, then she said: not really. I did a crazy thing: I *fornicated* with a complete stranger on the train.

Tarita joined her on the bed and said: my God! Wasn't there anyone else in the carriage?

No. We were all alone, except for a couple at the other end from us.

So where did you do it?

In the toilet.

O God! Tarita laughed.

But surely you found out something about him?

His name. But I've forgotten it.

Where was he going?

Cambridge.

Are you meeting him again?

Yes. That's the problem. I've arranged to meet him at The Eagle this evening. I was very tipsy. O, God, I nearly had his name then! Was it Riley? Something stranger.

Roly?

Yes, Roly!

What did he look like?

To be honest, quite attractive. In a villainous way. Looked like a gaolbird.

Then Tarita went to her travelling bag, took out a purse and from the purse a photograph.

As she struggled to get the photo out, she said: no one knows I've got this. I don't want people to think I want to see his face.

Then she handed it to Rose and said: I keep it for emergencies. In case I need to show the police.

Rose looked at the photo for a moment and then said. That's him. Is this....?

Rolcord. My husband.

O shit! You'd never told me his name!

Well, not his shortened name. He's coming to get me!

We need to talk to Will. What if it's not him? Identifying people is not one of my strong points!

There's one thing that could only be him.

Yes?

Did you get a look at his thing? His dick?

With a note of eye-opening, Rose said: shit, yes. The snake.

He had it done as a birthday present for me.

You?!

Said I could imagine the snake's tongue flicking my clitoris and driving me mad with it.

Rose said: and the spit of a poisoned sting. Do you think he could have any disease? The clap?

Could have. Though he's been away from women for months.

He's not shy about the anal road.

Then Tarita, suddenly sorrowful, said: he's come to kill me.

Tarita, that isn't going to happen.

And Rose kissed Tarita and Tarita reciprocated.

Chapter 39

Obsessions

In the days following the incident in the cathedral, Will became increasingly obsessed with Carla. All the selfless emotional gestures he'd ever extended to the women he'd known, including Rose, now gathered in a debilitating assault on his nerves.

He would calm himself by considering that he couldn't really be sure that the man he saw in the cathedral with Carla was actually Sternbend. The man in the cathedral looked a lot younger than the man who was his landlord. But he'd soon counter that with the argument that anyone living with Mrs.Sternbend would look old, while Carla could knock years off a lover with the ease of a Bob Willis knocking off an Aussie batsman's bails.

On the fourth day after the bitter knock at the cathedral, on the day Rose's adventure in London, Will arrived home to her and Tarita waiting at his door. They looked apprehensive.

Shortly after I arrived at Will's, he turned up - the scorned lover, but I have no delight to pass away the time on that. Though it did cross my mind that the bubble of self-regard of the successful lothario had been truly burst by the rejection he'd experienced. I know that's harsh: he was hurt. And I know he's a young man and that's how good-looking free-spirited young men tend to be. Good, trustworthy lads, by contrast, those who never roamed would more than likely be boring as hell. Young women will often go for guys like the former and then try to get those guys to settle down and become the latter and if they play around a little, the women go crazy, not realising that the guys are only doing what made them attractive in the first place. As for screwing Rolcord, I felt I'd arrived at the last stop on a line that's going nowhere. It's time to recognise that you sometimes need to check things out with the conductor.

Will said: what is it? What's happened?

Tarita said: Rolcord, my husband is here.

Here? Where?

I said: who knows? But we think he's looking for Tarita.

How do you know he's here?

I said: I met him.

Will said: Let's go inside. Sternbend's car's not here.

Inside Will's room, the two women sat on his bed and Will asked:

What do you mean when you say you met him?

I said: I met him on the train. Coming back from London.

But how did you know it was him?

I didn't.

Hang on. So you met him on the train, but you didn't know him.

Yes.

So, when did you find out that it was him on the train?

When I was telling Tarita about a stupid thing I did on the train by fucking this guy who told me his name was Roly.

You fucked him? Where?

In the toilet.

In the toilet?!

I knew at a moment like this his anger would be tempered by a growing desire to fuck me himself.

Yes.

Is this a thing with you?

You don't plan these things.

Have you learned anything out of it? For your research.

Yes. I've learned that a guy with a snake tattooed on his dick is going to have a history.

A tattoo on his dick?

Tarita said: a viper.

I said: I thought it was more like a mamba.

Viper. He said. He said what distinguishes a viper is that the head is very different from the body.

O yes!

Then Will said: ok, fuck all this! Does Dewey know?

He wasn't there.

Will said he'd go and see Dewey and we worked out that to make sure the guy I fucked was actually Tarita's husband, I would go to The

Eagle at 7.30 and make sure I got him to sit at a table with his back to the door so that Will and Tarita could have a peep to check him out.

And before we left, I said: it doesn't help that you're so obsessed with a middle-aged woman! I may have many men, but I only love you!

Chapter 40
Rolcord at Groyne's

Rolcord Wyre finally found his way to Jesus after a wearying trek. It was 5.37. At the porter's lodge, he asked for Farquhar-Groyne and was shown the way to his door. Groyne opened the door, looking groomed and quite magnificent. He was wearing a dressing gown and probably nothing else.

Mr Wyre!

He looked at Rolcord with a calm hunger.

Please come in.

Rolcord felt a little diminished by the room but certainly not overwhelmed.

F-G said: whiskey?

Ok. Thanks.

Sit down!

He sat.

To F-G, Rolcord looked like a plausible piece of rough. He sized him up: a lean, muscular torso. He was pretty sure of that. And he could imagine an assertive, strong, big cock.

I was hoping you could help me find my misses.

He swigged the whiskey down.

Oo, look at that. Another?

Yeh. Ok.

Your misses?

My buddy Fordham Creek came here last week and met a Swedish guy who seemed to know something about her and he gave me your name.

Right! So the Swede went? What's her name?

Tarita. Tarita Wyre. You probably know her as Tarita Begrum.

Groyne had poured the whiskey and Rolcord swigged it down again.

I may as well bring the bottle over!

Groyne fetched the bottle and put it on the table.

Farquhar Groyne sat on his bed. He said: Do you know Cambridge?

No.

It's a complex of clubs and societies, all having their own initiation rites. No one helps anyone without membership. You can see it especially in the Tory party to which my particular club is affiliated.

Wyre drank more.

What club is that?

The Apostles Volume Two. We are the apostles of Mosely.

Who's that?

Oswald Mosely, Britain's great Nationalist leader of the 1930s.

By now, Rolcord had swigged a couple more whiskeys and was feeling relaxed and even adventurous.

Wyre said: you going to be able to help me?

Once you're initiated, I'll put out feelers. She can't hide once I've done that.

Rolcord poured himself another whiskey. What's that? Initiated.

I understand you've recently been in prison.

How d'you know that?

I know.

Fucking Fordham.

Your wife is a Jew?

Yeah? I don't think so.

I was led to believe so. The Apostles don't like Jews because they reject Christ.

So you do know her.

How you feeling?

I'm feeling ok.

When you were inside, what did you do for sex? Much wanking?

Well.

Did you ever share your need with another?

I know what's coming. Is this the initiation?

He undid his dressing gown to reveal an erection.

Groyne said: my, my. Big fucker.

Want a bit of lighthearted fun?

Rolcord stood up and in imitation of the histrionics he'd developed in prison, quickly took off his clothes.

Chapter 41

Once More The Eagle

(Hail Bellow!)

A little before 7.15, Rose came from behind the bar at the end of her shift and arranged a small table and chairs in the corner, ensuring that Rolcord would have to sit with his back to the door. She then sat in the chair and waited.

At twenty to eight, an oiled Rolcord turned up and seeing Rose, went to the table and sat with an ambiguous giggle.

Rose said: did you get your business done?

Not what I came for, but yeah, got something done.

Sounds mysterious.

A room in a college.

What's the stain?

Red wine.

O

Yeah.

That's where you've been?

Yeah! In a room in a fuckin college!

Ok! Which one? Which college?

Jesus.

Hmmm. Who do you know there?

I didn't know him. Not when I got there. But we found out we had things in common.

What, intellectual things?

Nah. Fuck that. More on the non-intellectual, animal level.

What was his name?

Don't know. Smiley. Left him with a smile on his face.

Hmmm. Let me get us a drink. What d'you want?

She went to the bar and saw, as she got there, Tarita, Will and Dewey in the doorway all making affirmative gestures.

Will said to her quietly across the space between them: go to the toilet!

As she was about to move, the door opened and Chatterton came in, pushing past the other three. He went immediately to Rose and said loudly: I need to see you!

Rose said: I can't!

Why?

I'm going to the toilet!

I'll wait.

Seeing Dan as Chatterton, in Chatterton's garb, caused a stir among the few punters in the bar and caused Wyre to turn in his seat to see what it was all about and in the process see Tarita at the door.

He suddenly got up, shouted Oy! Jew whore! and made for his wife.

Chapter 42
Woman on Woman

(Hail Djuna Barnes!)

The exact details of what happened after Dewey and Will intercepted Rolcord Wyre on route to his wife, I don't know – it all happened so quickly while I was in the toilet! In the toilet with Dan (Chatterton). It seems that when you have something to do in haste, the toilet is the place to do it. But he didn't *do* it. I told him I wouldn't let him and I couldn't see him again. Shit! I needed to see what was happening! He said: why? I said: it's sleazy. He said we could do it somewhere proper. I said no! It's too complicated. He said: never see you again? I said no. I left him on the toilet seat, weeping.

About what happened, I only know as much as they told me.

What I didn't know until the events of that night were revealed was that Parfitt and Buckland had become lovers. The business of Parfitt being accused of plagiarising Buckland's work seemed to have brought them together. One began to wonder whether the rumours about the anonymous Buckland and Farquhar-Groyne had been the truth; that the manipulative Groyne had turned Buckland onto his sexuality.

After Will and Dewey had left with Rolcord Wyre and I returned from the toilet, I found Tarita at the bar waiting, I think, for me. She was deeply shaken and so I got her and myself a brandy and we sat and drank them. I held Tarita's hand. I said:

I don't think he'll be back.

She said: he'll never be gone. That's my life now.

She seemed so small and powerless, like a young woman yearning for love who's been stood up outside the cinema on her first date.

I said: drink it down, it'll do you good.

She finished the brandy in one swig and said:

It burns.

I said: it burns because it's working. It's doing you good.

I think I want to go home. Can we?

I said: of course! You need to feel secure.

Yes.

On the walk home, she was as nervous as a kitten. The merest noise would startle her and she would hold onto me. In the twilight with the shadows on her linen white skin, she looked more beautiful than ever.

When we got back, we said very little. She took me by the shoulders and we began to kiss. She led me into her bedroom. Soon we were naked and on her bed. What we did was whatever two women could do in this superior passion and we did it all night and for hours, we couldn't stop coming. As I lay awake in the first minutes of her sleeping, we laid side by side both naked me looking up at the low artexed ceiling in her room on which had been traced in a deeper tone, a huge circular feature which took up most of the ceiling and with the surrounding white had the effect of suggesting a world, a planet just above our heads; us powerless and ecstatic beneath the descending world. I was surprised that I hadn't registered the ceiling before. And laying there in a temporary silence, I suddenly asked myself: who do I love? Is it Will? Perhaps Dewey. This girl? Is my story a love story? Or am I simply obsessed with self-gratification? Like, for example, with Dan: simply overcome by his majestic cock – belied by his general appearance. And then I had these thoughts – not meant to be the final word - just what I felt:

When a man fucks a woman, the benign account is that he is doing nature a favour by fertilising her seed; the reality, most of the time, is that he has an overwhelming, burning reality to shoot into her. That mad, crazy need to fill the welcoming hands of the devil with his cum, the moment when he has so much power he can deliver his powerless being into the euphoria of death. Whether sublimated or not, it is an act of aggression.

When a woman fucks a woman there is no benign illusion about fulfilling the needs of the future, serving posterity: to fuck to bear the future, there is the desire to become the other; to realise in the delicate hand inside you searching for the place that triggers the deepest philosophical truth the journey of your own hand inside her: you bring her soul into your brain as your soul enters hers, and when you manage that scissoring position where your legs as scissors replicate her scissoring legs on you so that the lips of your cunt can kiss the lips of hers and the consequent weeping remind you of the joy in sorrow, then you become truly transcendent. Then you become the deniers of any of those instincts in man for aggression.

In the night, half asleep, I was sure I heard the door open and I became aware of someone looking in and then closing the door ever so quietly. The only person who has my key is Will, so I assumed it was him, which would make sense because I was expecting him.

In the morning, as I got ready for work, I looked at her sweet face and realised that I'd fallen in love with her. It seems that the unrevealed and maybe fearful mysteries of sex can be the most powerful and transcendent.

Chapter 43
Nightmare on Jesus Green

(Hail Poe!)

As Wyre began crossing Jesus Green in the dark after his run-in with Will and Dewey and several pubs on a crawl about town, he could feel his anger solidify and his conviction that whatever he did now, he could justify, accompanied by his reasoning that in this now dark place, he could probably get away with it. He felt that, as soon as he got the opportunity, he would want to cut off someone's balls, for the second time, as a gesture against those two fuckers who took those liberties with him, humiliating him in the process. He had anyway broken a leg from a chair abandoned in an alleyway. He knew that there were Jews around here: he could smell them; the chances were that anyone crossing this green coming towards him, would be a Jew. He put his hand around the long-bladed, unflicked flick-knife in his pocket and threw away the chair leg. As for that tart of his, she'd kept from him that she was a Jew, grounds for whatever final divorce he meted out to her.

As he approached the centre of the Green, where it had become a little misty, he saw coming his way the shape of someone walking. He had felt utterly devoid of any aspiration or desire to do anything useful and felt only a vacant anger that needed to be humoured.

He stood perfectly still for a moment to be sure that there was no sound of kids playing or dogs playing, started walking again and soon saw that it was a young man. He shouted at the young man as he passed: evening! The young man replied: good evening! Got to be a fucking Jew! Wyre carried on for about fifty yards and suddenly turned, took the knife out of his pocket, unleashed the six-inch blade, raced after the young man and as he reached him, shouted: fucking queer Jew scum! And slammed the knife blade into the walker's head. The young man fell. Wyre fell on him, furiously stabbing him and then pulled the young man's trousers and underpants down, took his shoes off and yanked the trousers off. In the quiet after Wyre had buggered the dead man, a dog barked. Wyre looked up and saw coming towards him a huge and clearly annoyed Doberman. Instinctively, he cut the walker's genitals off, threw them at the dog and sprinted away across the Green.

Chapter 44
The Russian

(Hail Pasternak!)

So much had happened of late that I'd been utterly remiss in not phoning Vladimir. So I did. He said: hello and I said: Vladimir? It's me, Rose. Rose? My Sonia? Yes. We will meet? Yes. I could see you this evening. He said: The Green Olive and I said: of course! His responses were so quick that it made me think he'd been sitting by the phone for the last few weeks, waiting for my call.

I said: what time?

Nine? It is too late?

No.

I guessed he was thinking that if we were out until about 10:30, it would be a good time to go to his place. No time to discuss options.

We sat at the table at the back of the café, you could almost say *his* table, the table he was sitting at when I first met him. His eyes were like Omar Sharif's in *Doctor Zhivago*, dark and passionate and a little wet with suffering. He reached his hand across the table and took mine.

He said: you have lost some weight.

Thank you.

And you look more beautiful.

Thank you, again! There's some sadness in your eyes that I didn't see before.

I am still hurting from when I hurt you.

It's ok, I said, I understand what you were going through. And I had no right to mention the Chilean. These are things I know little about. In the Soviet Union, women are equal – equal in marriage, which is anyway frowned upon as being against collectivism; equality in work, but also equality in suffering. Women are entitled to suffer as much as men. So men treat women as they treat men in *Nastoika*. Maybe without respect. Behaviour recognised by the state as correct. We were brought up in this way. So how have I escaped Soviet influence if I can treat you like this?

I'm sorry, Vladimir, what's this "nast...?

Nastoika? It is, you know, where you work!

A pub?

Yes.

O, I think men treat women just as badly here in our pubs. In this country.

So a man could hit a woman in a pub?

Well, no. Not really. But in Russia, it would be also reasonable if I was to hit you?

He said: do you think you may ever want to hit me?

No, of course not.

What you taught me: you can never be free unless you are free in sexual things, but through love. Because sex through love is way to freedom of emotion and freedom of emotion is only true freedom. In Soviet Union, only Politburo have freedom of emotion! Men or women who express freedom of emotion, then he drew his finger across his throat and said: *zakonchennyy*. I think only these things since I met you.

A waitress came and we ordered food and ouzo.

When she'd gone, I said: are you missing the Soviet Union? You've started to use Russian words.

No, I do not miss the USSR; I miss Russia. My home is in Russia.

Then, after a lull, I said: did you hear about the murder last night? On Jesus Green.

Yes. It is terrible. There was such a murder before I left in *Zaryadye Park* in Moscow. Do you know what happened? Last night?

No. They haven't even released the name of the victim.

After a while, a couple sat at the table behind us.

The waitress brought the ouzos.

Vladimir said: why have they not said who, do you think?

I immediately took a large gulp of the ouzo.

I said: Perhaps the victim was important. But how could anybody do it? Why?

Someone who likes to control and has lost control. Perhaps. Someone who is angry.

I've read that most victims are known to their murderers.

With this in mind, I was shocked by what I thought I heard the woman behind me say. I turned to her: I'm sorry I couldn't help overhearing something you said about the murder.

The woman said: that's ok.

I said: Did you say that the victim of the murder last night was a student?

She said: yes.

Do you know the name?

Was it Buckford? Something like that?

Could it be Buckland?

Yes.

Thank you.

She smiled as I must have gone white.

I turned back to Vladimir. He said: what is the matter?

I know who it was. The murdered one. Buckland.

Do I know that name?

I thought for a moment and said: I think you may! Do you remember the evening you gave a talk in my pub and a young man challenged you?

From the back of the room?

No. He was near the front. You were arguing about plagiarism.

O yes. I do remember that!

That was him! That was Buckland!

Then our food arrived.

We ordered more ouzos.

We were silent while the food was laid out. Except I turned to the woman again and said: I'm sorry, do you know any more of the details? I'm sorry, it seems morbid, but I know someone of that name.

O. Well, all I know is that they're saying there was something ritualistic about it.

Ok. Thanks. Thank you again.

I turned back to Vladimir and he said: if you're right, then perhaps he knew killer. The woman said they're saying that it may have been a ritual killing.

We began to eat and I said: you know, in Cambridge, there are many secret societies and clubs.

Vladimir put his hand on mine and said:

I think perhaps we should not talk about this business. It cannot be undone. We could be crushed by what we can't control.

Chapter 45

The Love Between Buckland and Parfitt

(*Hail Edward Bond!*)

Sometime after the insurrection evening where Parfitt met Buckland for the first time, Parfitt made it his business to get Buckland's details: address, phone number, where he studied, etc and found that the young genius used King's College library to work in.

On that evening, Parfitt had immediately felt something for Buckland. It wasn't sexual: Parfitt had always been horrified by the idea of body fluids mingling; rather, he felt something for Buckland's vulnerability made all the more acute by the simplicity of the young man with the complex mind.

Walking the length of the main aisle of the library and seeing no Buckland at a desk between bookshelves, Parfitt went to the library alcove and found him there. Feigning surprise, Parfitt said:

Mr. Buckland!

Buckland looked up and saw a young man in a slightly crumpled suit jacket from which extended *elocutionary arms from frayed cuffs* and unmatching trousers while exuding an imperious air. The trousers were baggy at the knees and the jacket shiny at the elbows. At first he didn't recognise him, then he said, O hello Mr. Parfitt.

Speaking *sotto voce,* Parfitt said: sorry to disturb you. Am I disturbing you?

No, no, it's ok.

Parfitt sat. What are you studying?

I'm looking at Wittgenstein. I saw a play recently about him and thought it was time I did some research. It's a fascinating play. *Wittgenstein's Daughter.* Do you know it?

'Fraid I don't.

You remind me of him. To look at. I thought that the first time I saw you.

He is something of a hero of mine. Can I sit?

Of course.

Parfitt sat and said: what was the thrust of the play.

It's about the daughter of the philosopher who returns to Cambridge from Paris in search of evidence of her father's life. As you probably know, Wittgenstein was gay, which was, as you also probably know, illegal and morally unacceptable. A disgrace that people had to live beneath that burden because of their sexuality. I'm sure you know that in his work, he said that the only things we can meaningfully talk about are things that can be scientifically proved. Or tautologies. So, for him, moral judgement couldn't be made about his sexuality. Unfortunately, society didn't see it like that and so, in order to satisfy public prejudice, not to mention the need for safety from the threat of prosecution, a daughter was conceived with the help of an ex-boxer and a whore as a means of making it seem that he was, in fact, heterosexual. The more she looks into his life, the closer she gets to the truth of her provenance. The thrust of the play is rooted in the argument made in some quarters that Wittgenstein fashioned his moral theories so that his homosexuality couldn't be discussed in any meaningful way.

So the man himself isn't portrayed.

His ghost.

Ghost?

Yes. Wittgenstein's Ghost is a character in the play. I have the book of the play if you'd like to borrow it.

Absolutely. And once I've read it, we can meet to discuss it. In fact, we should make a date and you can come to my room and I'll feed you! How does that sound?

Yes. Thank you. How shall I get the book to you?

You could leave it here. With the librarian. I'll come and get it tomorrow.

Parfitt got up to leave and said: do you mind if I give you a friendly little kiss?

He wasn't sure why he asked this, except it was Cambridge and quite commonplace to express friendship in this way.

Buckland said calmly: if you were Wittgenstein, you probably would. Parfitt giggled and said yes and kissed Buckland fully on the lips.

Two days later, Buckland was at Parfitt's. Parfitt greeted Buckland with a passionate kiss, took his coat, brought him into his room and invited him to sit. Parfitt sat beside him and took the young genius's hands in his.

I've read the play! It's bold and almost expressionistic and I think it gets to this truth about his sexuality, that, for him, it had no place in the world of his theorising, which is why, though it's not covered in the play, most of his urgent, sexual desires were satisfied in the toilets of the city.

Is that so? I didn't know.

O yes. What I'm proposing is that we follow his example.

Meet in toilets?

No, no! I was thinking, rather, that when we meet to do our own theorising, we keep it free of passionate distractions; unsullied by moral ambiguity.

Of course.

Tea or sherry?

I'll have a little sherry.

From somewhere came the smell of a professional curry in preparation. The frying of onions, garlic and ginger. And coriander and....

Buckland said: My God, where's that divine smell coming from?

That's charming, Chitrabhanu, our Keralan queen. He lives in this building. He's cooking (he sniffs deeply) Puttu and Kadala Curry. Why don't you linger, Neil? I'm sure I could wangle an invite to dine with him.

I have to be somewhere.

O, very well then.

Chapter 46

Snookered

Will couldn't rest; couldn't accept that he'd been rejected by a middle aged woman in favour of an even older middle aged man and while Rolcord Wyre was putting the finishing touches to the short life of the genius Buckland, Will was in the snooker room where he'd found Parfitt sitting at the bar with a glass of lemonade, asking Parfitt to take him to Goldstein's so that he could see Carla.

You know what you're experiencing, Slade? An absence of profundity.

What the hell d'you mean by that?

The profound thinker, the one who plumbs the depths, understands the banality of his own selfish emotions and rises above them. Christ, man. You have a beautiful woman. Rose! Incidentally, why do you think people wanted to believe Buckland was dead?

Since he's been around, the best brains have been relegated, if not humiliated,y someone from a lowly background. He reminds me of Chatterton, who was driven into poverty by the refusal of the poetry establishment to acknowledge him and allow him to earn a decent wage. Because of his provenance.

Ah, yes. Well, that probably is true.

Do you think it's too late to go around there now?

Where?

To Goldstein's

Christ, Slade, what do expect we'll say? Good evening, Mr. Goldstein, Will here would like to tup your wife? Anyway, I was about to have a game.

With who? Perhaps he won't turn up.

As it happens, with Neil.

Neil?

Buckland!

O! When should he have been here?

Half an hour ago.

He's not coming.

He may!

He's probably down some diamond mine of ideas immobilised by the wonder of their twinkling!

We'll give him fifteen minutes more.

At Goldstein's door, they waited. They rang the bell a second time and were about to leave when Goldstein came to the door. He looked as if he'd heard some challenging news.

Ah, Anthony, Will. I'm glad you've come. I've just had some disturbing news. A student has been murdered!

Chapter 47

A late evening with Dewey and Rose

(Hail Dostoevsky!)

I'd never thought of sex as an act of charity until one evening when Dewey and myself were alone.

I said: no luck with jobs?

No. I've got no confidence, so people think I'm hiding something.

I don't know why I haven't thought of it before, but do you want me to ask Quaid?

Sorry, who?

Quaid Laurel, my boss.

Doing what?

Bar work? Serving drinks. Changing barrels. We'd all be happy if you were to do that.

Dewey was silent for a moment, then he said: I would have to meet a lot of people.

Of course!

I'm not sure. Not sure if I'm strong enough. Not sure if I would have enough confidence.

What d'you think happened to your confidence?

The house of the dead.

Broadmoor?

When you come out, you realise just how dead you are. Your life has been cancelled.

There was something in the air of the room. Some pulse. Dewey was sitting on the edge of the sofa bed but couldn't get comfortable. Like someone waiting for the train that would take them to freedom, fearing it may not arrive.

What can we do to get it back? Is it the case that you haven't been with a woman since your release? Dewey could see in the way I spoke that I was about to offer myself.

You wouldn't say Dewey was particularly good looking: he had a heavy face and always almost too clean-shaven, but he had an almost saintly presence and he gave the impression that it was so important for him that each moment had a positive outcome that he would do anything for you in order to achieve it. We were silent for a moment. I knew from his eyes that he knew what I was proposing.

Ok, I said, moving towards him; tell me to stop if you don't want me to go on. He was sitting on the bed. I kneeled before him and undid his fly. I paused. Then I gently pushed him and he lay back on the bed. His cock was yearning for escape. I undid his trousers and tentatively pulled at them slightly pausing, then he lifted himself and helped me. Then his pants and as they passed the head of that mighty member, it sprang up. I must say it was one of the more robust and committed to the moment I had encountered. Almost up with Dan's. I put my hand to it and held it and immediately he came.

He said: O, god! What a mess.

No, I said, it's beautiful. And poignant. It's a plea for the lonely. And you'll be fine once you're ready to carry on.

I took a tissue from my bedside and wiped away his unload. As I did, he said:

I'm afraid. I think if we did it, I would fall in love with you. In fact, offering yourself to me means I already love you.

Dewey, this is about rebuilding your confidence. Healing you. I'm your nurse. Nurses fuck patients in cupboards without falling in love. It's part of your treatment.

What about Will?

He doesn't have to know. Anyway, he's currently under the spell of Carla Goldstein. As I said that I began to caress his loving fuckpiece, which, after a while, rose as his breathing grew stronger.

We did it through the night, through the undergrowth, beneath a blue sky, through the soaking of monsoon, through joy and fear, guilt and sadness, through triumph and remorse and hallelujah.

The next morning, I could feel the signs of predepression arriving. This is a term I used for that place of warning when you were given the opportunity to steel yourself against the worst: the need to understand the threat and where it was coming from. For me, it usually began with the coming together of three or four threatening prospects you feel you have no control over. The need is to identify them and understand them and take back control. I could see nothing like that. It wasn't until later that it seemed as if all three or four such anxieties were actually in Dewey and somehow he'd pumped them into me.

Chapter 48
What had happened that evening

(Hail Lorca!)

This is what I picked up from Dewey about that evening: as Wyre had lunged for Tarita, Dewey had put a hand to his chest and stopped him. Wyre was stunned: how had a single hand stopped him? And belonging to some knobby, brainy, probably poofter twat. Dewey was phenomenally strong, as we knew from the incident with the Alsatian. Tarita had stood behind Will and Wyre's instinct was to go for her again, and he was stopped again.

He said to Dewey: what's your game? That's my fucking wife!

You think so?

Yeah! I fucking know so!

Will turned to Tarita and said: are you this man's wife?

No. And he's not supposed to come near me.

Wyre went for her again and this time, Dewey clasped a hand around his throat and with the other, clasped a hand around his testicles and squeezed.

Wyre let out an outraged cry. In this way, Dewey removed him from the pub.

Will went with them.

Dewey said: get out of Cambridge and don't come back. He let Wyre go and Wyre pressed his face on Dewey's and said: I've got your number, mate!

If you do come back, bring an army.

Apparently, Will said to him:

This man has just come out of Broadmoor. He would do workouts with Frankie Frazer, the gangland killer. You will never come near Tarita again.

Have her. She's scum! And he left.

They say they had never seen a man so angry; full of the vim of violence.

As I came to the end of this reverie while laying in the bath, there was a furious knocking on my door.

I quickly climbed out, flung a bath towel around me and went to the door. It was Will. He came in. Solemn.

He said: it *was* Neil.

Buckland!

He had a stab wound through the top of the head into the brain; a load of stab wounds in his body and his genitals were cut off. They're missing.

Chapter 49
Repair to Chatterton

(Hail Mary Shelley!)

Once again, I found myself in Holborn on Brook St. heading for Chatterton's place and then climbing the stairs to his garret. And there he was, as in the famous painting, draped along his *chaise longue*; you'd think dead. The room smelled of nothing. Perhaps the inside of my head. I went to him and shook him. He woke. I said: some would think you'd died.

Why?

Because accounts have claimed you killed yourself. Committed suicide. With arsenic.

I took arsenic to cure my syphilis.

Did it work?

I didn't have syphilis. And I didn't take the arsenic. I wanted people to think I killed myself. But I died of a broken heart. I was murdered by rejection.

I gasped, recalling:

A friend of mine was brutally murdered on Jesus Green in Cambridge. Just the other day.

Sorry.

There was something ritualistic about the killing. His penis and testicles were cut off and as far as anyone knows, taken by the murderer. Why? He was a genius! People loved and respected him. They fell silent in his presence.

Then Chatterton was silent.

Then he said: *ignoratio elenchi.*

I'm sorry?

It is a fallacy in philosophy: where you think you're discussing one thing, but you're missing a consequence of your argument and unintentionally prove an unintended outcome:

Wherefore did Christ post hanging

wander to Kashmir taking alms from

goatherds whose profound ignorance was

like the sweetest life-sustaining water to one

made life-threateningly thirsty by the vinegar

of sophistication and then die again bemused

a pauper in Srinagar? In search of Israel's lost? No

to find understanding in the living world

of ignoratio elenchi

If Christ was a man, he died uselessly and cruelly like so many others and if he was a god, well….. he becomes a metaphor for the power of myth. Or was he the proof of the non-existence of God? A good, benign, caring God would not sacrifice his son to prove his existence. If there was such a god, we wouldn't want him!

Christ, who refuses to give in to his dying, died a third time, sucking the sand around Timbuktu searching for the proof of *ignoratio elenchi* when he'd already found it and proved it!

in the churchyard of St. Thomas the Martyr

within the mortmain of St Dogmaels Abbey

long laid waste by Henry's Cromwell, in a

collection box screwed to the wall there lies a

penny i had prized left by me

not as an oblation, homage to infinity and the cosmic

influence of ruins on blue but for

missing the point about Christ!

I said: missing the point of Christ? What was it?

The point of Christ was not to prove the existence of God but to disprove it.

O! Is that your idea?

Yes. Of course.

And the piece you just recited?

Scribbles. I spent so much time creating fictitious medieval undiscovered work, now I'm trying to write a fictitious work of the future. But I won't bother making it public – they'd only scoff. They may call me pretentious.

I wasn't sure what to say, but I did say that I thought his language was ahead of its time. He said thank you and I said but the "wherefore" at the beginning of his poem seemed to belong more to his day rather than the future. And he said Oh.

I said: I've met you before, you know?

We are all of us only here by the grace of subjectivity.

Why did you say that….what is it? Latin? *Ignor……*

Ignoratio elenchi.

Yes. Why did you say that after I told you about my murdered friend?

I'm sorry. I've often been criticised for apparently missing the point myself. *You* missed the point because you think you were talking about your friend's death, but, in fact, you were talking about your own. You see? You missed the point. It's a universal fallacy. You see, you wanted to prove that you can be devastated by your friend's death, but succeeded in proving that you're actually devastated by the little death it produces in you. All our emotions, finally, are selfish.

Then we did it.

And we did do it. It was true. We really did it because I could feel him moving around in me with all the power of death. Filled me with all the mystery of the cosmos. When he came, it was like a torturing electric strike.

Of course, it didn't prove that you can fuck in death, but rather the opposite: that all dreams of life in death, death after life, is sentimental pap. That's what Thomas would say.

Chapter 50

What the Fuck?

The next morning, Will told me about Farquhar-Groyne.

He said: He was found in his room. About the same time as Buckland, but the college authorities kept it secret for a couple of days.

What the fuck?

Yeah.

Will put Debussy on, then sat on my bed.

It was the same. Groyne's genitals were removed, but his were stuck in his mouth. They think it was done by the same person.

God, Will. Do you think we're in danger? Might the killer come for us?

Why? We don't know him.

Not specifically us. Say, people who knew Neil. Why Buckland and Farquhaur-Groyne? And what about Anthony Parfitt? It was Farquhar-Groyne who published Neil's paper and said it was Parfitt and that Parfitt had stolen it.

I don't know. And Parfitt and Buckland had become very close. Almost lovers.

O Will, put your arms around me.

He did. And he said: Rose, I've missed you.

Because you've been chasing after Carla. Becoming obsessed with her. Jealous!

That!

Then he got into bed with me. One of his furious ones. As if crazed. Strangely, as he entered and re-entered, I imagined I was with Chatterton – Dan, not the dead one. Afterwards, I thought I know this sounds obvious, but most times when we make love, we're missing the point. Love, you would imagine, is about sharing experiences so that we're mutual beneficiaries when actually we're doing it for ourselves. That's been my experience anyway. Most times. And I can't seem to stop doing it. Lately, perhaps the only time I made love was when I did it with Dewey, because I was doing it mostly for him.

Ignoratio elenchi!

Chapter 51

Strangers on a Train

(Hail B. Traven!)

After the news about Buckland got to Bubovsky, he asked to see Rose. He was in a state convinced he was next. She sucked him off to settle him down, then he told her he was taking a late train that evening, to London. He was leaving it till late so that, hopefully, he wouldn't be recognised and bothered with questions about the brutality of the Soviet Union.

There was a train around midnight, but he told her it was leaving earlier. He needed time between the exertions of ejaculation and, he hoped, an hour of reflection before the train and maybe on it.

He sat in the almost empty waiting room. A waiting room is just that. A place to wait; a place where you may feel alone, even lonely. A place where you suspect the rising of panic. Vladimir felt that uneasy. He felt he may be coming to the end of his relationship with Rose: the fizz he'd found with their sex had suddenly become a parochialism. Now he wished he'd timed things so that he could have immediately caught the train. He realised he'd sat in a place like this one time a long time ago, in a forlorn Bolshevik outpost and his spirits slumped. And in that slump with images of Rose and what they'd done in his peripheral thought, he felt disgusted and nauseous.

When the train turned up, he found an almost empty carriage and settled down for the journey. But just as the train was about to pull off, a young man struggled onto the train, threw his rucksack onto the seat across the aisle and flopped down into it.

He said: almost missed it!

Bubovsky smiled.

The young man looked a little wild-eyed. Bubovsky thought that was probably because of his rush. He was wearing an unconvincing overcoat that must have belonged to someone else. Bubovsky thought that someone must have kindly lent it to the young man for the night's travel. In fact, one could tell from the cut of the cloth that it was an expensive coat and Bubovsky missed the point that the coat was stolen, stolen from someone whose blood stains on the young man the coat was hiding.

The young man was Wyre.

It was likely to be a cold night and if Wyre was going to lie low for a couple of them, he would need to be wrapped up.

When God kicked the lovers out of Eden, His intolerance and lack of compassion justified all acts of dispatch: throwing out of gardens, doors, windows, land, nationhood, life, war and murder. When He banished knowledge from the garden, He justified fascism. Rolcord Wyre was God's warrior banishing knowledge from Cambridge, dispatching the genius and the Don. Farquhar-Groyne, victim of war in the Kingdom of Wyre.

The young man said: on a winning streak!

Bubovsky smiled.

Then the young man said: been visiting?

No, no. I live in Cambridge.

You foreign?

Russian.

O right. Commie bastard. Then, after a very short pause in which the Russian looked anxious. It's ok, mate. Joking.

I live in exile.

Wot, they kicked you out?

You could say.

Naughty boy?

Vladimir said with a smile: yes.

The young man said: we've all been a bit naughty. It's my middle name. Naughty. Then, with a gesture as if indicating his name in lights: Rolcord Trouble Wyre. What's your name?

Vladimir.

Bubovsky was sure he'd heard the young man's name before. Perhaps from Rose? It made him uncomfortable. He said: have you been visiting Cambridge?

Yeah. Just today. Had a bit of business. Hell of a day. Ha! Ha!

There was something in the young man's laugh that caused Bubovsky another moment of anxiety. He had heard that laugh many times in the psychiatric ward they'd locked him up in, not among the politicos but the truly ill.

Rolcord Trouble Wyre said: I visited the university!

What college?

Cambridge! Cambridge University.

But there are many colleges: Kings, Trinity, Emmanuel, Jesus....

Jesus, yeh. Don't think Jesus would have much to do with me! Ha, ha! Mind you, if you're talking about crucifixion!

Were you?

Wot?

Talking about crucifixion.

Well, I spose he had it coming!

Do you mean it wasn't wise to call yourself king in country where they have king?

Something like that. It's like these homos going round spreading disease in a place where it's not normal to be a homo. I bet they haven't got homos in Russia.

I am sure they have, but not so open as in the West.

What's the Russian for bum boy, hey? Ha, ha.

Now Bubovsky felt distinctly uncomfortable. The murder of the student crossed his mind. He was reluctant to alert, say, the conductor. He remembered how going to someone in authority in the Soviet Union about someone else, perhaps something trite and inconsequential, could lead to their summary incarceration; which was not the same as if, for example, Razumikhin had gone to Porfiry Petrovich with worries about Raskolnikov. That would have been Razumikhin alerting the authorities as a matter of duty to justice. Surely, then, it would be the same in this case!

Bubovsky got up with his travelling bag and said: excuse me.

Wyre said, almost menacingly: you leaving me?

I have to go to bathroom.

Won't find a bathroom on this train, mate! Ha, ha! Taking your bag?

It would be unfitting behaviour leaving bag with complete stranger. May invite my own crucifixion.

Nice one! Ha, ha!

Bubovsky left his carriage and passed through others with a rolling sway until he found the conductor.

He said: excuse me.

The conductor turned to him and said after a very short pause, excuse *me,* Mr. Bubovsky. My wife….I'm quite overwhelmed. We've followed your story from the beginning.

Thank you. I'd like to……

Do you know Mr Solzhenitsin? My wife's a big reader. She's done Cancer Ward.

"Done?"

I say "done" because, for me, it would be a chore. I'm not a reader. Newspapers, yes. And that's where I've followed you. Daily Mail. I don't know how you put up with those communists for so long. I suppose they were everywhere. We have a few here, but not that many. Whenever I come on one, I get the creeps. The willies. What was it like, the brutality?

There is young man three carriages back who may be murderer.

Well, I suppose you would know, having lived amongst murderers and whatnot.

Perhaps you heard about this. Young student on Jesus Green in Cambridge.

O, yes!

I think, perhaps, you should alert authorities.

Three carriages back? Maybe I should check him out.

Well, I think he may be dangerous. He told me his name, which I'm sure I'd heard in context, which could connect him with murder. And he seems, you know, unstable.

What's the name?

Rolcord Wyre.

Funny name.

Just then, at the end of the carriage Bubovsky came from, he heard: so there you are, Vlad! And as he approached, said to the conductor: watch him, he's Vlad the Impaler! Ha, ha!

The first thing that crossed the guard's mind was: unusual to see murderers wearing rucksacks! On the other hand, that may have been designed to distract the suspicious. But not him. Not the guard. Not the conductor.

Chapter 52
Talking About Crucifixion

(Hail Carver!)

When the news broke that Rolcord Wyre had been arrested for questioning about the double murder of Farquhar-Groyne and Buckland, Rose heard it alone.

She couldn't believe it and then she could. On that dreadful day, she'd let him pin her to the wall beside a sink, travelling at 70 miles an hour. A grub of menace rose in her anxious mind, causing her to think that she may have made herself an accomplice. But what, then, seemed worse was that her blind devotion to her investigation into sex had driven her into the clutch of the criminal. Like some demotic nymph! And then, to top that, *ignoratio elenchi:* that the deepest sexual experience in performance counters knowledge; that when you're about to do it, you don't want to know anything about the one doing it to you; you don't care if it's a murderer or priest! She wondered: isn't the point she missed that sex is about *ecstasy*! Beyond stasis; beyond reality and the world of knowledge. *No, no, you're panicking! What you're searching for is precisely acknowledging the state of stasis and sex's role within that!*

And then she thought: I need to give more time to this. You're shocked. And there is that frisson of thrill.......

She got herself a glass of wine and settled down. And then the torment really began:

If she hadn't fucked Rolcord Wyre, she wouldn't have mentioned it to Tarita who wouldn't have identified him, they wouldn't have arranged the intervention of Will and Dewey, who wouldn't have been so frustrated by Will and Dewey's ultimatum and wouldn't have taken it out on the first innocent he'd come across who he was able to kill. And that was Buckland. Put simply, her fucking had killed Buckland!

But then she thought: isn't the real point I'm missing that he'd already killed Groyne?

All these thoughts caused Rose to panic. And the discovery of *ignoratio elenchi* began to eat away at any sense of security and she became aware of the deep black lake threatening.

Chapter 53
Mourning Becomes the Goldstein's

(Hail O'Neill!)

Carla felt Parfitt's pain.

The whole city, of course, was in a state of shock. Two murders: a Cambridge don and a boy genius! Word had got around that Bubovsky had alerted the authorities to Wyre and when he returned from London, it was to a hero's welcome, which meant that Rose couldn't get close to him through the high tide of his new fame.

Parfitt had gone round to see the Goldsteins the day after news of the calamity. He had shared with them certain details of his relationship with Buckland and confessed that he was devastated and inconsolable. They took it on themselves to attempt consoling him and invited him to stay with them for as long as he wanted; until he could face his life - now without Neil - again. What most disturbed Goldstein had not been the revelation that Farquhar-Groyne had been a rabid anti-Semite - he kind of knew that anyway - with his collection of roughnecks who weren't all low-life lumpenproletariat but some of a higher order: lord's sons and earls' bastards, a little like Rogozin's crew in Dostoyevsky's *The Idiot* but given his profile, who would have done it? A Jew?

At this time, Will had tried to contact Parfitt and been unable to and figured that this would be a good time to call on the Goldsteins with the excuse that he was looking for his friend (and maybe freshen things up a bit with Carla!)

The door was opened by a sombre Carla who said quietly: hello, Will. Please come in. Anthony is here. Goldstein said: come and sit Will.

Parfitt muttered: Slade.

Carla said: would you like a drink?

Will looked at her longingly. He was lucky she wasn't the kind of person who would take offence at someone deploying such a look (inappropriate) at such a time.

Yes, please.

Red wine?

Yes. Please.

Goldstein said: Farquhar-Groyne…..I think they call it rough trade.

Will said: do you mean someone picked up, say, in a toilet?

Yes.

Parfitt said, glumly: Wittgenstein indulged in that kind of behaviour. Some men are so disgusted with their sexuality that they'll satisfy the need and then turn on the person they did it with, blaming them for what just happened.

Goldstein said: not Wittgenstein!

Parfitt said: no! Although perhaps in his own way…..through his philosophy….

The phone rang.

Carla answered it.

It's for you, Will.

Me?

It's Rose.

Will took the phone: hello?

I need to see you, Will. I need you. I guessed you'd be there. Obviously.

What is it? What's happened?

They've arrested Rolcord Wyre. For the murders.

Will was silent.

Hello? Will?

Hang on a sec.

Will addressed the others.

Rolcord Wyre's been detained.

Goldstein: Who?

The husband of Tarita. He came to kill her.

Variously: What? Isn't that the woman you're helping? I don't understand.

Then Will said into the phone: I'll come now. And to the others: I'm sorry, I'll have to go.

Goldstein: Of course.

Parfitt: 'Bye, Slade.

Carla: I'll see you out.

At the door, Will suddenly blurted out: I saw you with Sternbend. Is he….

What?! Where?

I was in Ely Cathedral one day and, by chance, saw you.

You know, Will, if I didn't like you, I'd be furious now. The conclusions you jump to are determined by your state of mind, your emotional defaults and your temporary abandonment of logic that those predispositions determine. Never look into private mail because you will be predisposed to misunderstand what you read.

I'm…I'm sorry.

One thing I ask: say nothing to Mr. Sternbend.

Of course.

Will left feeling disgusted that he'd so offended Carla for a green moment. And at the same time, he'd been hurting Rose, whose ebullience and shameless determination to crush the age-old myths of sexual despair he so admired.

At Rose's, he suddenly had the urge to deeply fuck her. She was wearing only one of his shirts she'd nicked and he occasionally caught a glimpse of the trimmed hairs celebrating her pretty, pursed cunt. She had lost weight, he could now see, and was devastatingly beguiling.

Before saying anything, he lay her back on the bed, picked her legs up, held them apart and kissed and sucked those pouting, rosy lips. She was thrilled by this original way to say hello and thought the French must have a term for it: *bisou salut dans les lèvres de la vulve?* Except that would be clumsy – not reflecting the efficient charm of the act. Maybe *bisou de la vulve* or even just *bisou!*

Back at the Goldstein's, Parfitt said: you're not saying that Buckland was mixed up with anti-Semites, are you? Don't forget, in his paper, Buckland had argued contra Arendht who'd agreed with Eichmann that he wasn't an antisemite but someone simply following the call of duty, for Buckland, he was anyway guilty as hell. If you kill Jews, you're an anti-Jew.

Goldstein said: it's true that too avid a desire to solve a problem can invite what I call *the error of convenience* and the censure of the innocents. If anything, he was attacked because the attacker thought he was a Jew crossing Jesus Green after being at that small kosher place on the east side.

But if the attacker was an antisemite, why would he kill the antisemite Farquahar-Groyne? Because I don't think he killed Neil for being Jewish, I think he killed him for some other reason.

Goldstein said: perhaps it was because he perceived him as being homosexual.

Immediately, Parfitt thought that *this* must be why Neil was attacked. That, though they'd not done anything physical, he'd brought out the homo-erotic side of Buckland and that the killer must have been a repressed homosexual who was able to recognise the true nature of Neil.

Parfitt said: it must be Wyre. He's got a track record of violence. It all fits. And they wouldn't have arrested him without being pretty certain.

In a post-coital calm, Will said: do you think the whole thing is my fault? For helping Tarita?

More likely my fault for having sex with Wyre. You helping Tarita was a generous act. Mine was selfish. You and Dewey drove him off and maybe saved her life. Mine drove him to murder because he couldn't have that evening what I'd given him on the train.

But he killed Farquahar -Groyne *before* he came to meet you.

Did he? How do we know? When we did it, it put him on the roll that would lead a man like him to need to commit the ultimate act of dominance.

I think he did it because he was in a bad mood.

That's a bit of a straw man. That's obviously true, just as it would be true to say he's a psycho, but the point is, what triggered it? Me screwing him. That's why. Then me *not* screwing him later after he expected it.

Why do you do this? Why complicate everything? He did it! End of story.

But we need to understand things. We often miss the point because we don't want to face it!

Ok. Let me try this: Why do you like sex so much? In all its manifestations? You say that because you need to understand the philosophical roots of sex. Then I say: that may be true, but it's missing the point! The reason you like sex so much is because you're a nympho; if you weren't, you wouldn't have begun your quest into the logic of sex to begin with!

Rose was silent for a moment.

That's what we call a fallacy: You've introduced an idea that does not in any way advance your original assertion but is a hugely different argument. Totally without logic. It would be like me saying that you're doing a PhD on Chatterton because you're basically a lousy poet and you think that studying someone like that will raise your profile and give the impression that you're a poet of some weight! Did you come here because you'd be sure of an easy fuck? Because you can't fuck her?

Sorry, Rose. I didn't mean that you *are* a nympho. I was being hypothetical.

Both were silent, then Rose said: I just can't get how this happened in Cambridge! It's like Satan in Paradise. Maybe he didn't come for Tarita or Farquahar-Groyne or Buckland. Maybe he came for Cambridge itself. We know how fascists hate intellectuals!

Chapter 54

Dewey the Obscure

(Hail Schopenhauer!)

Dewey was alone with Tarita. As her guardian as much as anything. She'd heard about what her husband had done and couldn't really deal with it. She was in that hidden land between shock and indifference. She was pleased to have Dewey there: his calm authority was a welcome antidote to the horror story of her husband. Dewey had brought a bottle of Yugoslavian Riesling. He figured the sweetness of the grape would help remove the sour taste of their particular holocaust.

She was sleeping when he came. Not a deep sleep; a light slumber in the resonances left in the wake of Rolcord's arrest. Dewey left her alone and went to the bathroom and when he returned, she was awake.

Hi Dewey.

Are you alright?

I am, yes. Thank you.

She lifted herself and repositioned herself with her back resting against the headboard.

I've brought wine. Would you like some? I think you'd like it. It's a light, quite sweet white from Yugoslavia. Riesling.

O yes. Thanks.

I haven't had a drink for a long time, but I'll join you. He poured drinks.

He said: You seem calmer.

I think I am.

He gave her the glass and she drank half straight down.

Dewey said: how do you feel about him?

I'm not sure.

If you think about how he hurt you, insulted you, and robbed you of your purity, then you'll never be free from hate. So put him out of your mind.

I'm sure that must be true. I think I'm getting there.

The Buddha says: *Through perseverance, vigilance and self-restraint, a wise person creates a safe harbour for herself that no storm can overwhelm.*

Buddha?

Yes. I've been studying the Buddha.

Dewey sat on the bed beside her. They drank the almost flowery drink and he refilled the glasses from the bottle standing on a small table.

The wise one does not judge others, not their words or their deeds or what they have or haven't done. The wise one only contemplates her own words and deeds.

Are you saying I shouldn't judge Rolcord?

Would it do you any good? *A spoon never knows the taste of soup.*

Ha, ha. You make me feel calm, Dewey.

Good.

Yes, good.

Then Tarita said: could you comfort me, Dewey?

Yes. What would you like me to do?

Just put your arms around me.

Dewey embraced her, his arms like a down stuffed collar. He held his face against her hair, which was soft and luxurious. He didn't know the identity of her perfume, but it filled him with that incongruous hope he would occasionally experience in the darkest hollows of the hospital.

Tarita said: how do you feel about me? Do you think you could love me?

Yes.

Physically?

Dewey paused.

Is that not something you'd expect me to say? I think I feel stronger and liberated now that Rolcord's been arrested.

You're beautiful and I'm a man. But I would be afraid to hurt you.

Could you hurt me?

I'm a man.

I think I could tell if a man would hurt me.

As the lotus is unstained by water, so is nirvana unstained by the defilements.

I don't get that.

The things of nature are pure. The highest state of purity is nirvana. Everything else, all that might seem pure, may be defiled. People can get hurt despite the purest of intentions.

Do we have to get to nirvana?

No.

They kissed.

Chapter 55

You Were on Fire, Rolcord Wyre!

(Hail Kafka!)

INTERVIEWER: So, Rolcord Wyre, how does it feel to be a celebrity?

WYRE: Great!

MAN: People say you were on fire.

WYRE: They know.

MAN: And in here? In prison?

WYRE: They're in awe. Full of admiration. The guys are great. I get treated

like a hero. Lots of perks.

MAN: Perks.

WYRE: The young uns – the boys - let me fuck 'em. No problem.

MAN: (To off) Can we cut that? (To WYRE) Sorry Rolcord, Today's

Celebrity

Is:........*is a family show. Need you to be a role model.*

WYRE: (Shrugs) Ok.

MAN: Your perks?

WYRE: The young guys are nice. Very friendly. They'll do anything for me.

I'm

the boss.

MAN: Was it difficult?

WYRE: What?

MAN: *The undertaking.*

WYRE: *Well, you know, in this game, we can't afford to feel sorry for ourselves.*

MAN: *What was it like? Can you tell us? I'm sure the viewers will be interested. Excited.*

WYRE: *Difficult to pin it down. When you're in it, doing it, you're like something else, a different entity. You're almost like a god. I'd practised my thrust*

for a long time. Into the top of a watermelon.

MAN: *Like God? Our viewers may find that a bit of a stretch.*

WYRE: *No. A god. Like one of those Roman ones.*

MAN: *Do you need to psyche yourself up before….before the moment?*

WYRE: *What helps is if your bird's just shat all over you. Oooops. Something like that.*

MAN: *Bird?*

WYRE: *Yeah. Your bit of arse.*

MAN: *And that fires you. Makes you determined to conquer the forces that seem to conspire against you.*

WYRE: *Makes you fucking mad!*

MAN: *I'm sorry, Mr. Wyre, I must ask you…..The language?*

WYRE: *What language? Fuck? The fucks? Well fuck you. I didn't want to do this! You lot started this!*

MAN: I'm sorry?

MAN: The BBC! Let you into Scrubs for the day. I'm not a fucking saint, you know!

MAN: It's ok, we can cut. Do you have any regrets?

WYRE: Regrets?

MAN: Well, that you may have……..

WYRE: Regrets? What the fuck?...........

Chapter 56
Carla & Sternbend

(Hail Neruda!)

In 1973, Carla Hernandez, already married to Goldstein, was in Santiago, Chile, the city of her birth. She left Chile for England when she was eight; her father had been sent to London by the company he worked for.

She had arrived in Santiago a week earlier in response to a promise she'd made herself at the time of the Leftist victory in 1970.

On this late summer evening of 10th September, enthralled by the fiesta atmosphere in the plaza de la Constitución and the plaza Bulnes, no one could have guessed what would happen on the following day.

Carla had stayed over at her friend's place on Alameda Avenue, a few blocks away from La Moneda, the Presidential Palace currently occupied by Salvador Allende. Out of the blue, at ten past eight in the morning, the voice of President Allende, broadcasting from the radio stations of the Left forces, announced: *The Navy has mutinied. Valparaiso is cut off. The situation in the rest of the country is under the control of the legal government.*

Carla said: What's going on? What's happening?

Her friend Isabel said: it's ok. They tried this on June 29th when tanks surrounded the presidential palace. At that time, the rule of law prevailed. The same will happen today.

Perhaps that was a trial run.

Carla, just six months ago, Allende won a second election with an increased share of the vote! He's not going anywhere!

I'm going out.

Mind you, don't get run over by a tank! Ha, ha!

That's not funny!

Listen, my brother works at Radio Recabarren. It's not far from here, in the Ministry of Labour building on the corner of Huérfanos and Teatinos Streets. Go to him and you'll find out everything you need to know.

What's his name?

Rolando.

It was 9 AM when Carla reached the studios of the radio station. In the streets, the atmosphere of unease was intensifying. Office workers were leaving their office buildings, pale-faced, buttoning up their jackets. Columns of infantry were moving up Bulnes Avenue. Carla found the building of the Labour Ministry, went in and a plaque told her she needed the thirteenth floor.

Things were a little chaotic as she asked for Rolando. When she got to him, she told him she was Isabel's friend.

He said: British?

Well, I was born in Chile. Here in Santiago. We left when I was 8.

You should leave now. It's not good for you to be here. The junta has given the President an ultimatum. He can leave the country – they have a plane waiting for him. But he won't go. He's too honourable. Anyway, they would kill him.

Another voice said: I doubt the plane would leave the runway.

There is an explosion close by.

Carla is scared.

Rolando said: the soldiers are everywhere. At a window, he says: look, the tanks are coming. They will surround La Moneda. Again. Let's hope, as before, the rule of law holds.

She knew how brutal the army of the ruling class could be against the workers and those who support them; how at the turn of the century, as a result of joint action by workers and peasants in northern Chile, the workers were herded into trade union headquarters and burnt alive; in Antofagasta they were driven out to the pampas, invited to run and shot in the back; in Valparaiso put into sacks and thrown into the ocean to drown alive; in Temuco and Colchagua tied up in pigsties and left to be eaten alive by the pigs and untold numbers simply shot; whole villages murdered.

He said to Carla: go with Mateo. And to Mateo: take her to the Institute of Music. Quick. Things are moving fast.

The Institute is close. Part of the University.

As they left the ministry, they saw at the far end of the street an old man remonstrating with two soldiers. One of them shoots the old man. A desperate young woman, barefoot, clutching a baby, runs across the broken glass on the road. Her feet are bleeding. Tanks are moving down Alameda Avenue towards the palace. There is an explosion. Carla screams. Glass showers down on them. Carla is cut on the shoulder. Her flimsy summer dress.

Inside the Institute, Mateo finds Augustin Flores. The students are organising the defence of their classrooms. Many will be tortured and murdered by Pinochet's Junta in the Estadio Nacional in the following weeks.

Mateo arranges for a dressing to be put on her shoulder; no need to hide the blood on her dress, there is already so much blood on the street.

Mateo says to Carla: wait here. He leaves.

Carla sits. She watches the students. Corpses.

Mateo returns. Follow me.

She follows Mateo to a side entrance to the building. There is a truck parked there with its engine running.

The lorry will take you to the border. The lorry drivers are on strike against the government and the military will be sympathetic to them. You won't be stopped. You will be helped to cross into Peru.

But I don't have my passport. I've left all my things where I was staying.

It's ok. We can get you across the border. Once you're in Peru, you can send for them.

But I don't understand! How do you know all this? It's all just happened!

After the June coup attempt, we prepared for the worst.

Carla was put in the back of the truck and covered over. It was a long drive to the north with many stops: Carla guessed soldiers. When the truck finally stopped and Carla was let out, she was already in Peru. They were on the outskirts of Tacna. They had stopped outside Tacna Cathedral. The driver told her, with only minimal English, to go inside where she would be contacted. She couldn't understand all the cloak-and-dagger stuff unless it was because she had entered the country illegally.

There was a large walkway leading to the entrance and as she crossed it, she felt vulnerable; that maybe she was being watched. She was. From a point just inside the doorway, a man called Powell was tracking her.

As she entered the cathedral, he took her to one side and introduced himself.

My name is Powell.

You're English.

I am. I will arrange shelter for you from where you can phone. Are you married?

Yes. My husband is in Cambridge. We live in Cambridge.

Powell was a slight, unimpressive man, to look at, of about 45.

My home too.

O. How strange. But why all the mystery?

Because Chilean soldiers have been seen near the border, we have to take precautions so that you don't get snatched! We have a safe house just off the Avenue Humbolt. It's quite close to here.

As they walked, Powell greeted the occasional individual of the PNP, the Peruvian police.

Carla said: you know them?

After the coup, I worked for the international office of the government.

Anxiously: coup?

Yes. In 1968, it was a Leftist coup which carried on the policies of the previous Leftist government.

That's strange. And why a safe house?

It was set up after the June coup in Chile in case any future coup was successful. To help people like you.

In the shock of her coup, she had seemed to be hanging onto life in a place beyond reason. Living from one moment to the next in a place beyond fear and meaning. Now the world had returned and all the understandable anxieties. What if Isabel herself had been arrested? How would she get her passport back? And her notebooks.

At the safe house, Carla phoned her friend.

Isabel said: where are you?! I thought they might have taken you!

Your brother got me out. I'm ok. But look, can you send my things? Especially my passport, my notebooks and my traveller's cheques?

I'll try.

Now there's panic and tears: they're arresting everyone! The Presidential palace has been attacked: shelled and bombed. The air force! I can't believe they've done it! And poor Allende is in there! He had trusted Pinochet! Made him head of the army! Where shall I send your things if I'm able to? This is the beginning of the darkness! These are the days of Nixon!

Carla said: can you send them to Poste Restante, Tacna, Peru…

Peru!? You're in Peru?

Yes.

O, thank God! You'll be safer there.

I hope. But every time I see a uniform, I shake. But you? Will you be safe?

I'm going to hide. They have no reason to search for me, unless they connect me to my brother. To Rolando.

The day she posted Carla's goods, Isabel was arrested. She died before the month was out.

Carla had phoned Goldstein and told him about Powell.

He said: I know Powell.

Carla asked him: How?!

Have you heard of the International Jewish Conspiracy of the Left?

Well.….

It's me! He laughed.

Mr. Powell lives in Cambridge.

Yes.

There was a momentary silence.

Goldstein said: hello?

Hello.

His real name is Sternbend.

Chapter 57

Mourning Becomes Rose

(Hail Auden!)

Will said: Perhaps you're right. Perhaps he did come for Cambridge itself. In which case, you're not responsible. In fact, you could say that by screwing him, you indirectly alerted us to his presence. And if it is the case, he would have murdered those two anyway. You seem to relish mourning, Rose, and want to blame yourself. I noticed something like this when we went to visit your dying father. You seemed to carry guilt for his condition so that you could more deeply grieve and more impressively mourn. In fact, your fucking Mr. Wyre revealed the monster and ultimately prevented him from carrying on with his killing. So, your penchant for sex provides a societal service.

Nice one, Will, but I'm strong enough to handle my guilt. Anyway, you began this by wondering whether *you* might have been responsible.

She got up and began to dress.

I have to go to work.

Mine was more idle speculation. It's all too big for us. I'll see you in the pub later.

I do mourn, Will, but it's not a pose. I mourn for every good thing that's lost.

So, you wouldn't mourn Groyne, but you would mourn Buckland.

Yes.

Because Buckland's good.

Yes.

How do you know?

Don't we all? *You* knew him from L.

I don't think I ever really knew him. No one knew Buckland. No one knew in what capacity Buckland knew Farquhar-Groyne!

After a thoughtful moment, Will said: how well did you know him? Buckland. Did you fuck him?

No!

But you would have.

Don't you think I would have learned something? When people have unwrapped themselves during the sex act, they don't care what's seen beneath the skin. All coyness and restraint have succumbed to freedom.

Chapter 58

Are you with us?

(Hail Tolstoy!)

Later, Will turned up at Goldstein's. Carla ushered him into the study.

Goldstein shouted from the lounge: who is it, *bubbeleh*?

It's Will. I need to show him something.

In the study, Carla pulled the blouse down from the shoulder that was wounded in her escape from Santiago years before. She revealed a deep scar where an amount of flesh had been removed.

Will said good God! What happened?

I was wounded escaping Chile on the morning of the Pinochet coup.

She readjusted her clothing.

She said: I got to Peru, where an Englishman named Powell helped me. I didn't know, but the wound was already becoming sceptic. Powell got me to a hospital in time. They had to cut the infected area out. Powell was from Cambridge. It was Mr. Sternbend.

Sternbend? Wow. So that's…..

Yes. That's why I met him in Ely Cathedral.

But Sternbend isn't anything like the person you describe. Mr. Powell.

Mr Sternbend wishes to keep a low profile.

But I don't…does Mr. Goldstein know about you and Sternbend?

Of course.

But….

Will. Are you with us?

Well, I suppose…

Come with me.

Carla took Will into the lounge.

Chapter 59
Desire On The Backs

(Hail Kundera!)

One evening when Rose wasn't working, she and Will got pissed in The Baron of Beef, a pub on Bridge Street. Leaving, they made their way trippingly across the Bridge of Sighs to The Backs - as far as he could make out, the Back of St John's College, and fell giggling onto the grass at midnight. The air was warm; Cam and it carried the mysteries of the river.

Will was almost at that place where the intoxicants bring conviction to irrationality and felt it an imperative to say: something I haven't told you. Sten. Sten wasn't Sten but Stig. I made a porno film with him. I was seventcen.

Riveted to the lawn – backs on Backs, silence while Rose reflected in her fuddle.

You mean he filmed you while you fucked some actress?

No, he filmed us while we fucked.

You and Sten?

Stig. Yep.

Filmed it?

A camera on a tripod. He paid me 100 kronor. I needed it!

I knew it!

Knew what?

Knew that you knew him! So, Mr. Will Slade, you are a prostitute!

I was out of my head.

My God! I guessed it. You're bisexual! Ha, ha! Fucking hell.

They laughed.

She said: what happened?

You want the ins and outs?

Ins and outs! Ha, ha! Yeh, why not?

So he told her. Every detail. At the end, she said: what did it feel like?

I felt enslaved and free at the same time.

But what did you feel?

I suppose the inside of the anus is covered with sensors that are triggered as the penis goes in and you feel an exquisite tingling and when it hits the prostate, that feeling is intensified and your whole body is electrified and your teeth are clenched in the rush of the mysterious feelings you don't fully understand.

Do you think women enjoy it? They haven't got a prostate.

I suppose that for men and women, men doing it and men receiving, everything is intensified because the passage is tighter.

She was silent for a moment, then she said: do you think you could bugger me.

Want me to do it now?

Now? Here?

There's no one around!

Bugger me, Will.

Ok.

When we do it, you'll travel. You'll imagine all the mysterious, exotic and erotic places in the sweating world.

With the aid of some spit, he did it. On St John's Back.

They came in Bangkok, Bali and Tahiti and rested he by the Tumtum tree. As they rested, the tempo of their drunkenness turned down accordingly. Rose said breathlessly: I'm glad that was you.

They lay in silence

Well, when you fucked Stig in that toilet, I think he really wanted me, so I'm glad *that* was you!

Ha, ha!

He'd seen us in Broadmoor – a simple coincidence – but then followed us.

Then Rose said: And then he followed us to Cambridge.

You didn't tell him where he could find you.

No. When you saw him in the Eagle, did you know him? Recognise him?

I wasn't sure.

But later, you were?

Will said: yeh.

Didn't you want to do it again with him?

He seemed different. Psychologically deeper. Worrying. Had you ever experienced it before? The anal sex?

She lied: no. She didn't want Sten to become a part of this moment.

What did you think?

She giggled. Now *you* want the ins and outs!

He laughed.

Well, I orgasmed as you put it in. Just the thought of doing it. It's a lot like vaginal sex. Lots of sensation when you first entered. Slowly. That's when I came.

I didn't want to hurt you.

My coming gave me natural lubrication.

I thought it was easier than I expected.

She said: o, frabjous day! Callooh! Callay! Would you want to do it with Carla?

God, no.

Why?

I can't imagine it.

You could imagine it with me?

Often thought about it.

Why?

It's the way you walk.

What about her?

He didn't really want to carry on with this conversation.

He said: I think of her old man. Goldstein.

Isn't she sexy?

I did think so. But to say that doesn't necessarily mean anything. Shall we go?

Rose said: I feel like a drink.

Ok. First place we come across.

In The Punter's, they found a table. They were both smiling, reflecting on what they'd just done and their residual tipsiness.

Will said: do you want a whisky?

Ok.

Will went to the bar. When he got back, she said: why did you say that saying Carla was sexy wouldn't mean anything?

Because you can't prove it. If you can't, then there's no objective truth and so it's meaningless. Everything we say about sex is meaningless. No truth.

Rose said: Truth?! What *is* truth?

That which is provable.

Wait a minute, Will. I need to think about this.

They began to walk home and Rose said:

Why do you want to prove it? Why do you want to *prove* anything about sex?

One wants to believe that there's some logical basis to it.

What do you mean? Something scientific? Shit, Will. This is all a bit heavy.

Is that why you changed your mind about her? Because you can't say that it's meaningful to say she's sexy? What about what you feel?

Carla, I discovered, belongs to the kind of person elevated and purified by having been at the heart of historical events and escaping inescapable death. She was in Chile the morning of the coup. That's where she met Sternbend. They've got a thing called ICOJOL. The International Conspiracy Of Jews On The Left. Goldstein's the main man. Then there's Carla, Sternbend and Parfitt. And others. Your friend Quaid Laurel is also involved.

He's not a Jew. I know!

I've joined too.

Fucking hell, Will, you're not a Jew either!

Think of non-Jews as associate members. They help plan the group. My old college philosophy professor…

I thought you did English.

Joint honours. He told Parfitt I was coming to Cambridge. That I was on the Left. Parfitt told Sternbend to prepare a room for me, then Parfitt told a student we both knew called Piers Stanley, in L, who also knew I was coming to Cambridge to recommend Sternbend's place. That's how I got my room. Carla told me all this. They prepared everything well. Carla even swotted up on Chatterton - who she hadn't deeply studied – when they found out through Piers Stanley that Chatterton was going to be the subject of my dissertation.

After Will told me all this, I decided I had some thinking to do. Talk about missing the point! I missed an iceberg!

The next morning, I was hungover. The next morning, I had a panic attack. The next afternoon, I needed help. Prosac.

You feel it coming on for a day or two. A beast slouching towards Bethlehem. As it gets closer, you begin to recognise what it is and desperately try to fight against it. Distract yourself. Think of anything as detached as possible from you. King's Chapel. Dewey. But it's a swamp. Sinking sands. The order of the beast is upon you. And then that ache in the stomach. And in the morning, the shakes.

Chapter 60

Left v Left

(Hail Greene!)

When Rose turned up for work, she was surprised to see Quaid and Parfitt in excited conversation. It was quite early and though as busy as one might expect at this time of day, there wasn't yet the plethora of students that usually turn up.

It was Quaid's day off, and he looked to Rose a bit drunk; Parfitt, too, was not his reticent self.

Parfitt said: you remember when we thought Buckland had been killed, but it was a case of mistaken identity? It was an actor called Boldo Gribbs. Slade actually met him in here when he came in with a troupe of actors. Boldo Gribbs, it also transpires, was our London recruiter! The van that killed him belonged to Farquhar-Groyne and his storm troopers.

Quaid said: You seem angry.

Parfitt said: I am! WE ARE INACTIVE!

You see? The Trot!

That's offensive.

I perceived a Trotskyite anger born of frustration.

Parfitt said: What's that got to do with the cause of my anger? What the hell are you talking about? My friend was murdered! Didn't it move you? What I'm trying to explain is that they tried to murder him earlier and we could have done something but did NOTHING.

I didn't really know him!

How well did you know Farquhar-Groyne?

You see? This is your mood! Trotsky is your guide! Simple as that! Isn't he? His intellectualism was almost a perversity in the real world. Perhaps like yours? And you can't escape that burning reality.

So this is what you…… And Stalin? The sentimentalist and fake emotionalist?

He loved the people!

O yes, crying crocodile tears over Bukharin – the originator with Stalin of Socialism in One State and his greatest ally – as he unavoidably had to execute him.

He loved the people! Had to save them from traitors.

Traitors! Those who disagreed with Stalin's own treachery!

He saved the revolution. All he did was necessary.

He destroyed the democracy of the proletariat!

There never was!

And the *kulaks*.

Bourgeois!

The enforced famine?

Kulaks! Their refusal to collectivise!

Trotsky was the true Marxist!

He was anti-Bolshevik!

On what grounds do you claim that? He created the Red Army! He won the Revolution!

A Menshevik! Originally a Menshevik! Once a Menshevik, always a Menshevik!

He was anti-revisionist. On the left/right spectrum, on the extreme left. Stalin on the same spectrum on the extreme right. He betrayed Leninism! How well did you know Farquhar-Groyne?

He was a raging queer.

Precisely!

What do you mean by that?

Well, either you were collaborating with him or having sex with him!

Parfitt was silent for a moment.

You've been seen visiting him! Coming out of his rooms.

Quaid Laurel said: Listen, Parfitt, you've got something to say, get it out!

By now, the two were drawing attention to themselves.

Who was the link between Farquar-Groyne and Rolecord Wyre?! What are you, Quisling or queer?

Quaid Laurel suddenly jumped up and punched Parfitt in the corner of his eye, breaking his glasses, cutting him just below the eyebrow and shouting:

You mad, crazy, Trot bastard!

Parfitt knew before he spoke that if Laurel attacked him, it would be proof that Laurel was guilty of something.

Parfitt cried out and placed a hand over his eye with the bewildered shock of an academic: you've blinded me!

A couple came from a nearby table and said to Parfitt: are you alright? But didn't get too close - more a gesture than an intention to help.

Rose came from behind the bar with a cloth and said to the couple I'll take care of it.

Quaid said: sorry, old man, I lost it.

Rose took Quaid by the arm and said with managerial authority and urgency: you'll have to leave! Come on. I'll see you later.

Parfitt said loudly: It's alright! I forgive him.

Quaid began to leave.

Parfitt called after him: Wait!

Quaid turned back and said: It's no good. I'm finished here. It's obvious.

Quaid left for the last time. Before seven o'clock, he was fired.

Rose said to Parfitt: can I look at your eye?

I forgive him. It's his job. It was my fault, I provoked him!

At that moment, something happened to her. As she looked into his good eye, which she could see free from his distorting glasses, was quite beautiful, her anxiety faded, becoming a faint departing wave and the threat from the advancing darkness left. This was a man who loved the truth. More. A man who loves reason and logic. A man, perhaps, with the answers. A man, she was sure, at heart, free from posturing.

She said: let's go into the back so we can get a better look at it.

The other girl behind the bar on Rose's shift, indicated that it would be ok for Rose to take him into the room used by the staff. That she could manage.

As they settled, Rose said: I probably shouldn't say this, but I always thought of you as a bit pompous.

I understand that.

Rose looked closely at the hurt eye.

She said: But that's not as I see you now.

I suppose my pose is down.

Ah, and now he was without the pose. She looked closely into his eye. It looks ok. The glass missed the eye, thank God.

I don't usually drink very much. Are you Will Slade's young lady?

Well, we have a very loose relationship. Did you know him in L.?

Not so well. I was a couple of years ahead of him.

That's where I met him.

Were you at L.?

I wasn't at the university; no. I went there with someone I thought was my boyfriend. He was supposed to study there. But almost as soon as we arrived, he chickened out and left. Left me there. The best I could say about it is that I imagined he ran because he was too embarrassed to face me after dragging me there.

Rose was feeling almost a sense of privilege being this close to this well-known intellectual. Who'd suddenly become for her a paragon of those things she valued most.

I can't believe that Quaid behaved like that.

I think he was quite drunk. We often discuss politics. This time, it got a little heated. Did you know Neal?

The student who was murdered?

A little comfortable: I didn't, no. Not really.

I loved him. We weren't lovers. I was just drawn to him. Perhaps because of his genius.

A curious thought then came to her: what if she ended up with him, Parfitt and she had to say farewell to sex, because he could well be homosexual? Would she be ready? For that journey into a new unknown? She'd already thought that he could be the one who provided the ultimate answers. But had she done all the groundwork? She hadn't, for example, fucked a woman with a dildo.

And then he said: my time of grief is not yet over.

Rose said: what do you mean?

My dear friend, Mr. Goldstein, is terminally ill. And it will happen soon.

Rose couldn't hear this now.

She said: I have to go back to work. Could we meet soon and talk about it then?

Chapter 61
Broadmoor again

After his detention in Wormwood Scrubs, awaiting trial, undergoing psychiatric investigation, Rolcord Wyre was committed to Broadmoor.

Rolcord Wyre was laying on his hospital bed. He'd been medicated. They'd said he was ill. At first, he thought they meant mumps – he had a lot of mumps when he was a kid. But they meant in the head. To be honest, he could remember very little about his killing spree and now he felt normal. Could use a pint. He had a strong feeling of being in the shit. Made him very uncomfortable. He wondered if he was smiling. Not one of those sarcy, not-really-smiling smiles. When he was a kid about sixteen, he worked in a café – a bit more than that – almost a restaurant and he always noticed how when middle class or higher-class people came in they'd always have a smile like everything had been laid on for them whereas lower class people would have something more like a worried frown as if they shouldn't be there. From now on, he wanted one of those middle-class smiles as if to say: this is a nice hospital; they're going to make me better, then I can go home. The trouble was that his medication was already making him better to the extent that he felt it was time to leg it.

Also, he couldn't stop thinking about that girl he fucked on the train. She was something. Looked kind of Spanish. Lovely arse. Not much available fanny here. Anyway, for now, he was happy to think about the girl on the train. When they let him out, he'd have to look her up.

Then a geezer with a black beard came in from another ward.

He came up to Rolcord and said, with a broad Yorkshire accent: you're new.

Without thinking, Roly said: what you telling me for?

(Ironically): Wise boy. You know who I am?

No.

Never seen my picture? Wyre certainly became aware of his eyes: black and deep like the deeps of the ocean where no one had ever been.

Roly said: haven't been around much.

TV?

Don't watch it.

Papers?

Fuck them.

Jack the Ripper?

Sorry mate. Never met him.

Sutcliffe. Ring a bell?

Cricket?

You taking the piss? Peter? Peter Sutcliffe?

Blank.

The Yorkshire Ripper.

That rings a bell.

What d'you do?

They said I snuffed a couple of poofters.

How?

Knife into the top of the head.

Big knife?

Flick.

You say they say you did it. What d'you say?

I say the guilty party was a tart I fucked on the train to Cambridge. She's got a price to pay. She got me into this shit.

Are you saying she wielded the knife?

Wyre said: This is the point. Who's guilty, the one that did it or the one that set it up? Don't forget, Charlie Manson didn't touch anyone!

The trouble is, the one who set it up doesn't get the pleasure of popping the bubble of that head. Letting life out like gas. So, they've already paid a price.

I would think that was for the judge to decide.

You want her taken out?

I was hoping to fuck her again after getting out.

You won't be getting out. Think about it. I can arrange it. I'll be around.

The serial killer left Wyre, who immediately began to blow the fog from his mind by concentrating solely on an image of the act of fucking Rose – a kind of meditation. His ability to even attempt to meditate must have been because of the drugs; the medication. He managed to put most things out of his mind for a short while until questions about the conversation with Sutcliffe began to encroach. Never be released? Bollocks. And what kind of nutcase would offer to snuff your misses (not the Jewish cunt) because of something you said in a moment of weakness? And what would he want back?

Chapter 62

The education of Parfitt

You don't drink much, do you? You don't seem used to it.

That's why I got so quarrelsome with Quaid.

It was two days before Godstein's funeral. They'd just had a drink at The Baron of Beef and were on the way to Parfitt's place off Emmanuel Road. You seem quite relaxed now. It was the beginning of that crepuscular time.

Parfitt said: I think I'd drunk a little too much when I roused him to violence.

Don't blame yourself. Quaid *was* drunk and totally out of order. And he knew it straight away. It's usually how guilty people behave. Can I ask you something? Have you ever been with a woman?

You know the answer, or you wouldn't have asked.

Do you like women?

Of course. I like you. But I've only known boys.

Can I ask? Have you ever had sex?

He said, with a nervous giggle: you shouldn't ask that. Sexual practices are not universally uniform.

Wow. I suppose that's true. Have you ever masturbated?

Tony was silent for a moment. He could never expect anyone to ask him that. But perhaps this was how Rose would prepare his road to freedom: with outrage.

You ask the most intimate things! When you grow up with boys, you're bound to.

She brought him to a stop at a recess with a garage door. She pushed him into the recess. She began to kiss him and felt between his legs. Then she rubbed gently up and down between his legs.

He was thrown into confusion.

His penis hardened.

She said: are you embarrassed?

He whispered from a contracted larynx: no.

He's thinking: here we go. I knew it would come to this.

She unzipped him and he didn't object. Then she took it out.

Now her hand's there. And it's in her hand. Her flesh on my flesh. *That* flesh. Even if I don't approve, I can go along with it. It'll be….

Suddenly, a feeling he'd never experienced before with another person shot through him like an arrow leaving a bow and flying without restraint and he soon ejaculated and it flew up like an arm flung up in an unrestrained tarantella, taking with it all his own restraint. And it was nothing like anything he'd ever experienced when he masturbated: it was almost like you could imagine a holy communion.

And then he suddenly felt wretched. O God! Now there's a mess. He said: I'm sorry.

What for? Most of it's on me.

Well….that's what I meant.

You've got a hanky?

He produced a clean white handkerchief from the top pocket of his jacket and hoped that she would clean the mess in case any of it had been deposited on him. On his trousers. This she did, rubbing against his still hard but retiring cock.

Oooops! They both giggled. That giggle led Parfitt to feel he'd joined a secret pornographic order. And he liked it.

She wiped his trousers, then wiped her own jeans.

I'll take this and wash it.

She wrapped the hanky into a ball around his erection's secretion.

Do you still want me to come with you?

You've been very kind. But I don't think I can go any further. Further this evening.

That's alright. We can have a cup of tea. You do have tea, don't you?

O yes, I have different flavours.

Chapter 63

Intermezzo

(Hail Mozart!)

Two days later, on the day of the funeral, in the evening, Carla said to Will: wait here. I must go down and show my face.

Will said: and when you're back, I'll go down with mine!

They laughed. Will saw in Carla's eyes the dreaminess of the enraptured lover as if she were fainting helplessly into another reality. When she returned, they repeated the exercise and Will left her, promising to return, eager to get to Rose's place to share with her what had happened.

When Will got to Rose's place, she wasn't there. He'd tapped on her door, not wanting to barge into any scene of sexual congress. Tarita had come to the door and told him that her friend wasn't there.

Of course, he said to her, she's with Parfitt.

Could she have gone back to his place after leaving the *shiva*? Certainly not for fuck games. He was pretty sure Parfitt was fully gay. But was that just speculation? There was enough speculation that Chatterton was, but who knows? But that's all by the by: his preoccupation was and should have been with Carla. He could hardly believe what had happened.

But we're jumping ahead.

ROSE: Gonorreah. Ugly word (*description*). I'm a young girl kicking up leaves in an Autumn park. A storm arrived last night and I'm wrapped up against the chill. I've had to get away from the house – there's a bible reading. It's beginning to get dark! I hadn't noticed. There's an exit in the south of the park next to the toilets, hidden behind bushes. If I use that exit and not the entrance to the park, where I came in, I'll be amongst the shops. I was beginning to get a little anxious. I could see the lights in the shops. Tension eased. From the bushes, a rustling. It could be a fox. Have a look!

It's a man. Middle-aged. Older? He's got tattoos on his face! Never seen that before! I know what he's doing. I'm not that young. He's masturbating. It's ugly. Because he wants it to be. I don't like it. Everything seems black. Grotesque. And then he comes. Looking at me. Leering. Mr Gonorrhea. His onanic seed flying uselessly like vile bacteria. At the same time, I couldn't deny I was a little excited.

This illness. Ugly. Like the man in the park. The man with the painted face. The man leered as he came. I'd never seen that before. Later, I would fantasise about it. Until I caught the infection he embodied.

Who gave it to me? Who knows? As soon as I knew I had it, I got it fixed. How did I know I had it? I know my own vagina. If you don't, don't let anyone in. Everyone I biblically knew I told to get checked before I would next entertain them – unless it was Wyre and I wouldn't be touching him again. And anyone else? Who are they?

Chapter 64

Rose And Parfitt Compare Notes

(Hail Henry Miller!)

I could hardly believe what had happened. After I'd brought him to orgasm in the garage doorway when I felt sure I'd awakened in him biorhythms he was previously unaware of, we continued our walk to his place.

I said: I thought you were brave then.

I don't understand.

Well, you let me introduce you to something you were unfamiliar with. With a woman, anyway.

Easier to talk about these things while walking rather than when sitting eye to eye, drinking tea.

He said: It's almost like discovering a new philosopher. Well, one you'd been unfamiliar with.

I said, mischievously: might I qualify as a new philosopher?

What's your philosophy?

She paused. Then: you ready?

So, you have one?

Yes.

Ok.

It's about sex and knowledge. That in order to understand sex, you need to understand the world and to understand the world, you need to understand sex.

Sounds a bit like Freud.

Maybe, but didn't Freud instruct others? I'm talking about instructing yourself.

Anaxagoras? Know thyself?

Never heard of him. But see? This is what I'm talking about. We've had sex and I've learned about your man. Ana…

Anaxagoras.

Know thyself.

Then he said: not yet.

What?

Not real sex. Between two.

But I thought…

We'd reached his place and climbed the steps to his room. Inside, I was surprised at how orderly it was. And posh. There were two leather armchairs, an oak desk and panelling which I guessed was oak on one wall, a bay window with window seats overlooking Jesus Green and on the other two walls, papered with a deep red influenced terra cotta, framed photos of mostly men. And everywhere, books.

He said, please sit.

I sat in one of the leather armchairs.

In Ancient Greece, philosophers' meetings would be called symposia. Plural. They would drink wine during the symposium. Singular. I don't have wine, but I have whiskey. It's something I learned from my father. There would always be a bottle of whiskey in case of an unexpected need. Would you like some?

Yes. Great. Who are all these photos of?

He took two glasses and the decanter of whisky from the desktop and put them on a small coffee table between the armchairs.

He pointed to a photo and said: that's Wittgenstein; here, Schopenhauer, Nietzsche, Sartre, Kierkegaard, Popper, Russell, Moore, Ayer and many others. All philosophers.

And there's Buckland.

Yes.

I said, taking a risk: you loved him?

Yes.

But not sexually.

No.

How did you love him?

I don't know. What does love mean?

Parfitt poured two whiskies.

I said: Who's the girl?

That's Carson McCullers.

O, I don't think I know her.

One of my favourite American writers.

We had sips.

Would I know what she wrote?

Ballad of the Sad Café?

What a great title!

Yes.

Then I thought: as it looks as if I've lost the argument about a new philosophy (I wouldn't know if the Greeks were into sex), I'll try……

Tony put a record on his turntable. A rich, profound orchestra played. And a sensuous rippling piano.

I asked what this beautiful music was. He said: it's called *Nights In The Garden of Spain* by de Falla.

Never heard of him.

He's Spanish.

It's beautiful. Have you heard of *Ignoratio Elenchi?*

Vaguely. Doesn't it mean different things?

Shall I tell you?

Certainly.

I've learned this by heart: one translation is: ignoring the issue. Another is that it's a logical fallacy which consists of apparently refuting an opponent while actually proving something not asserted. Or: missing the point.

Can you bring it alive?

What do you mean?

How it works. In our everyday lives.

Here's a simple one: if I say: are gays allowed to marry by law? and you say they should be, that's *ignoration elenchi* because you're ignoring my assertion/question: the question was not should it be allowed, but is it.

And my assertion proves it does?

I'm not sure. I think that could be the fallacy. The point is, we miss the point and get things wrong. We're always getting things wrong – humanity - because we can never see the point we're making. That's because we always make assumptions that are favourable to the outcome we want and, in the process, we prove the opposite. That's because it's self-interest that guides us, not the need to find the truth. Human nature always gets in the way of reason. We're born to make mistakes; to miss the point and that's how we learn but it so often produces untold misery in the process. It's like marriage: you would think that it's done to complete a relationship and bring happiness; I may say it never works; marriage never works, which just seems like a cantankerous reply. Actually, the opposite of the original proposition is all too often proven: that it can't work and all too often it produces misery.

I think maybe you're stretching things. And watch it always.

What?

You're using the word always too rashly.

O.

He said: Mightn't this be a better example: I say: God gave the world his only son, you say: that's what Jesus himself says, but Jesus may have been a crackpot. We only believe in God because of Jesus. I say: it's what we believe. You say: that's because we're stupid. Jesus says he's God's only son and I could say what kind of God does he think it is if he's given his own son to have him killed on the cross? We might conclude that Jesus proves the non-existence of God. You see? The existence of God is not what was being talked about, but because you argued with my assertion, we arrived at our conclusion. The point I missed was that you can't make the assertion I made without questioning the existence of God.

I was shocked that Tony's argument seemed to echo Chatterton's!

I said: that's brilliant!

Coming back to your example: what about happy marriages?

Mostly, the only marriages that appear to work are those in which one partner is living the misery of subservience to the other. Marriages that really do work are the exceptions that prove the rule!

Bravo! Well argued!

He drained his whiskey.

I asked: what about my sex and knowledge philosophy? Is it new?

He poured himself another drink and filled mine. We both took a drink.

He answered (and this is as close to what he said as I can remember): Well. It seems you've taken the late positivism of Ayer and gone a step further: all knowledge is empirical, rooted in sense experience, but you've introduced sex, as if you've added Freud to Ayer. The psychology of sex to its physicality. You've set out to investigate the assumptions we make about sex and draw conclusions that provide us with knowledge beyond the purely biological by applying the rules of empiricism. I don't know of anyone who's quite done that. So I would say…

He raised his glass.

I studied his face and I realised that the reputation people carry with them, fairly or unfairly, can colour the way that you assess their look. What I saw was not the arrogant, pompous intellectual but a handsome young man with high cheekbones, those stunning deep blue eyes and a sensitive, wide mouth.

…..Yes! You are a philosopher!

I thought: he might change his tune when he's not so tipsy!

He drank.

He said: we'll call it sexual positivism!

Yippee.

Then he said: as for your *missing the point,* you've simply borrowed Popper: the enemy of certainty! You're a doubter. You doubt that your experiments will lead to knowledge and often identify them as failures. And you can so easily find something that's proof of the opposite.

I said: my God, I need to think about all that! Then I looked at him closely and said: what's your philosophy?

He said: The Supremacy of Absence.

How does that work?

Nothing can be proved unless you can imagine it's not there.

I said: and if you can't imagine it's not there, then it must be there?

Well, yes. Except you have to be more rigorous. It's only by imagining it's *not* there that you can understand its importance and find the need to prove it *is* there.

I wondered if he had any examples that could help me understand? Then I thought: I do not want to get into this now and said: Oh, ok. Let me see if I understand:

He was sitting, so I leaned over and kissed him. He seemed uncertain at first. I prolonged it a little and tentatively introduced my tongue. Then I said: I could imagine that your genitalia are not there and that makes me mad with needing to prove they are there and so I say, respectfully and with just a little trepidation: Tony, I'd love to kiss your sweet balls.

I smiled broadly.

He almost choked on his drink as he finished it.

I think he was not so much surprised as excited to hear me say that; excited in a way that was beyond his control. He had crossed over to my world after I'd caused him to come. He already seemed a different person from the one I always assumed he was. I suppose that began in the pub with Quaid. And I'd been there to claim him.

I said: But I'll settle for your lips!

We kissed, he hungrily. I could tell he wanted to go further than we'd already been. We kissed more and he began to move his hands up and down my back. I took my light black sweater off. My black sweater. Beneath that was my bra. He rubbed my bare back. His breathing quickened. I guessed this may have been the first time he'd felt female flesh. I unbuttoned his shirt. I licked his chest. Sucked his nipples. Kissed his lips. Chewed his lower lip. Now his mouth was loose. Whiskey-flavoured, hungrily opened like a newly devirgined cunt. I took my bra off. His eyes were startled as if by a pair of diamonds. He tentatively felt the flesh. He was already hard and hardening. He sucked my nipple. Nipples.

I stood up and undressed. Standing before him naked, his face metamorphosed into a thousand quick-change sets of acceptance and uncertainty. And then he thrust his head between my legs.

And I'd thought that with him, I may have to settle for a life of celibacy! I'd once again discovered something: the mental health benefits of sexual freedom, which far outweigh the dangers presented by venereal diseases (including this new virus they know little about, except that it's prevalent among gay men with many partners and there's no one like that in our circle. Except, perhaps, Farquhar-

Groyne). After all, I'd already seen that Parfitt was changing, becoming more relaxed. And communicative.

Chapter 65

Dewey Cometh

(Hail RS Thomas!)

Dewey was chewing on a liquorice stick, a taste he'd picked up from a friendly nurse in hell who'd clearly seen that the dedrugged, sober young man was in the wrong place. He was sitting in The Anchor. Had crossed the Mathematical Bridge on his way to The Eagle and changed his mind. Decided he didn't feel like the importuning indulgence of Rose. Couldn't believe they'd made love. The nurse. Lovely to do it with. Seemed to know more about him than he did. He'd made the detour to The Anchor, where he'd sat on the riverside terrace.

On the riverbank, a black rabbit in a bed of clover was looking at him, staring at him. Was it a portent of something more, more death to add to the flood? The times were like a stick of sticky black liquorice.

He'd finished his lemonade and began his walk up Silver Street towards Trumpington Street, where he turned left and headed for King's College Chapel. He passed windows where coffee cups steamed. On the street, so many young people – mostly students, he guessed, some in gowns – so many whose intrinsic wealth, the wealth they were born into, showed naturally with a self-confident smile. The sons and daughters of the nouveau riche, uncertain, frowned.

Suddenly, the sky darkened and cracked and large drops fell. Thunder seemed to shake the altars of a hundred cathedrals. He put his head down and quickened his step. Students ducked into shop doorways to save their hubristic gowns.

Inside the chapel of Kings, he saw only black, black hangings, black notes dripping from organ stops and so many students in from the rain, preying bats in their black cloaks. This was not the chapel of his sanctuary where in spring the eucharis bloom; this was the chapel at Broadmoor where in the night beyond the walls mad dogs wail calling on the criminally insane to breathe free and let their mad saliva flow and flood and spurn the trinity. He needed to get out of here before his benign dreams were corrupted; he needed the breathing of innocents. He needed someone to bless him, to lift him; to neuter the threat of the madhouse.

In the street, blood and milk flowed.

He raced through the rain – imagined himself a flower thriving in the rain. Raced along the darkened streets and high above Cherry Hinton, a rainbow. He continued to run until he came to Rose's door, who he knew was not at home. He knocked and waited anxiously for the door to be opened by Tarita.

Chapter 66

Après le Déluge

(Hail Rimbaud!)

Tarita opened the door to a rain-baptised Dewey. A shaking man. A Shaker.

Dewey said: are you alone?

You're soaked. You're shaking. Come in and dry yourself. They went in. Rose is out. Said she won't be back till late.

Tarita got Dewey a towel to dry his hair.

Tarita put the towel around Dewey's neck. She rubbed his face against her face. They kissed passionately.

She said: take your clothes off so that I can dry them.

What if Rose comes back?

She won't!

Dewey undressed down to his underpants. His erection was clearly evident.

Tarita began to take her clothes off. He helped her. When he got down to her bra and panties, he paused.

She said: what's the matter?

I don't know. I don't want to hurt you.

You won't.

I met a man in a shop doorway. He told me…..

Tell me later.

She put her hand on his erection.

After.

She pulled his underpants down. When he was naked, she marvelled at the tautness of his body that still possessed a youthfulness and the splendour of his erection: the erection of a man in his prime. She put it in her mouth. He was immediately taken to the ecstasy of his coffin.

He said: wait.

He took her bra and panties off.

She had to do this even if she didn't like him. She had to break through the fence that Wyre had built around her. She thinks she loves Dewey; loves his sobriety; the care he shows her; his quiet strength.

He was equally overcome. Her beauty brought tears to his eyes: how could anyone hurt something so fragile and perfect? Her smoky skin and the unusual and exceptional mystery of the place between her legs.

Dewey. That's your eyes. They're dewey.

When he entered her, he entered an English country garden in the spring: Lily, Narcissus, Lilac, the scents of self-confidence and tears.

Later, now dressed and sitting on Rose's bed, Dewey told Tarita about the man, a homeless man, he'd come across in a shop doorway somewhere off King's Parade.

He said: you wouldn't expect to see the homeless in this part of Cambridge; you'd think the guardians of the colleges might deter them for fear of upsetting the rich students: our future legislators! I gave him some money and he asked me to stop for a while. He said: "Catch a falling star. Give the child a mandrake root." As soon as he said it, I remembered it, but didn't know what he was talking about. He just came out with it. I said I was very sorry, but I didn't understand. He said it was John Donne, the poet. In his *Song* Donne was talking about marriage or, worse, relationships with very beautiful women who will always be faithless: to hope that either of these could work is hopeless, you may as well try to catch a falling star or get with child a mandrake root. I asked him what a mandrake root was and he said that it was the root of a mandrake plant, which often looks like a human form.

Tarita was silent for a moment.

Then she said: Were you thinking you might want to marry me?

I wouldn't be good enough for you.

Let me decide that. What about the beautiful woman bit?

You are a very beautiful woman.

Do you think I could be faithless?

No. But what if I was?

She put her arms around him. He said: anyway, you're married. There was a rap on the door.

Chapter 67
Parfitt in Tenebris

(Hail Hardy)

Thick-headed, Parfitt woke. Beside him, the unpetalled Rose. He felt a mild panic. He didn't know who he was. He felt his penis. It was an ambivalent thing. He looked at her, the blanket back, the full roundness of her buttocks, the hidden anus alien, the small black hairs of her pubis appearing like a displaced painter's brush. He was absent. He didn't want the proof that he was not. She'd – he can say the word – fucked him (her him or he her?), but was it real? For things to be real, one must peel back ecstasy, peel back the absence and walk where your feet get wet, where faces may be consumed by fire. Was this her reality? He was sure. He could smell what they'd done. Was smell a proof of reality? Yesterday, he'd sat in the café off Mill Road, which he occasionally visited, and there he watched the clientele. There was an old man at a small table – the same table he would always sit at and every time Anthony had seen him, he would be eating a meat pie. Probably the same kind of meat pie. And every time his actions, every action would be the same. As if he didn't belong to himself. Parfitt could always smell the pie: *a* pie, but was that sufficient proof of the reality of the man? He wasn't sure because the man gave off no sign that he believed he existed. Parfitt's doubt was enough to suggest that the man was actually absent.

He suddenly had the awful feeling that he was on a ledge and about to fall into a deep, perhaps cosmic, pit. He sucked in a deep breath, sat up and found his pants on the floor.

Rose suddenly woke. She turned onto her back, threw off remaining blankets, revealing her naked self, her hair like a Chinese fan spread out on the pillow, black against the white. Parfitt couldn't avert his eyes from that sepulchre to fertility and the afterlife between her legs.

Chapter 68

Rose in Lux

(Hail Joyce Carol Oates!)

In general, Rose rarely slept with a man after they'd done it – except Will - but it would have been a long way to walk back to her place at night. They slept well, disturbed only by the sirens that often howled in the night and occasionally this morning.

She was always apprehensive about waking up next to someone – except Will! - who may have found, lust spent, the experience somehow cheapening. Especially someone like Parfitt, who had an almost religious disposition. And he had been a virgin, which was a new thing for her but maybe problematic for him. Anyway, he'd looked at her arse and she knew that the concave curve of her back rising to the convex curve of her buttocks was arguably sublime. Will had said it made him think of Boucher's *Blonde Odalisque*. So maybe Parfitt had had a moment when he'd wanted to recapture something of the thrill. But she might have expected that she'd feel his hand there and then, maybe fingers searching out her clitoris. Instead, she could feel that he was restless and as he got up to put his pants on, he sneaked a look at his back and buttocks and admired the tightness and the ever so slight outward curve that gave them a sweetness. She could understand why another man might lust after them. She guessed he was going to leave. Maybe he'd drained the dregs where once the froth was gold.

She would leave too. He turned away to complete putting his shirt on and then she said: look!

She hadn't drunk as much as he had, so she wasn't confused, but she thought she might have pushed him too far: maybe he had experienced for him another country but had not crossed any Rubicon.

She wasn't sure of his mood. Important was for her to make love with Parfitt and see this completely other side of the man. She recalled a motto on a wall she'd seen in a Brit bar in Spain when she was in her early teens: drinkers make the best lovers and she thought that certainly applied to Antonio, this lover who, in his cups, couldn't stop coming.

But was that the whole story?

This was different from what happened with Dewey. What had happened here was in danger of being missed. *Ignoratio elenchi!* She had liberated Dewey from an imposed celibacy; Parfitt's was self-imposed and much riskier to cause his release from. You release a young dog from a cage he'd been held in and he goes wild with his new freedom and for a while will be uncontrollable and he'll tear at and rip up anything attractive to his crazed moment. Parfitt's persona and character had been determined by the restrictions on his sexual development. When he first came into her, it was like a ragged explorer finding El Dorado. It was like a heterosexual man being entered by a gay fellow for the first time and realising that his whole life had been controlled by the mores of the sexually moribund, middling murderers, for as everybody in the academic fraternity of Cambridge would sooner or later come to learn that those who are not gay are bisexual. No one is purely heterosexual. In the frenzy of heterosexual sex, the need for same sex becomes overwhelming. That's the point that's often missed or denied. And in Parfitt, maybe the reverse.

She had worried that for Parfitt, with the reticence and poise of a cardinal, all his beliefs could be shattered and the character of the man destroyed.

As a consequence of this reasoning, Rose decided to leave before he came back.

She said: how are you?

I'm fine. Ok. Thanks. You?

Yes. I need to go.

Of course.

Rose dressed. He went to the bathroom to freshen up.

She called: I'm going, Tony.

He came out.

She said: it was great.

Yes, it was. I feel different. Good. But fuzzy.

Kiss me.

They kissed.

She left.

Chapter 69

White Roses

As Rose was arriving back at her flat, pleased to find something serious going on between Tarita and Dewey – a coming together she felt partly responsible for, Parfitt was sitting alone in his rooms. He had a copy of Genet's *Miracle of the Rose* in his hand, but his eyes were fixed on the photo of Carson McCullers.

Then he turned back to the book and the photo on the cover of a man in his maybe late forties, a miracle worker who found roses in arseholes and gardenias growing from the murderer's follicles, the real Harcamone, murderer, lady of the flowers. Genet, who wrote poetry on leaves of wrath. And curiously looked like Khrushchev.

And then he turned to the picture of Carson McCullers with the face of a child and mind bent on ragged boys, homosexuals and other outcasts sweltering in the heat of Southern Gothic ambition, later in love unrequited with the androgyne photographer Schwarzenbach.

Parfitt wondered if he was somewhere between the two, riding the rib of a whale or split-legged on Crib Coch on Snowdon? Or was he termite indefinable on a scrappy weald. Rose had knocked down all the pins of his assiduously placed frame with a mightily thrown flopper ball. He was quite simply, at this moment, nowhere, absent, subject to its supremacy.

He had a shower and masturbated using the shower head to stimulate his anus, testes and the penis, soon to be his clasped in his practised grip, shooting his sperm as from a mountain pinnacle. Acceptable practice for a man of his aesthetic and intellectual disposition, the great American poet Robert Lowell had once described how he often broke off from his writing to release his sexual tension, utterly proud of his flying floribunda.

Anthony felt calmer.

He dressed and went out.

Chapter 70

When Parfitt meets Chatterton (Dan)

(Hail Ginsberg!)

In the street, the morning smiled.

On Emmanuel Road, which was quite busy, he walked quickly, turned onto Parker Street and Parkside heading for Parker's Piece. He passed women who seemed to smile at him as though welcoming him into a masonry of sex. Images of Rose's interlegs place tormented him and words like cunt, whore and bitch in a kind of mental tourettes sprung to mind. And everyone smiled – kindly or caustically — and on the young woman's mouth had become pudenda. And the young men approached him with huge erections. He put his head down and sped on, coming to Parker's Piece and suddenly felt free.

In a bush, he found a young man with a ragged beard and long, tangled hair.

As he approached, the young man said: go catch a falling star, get with child a mandrake root.

Parfitt stopped. He was looking at a young man with a young man's equivocal beard and dirty, tangled hair. The young man's face behind the hirsute veil was intriguing. He was wearing an Oriental overgarment like the hippies would wear in the late Sixties.

Parfitt said: can I help you?

The young man said: I'm Thomas Chatterton. The poet.

That's not possible.

Parfitt squatted down beside Chatterton.

Chatterton said: Why not?

Because he's dead.

I am dead. All is possible. Nothing is impossible. You're in Cambridge. The home of Wittgenstein. Nothing is real and all is real.

Parfitt felt himself breaking free of his dyspepsia. The exercising of the brain over the discomforts of the body can do that.

The boy said: I was in love with a beautiful young woman with long, luxurious hair, what the poets today would call obsidian. Black like obsidian. Her face was pale, like a shade of sad white. She betrayed me for others. She was with me when I took poison and then left me in poverty.

Parfitt began to think about Rose.

He invited Chatterton to accompany him to his place. If only to clean up.

As they entered his flat, Chatterton ejaculated: Did you bring me here to show off? This place stinks of cum!

He had felt sorry for Dan. Had thought of letting him take a shower – generally freshen up, shave, maybe let him use some of his clothes. The curious 18th-century rags he wore, filthy as if he'd slept in a mud bath. But when they arrived, after Tony had thought, an amiable enough walk, Dan was almost violently disappointed; neither Dan nor

Tony knew why. Parfitt himself felt calmer once they were through the door.

Tony went to open a window.

What does that tell you?

Parfitt shrugged.

It tells me you're a heavy masturbator. Luckily, he'd cleaned up the crushed lilies of his orgasm in the shower room.

Parfitt went to get a glass of water, which he gulped down and then filled it up again.

He said: Do you think so?

O, yes.

Parfitt said: do you think you might like to freshen up? You can take a shower.

Sure. Thanks.

And use my razor if you'd like. He was pretty sure that his refugee didn't smell anything – he was just making a wild assumption. Or was it introducing a note of a once forbidden sex?

While Dan was in the shower, Tony suddenly thought, because of what the ferile guest had said: there's a naked young man in my rooms! What, he thought, do I think of that? And as if by way of answer, Dan emerged from the shower room entirely naked.

– Parfitt was sitting in silence in his armchair, looking at Dan, also silent, standing before him quite still and still naked, his cock hard. It seemed like a challenge, even an act of anarchy. He simply stood there, the faintest smile on his sensuous lips.

Dan said: that was a great shower. Made me feel incredibly sexy. Especially when I use the shower head to spray between my legs. Parfitt: my god! Am I part of an alternative fraternity?

Tony was hugely impressed by the boy's huge member and said: do you want to do something?

And then, in a sudden change of tone, Dan said: I'm a desperate man. I have tried to emulate Chatterton. This came from playing him a couple of times and trying to write some poetry. But I'm useless. But Rose! His erection began to go away.

Because of his hangover and his own increased sensitivity to the sexuality of the moment, Parfitt's own erection had begun to rise. But at this moment, he was distracted by thoughts of Rose. He said:

I'm sorry. I can't help you. Bergson's your man.

Bergson?

You need to get the strongest sense of the creative impulse that brings forth and animates life.

O, I felt like that with my lover. Rose.

He began to dress.

Parfitt said: Rose?

Yeh. She works in the Eagle.

O yes. Many love her.

I know. And after a pause: Are you saying I could write my way out of this?

At the moment, you're arrogant and vain. Humble yourself before the spells waiting to be raised by you.

It would be like a novice climbing the highest mountain.

Wait. Let me give you some trousers.

Parfitt went to get trousers and said to himself: I'm different. She's liberated me from my own vanity. From my own posturing. My haughty proclamations have become caring advice. *I* have climbed a mountain. He found a pair of cavalry twills he hadn't worn for years. He was taller than Dan, so they would be a little long. But presentable! And a clean, white shirt

Dressed, Dan was the dude. Now Parfitt felt something a little deeper than simple affection for him. He was quite aggressive when they'd arrived and now seemed cute and vulnerable. A pretty boy.

Tony said: would you like something to eat?

Yeh. I would.

I can make you an omelette.

Prize! Cheese?

I always have cheese!

Parfitt put the ingredients together. He cracked the egg into a cup and began to whip it. The gooey mix suddenly made him think of some kid he heard about when he was a kid who lived on the council estate in his village. His friends used to call him Danker, which apparently was a euphemism for wanker. They said this, Danker, when he was still only fourteen, would masturbate up to four or five times a day and deposit the semen in a jar which he kept on the windowsill in his bedroom. Parfitt didn't know if it was true, but he was disgusted that he thought about it now. (Didn't Rimbaud do something like that?)

Finishing his omelette with its bitter taste of aged cheese, Dan suddenly got up, asked Parfitt if he could stand his bus fare to wherever he decided to go, took the fiver and left. Parfitt, bewildered by Dan's brief visit, suddenly experienced a churning in the area of his groin and wished Rose were there. He felt ready for whatever she would offer.

Dan made his way to the bus station.

This short time he spent with Tony Parfitt seemed to bring Dan to his senses, especially when he stood naked in front of his host with an erection. Perhaps it was the shower and the cavalry twills with their Apollonian croon of order. Most of all, he needed to figure out how he ended up on the streets of Cambridge; the whole age had been a time of confusion as if he'd been out of his head. He desperately wanted to see Rose but couldn't bring himself to go to the pub, especially not after the toilet session, which had been so clumsy and desperate and, frankly, demeaning. And then things had begun to fall apart. A week after the toilet episode, he'd phoned the actress Judy, crying into the phone, pleading for restitution. Begging her to help him get his job back, which he'd lost after missing three consecutive performances. She said she couldn't help – he'd blown it. How could this Rose have such a profound effect? To virtually ruin his life!

A quick look in one or two shop windows revealed to him how good he looked with washed hair and clean shaven; smiles from a couple of female students confirmed his assessment. Today, he would not go straight to the bus station but would walk around Cambridge, see if he could reconnect with the community.

Somewhere near Peas Hill, on a whim, he walked into a pub and asked for a job. The manager told him he could start the following Monday and he left the premises with a swagger. He felt he was getting closer to the point where he might visit Rose at The Eagle. The street had a romantic hue – almost as Waugh had said of Oxford, a city in aquatint. A city where his alter-ego, Chatterton, may have once walked, now here he was a latter-day *flanneur* in his cavalry twills with an optimistic bounce missing only the gold hat; to his lover, he bounced now high who will cry when he comes: *"lover, gold-hatted, high-bouncing lover/I must have you!"*

Soon he was on Bene't Street. He could see The Eagle's signage swing in the soft breeze and he felt anxious and stimulated. And now the aquatint was gently coloured. He had, of course, decided to go and see her.

It was mid-afternoon.

Chapter 71

Mourning becomes Carla, Parfitt and opportunistically Will

(Hail Camus!)

On this day, Goldstein, who had died from a stroke, perhaps brought on by the cancer he'd been diagnosed with, was to be buried.

As Parfitt, Rose and Will arrived, Parfitt with a black patch over his eye making him sexy like the Ogilvy shirt advert that revolutionised the products of Madison Avenue in the early fifties, there were others carrying food, in fact an almost continuous stream – there was a lot of bread, boiled eggs and stews made of vegetables or lentils, dried fruits and chocolates. This, they found out, was for the meal of condolence after the burial. Neither Buckland nor Farquhar-Groyne had been buried yet. The police had held onto the bodies.

Everyone removed their shoes. Someone was chanting: *Hamakom yenachem etchem betoch shaar avelay tziyon veerushayaim.* Goldstein's body, lying in a plain, pine coffin, the body clothed in a simple white shroud, was to be taken to the cemetery a little later in the day.

Carla met and welcomed the three, paying special attention to Will and even giving him a tired, sad smile when the others weren't looking.

To Parfitt: your eye?

I fell.

O, Tony.

A tide of warmth and daring surged through Will. In fact, Rose saw it, but rather than feel anger or jealousy, she also felt a sweet warmth for Will's moment of gratification.

Will said about the wake attendees: Mr. Goldstein was well-liked.

Carla said: it's a Jewish thing. It's as if all the Jews in Cambridge and beyond are one family and honour and support one another. I think that among those who revile Jews, many are simply envious of this brotherhood and community. Then she said to Parfitt: I must speak to you, Anthony. Not today, but soon.

He said: certainly.

This attention on Parfitt made Rose, who now felt responsible for him, almost proud and excited to be with, clearly, the most important person in the room. The house!

Carla then said to the three: would you like to see Leonard?

Parfitt said with authority: absolutely! While the others seemed a little less certain.

She took them to where Goldstein lay. All were astonished by the sweetscented smell of the white shrouded body and on the face the Goldstein smile! Perhaps he's smiling from *Shamayim*, for what he's found in the halls of heaven!

Rose said: look how he's smiling! That's beautiful.

Will said: I wonder what his last thought was.

Goldstein's last thought was, actually: I hope I don't give off the odour of corruption like Zossima in *The Brothers Karamazov*.

Carla said: his last words were: I've lost my life but gained the truth.

Rose said: what did it mean?

Parfitt said: one thing he would say to me was: better to lose with truth and right rather than gain with falsehood and wrong.

Rose gasped: so he hasn't lost at all!

Carla: When you've lost your family in the holocaust, you'd be a fool to think that you're doing anything else but visiting.

Rose: Of course!

Will: Perhaps the smile was a smile of gratitude for leading such a peaceful and blessed life.

As they left the body, Rose said to Parfitt: I don't want to go to the interment.

Parfitt said: If you'd like me to, I could tell Carla that you're not well. She'll understand. I would take you home.

O yes! That would be great.

And so Parfitt went with Rose to her flat: that place of Amazonian heat and plenty; arctic sharpness and clarity; mythical priapic gods; breathless lesbian encounters; ICU for the emotionally betrayed; café for the capture of Portuguese roses and bathroom of Debussy-esque delights.

But as they entered, Rose said: you know, should we maybe go back to your place? I was comfortable there. I'm afraid someone may turn up here.

Chapter 72

Halleluja!

After the burial of Goldstein, Will sought out Sternbend. He found him at the back of the house in the shadows. He had been crying.

Will said: hello, Mr. Sernbend. O, I'm sorry.

No, no. It's ok.

He took out a handkerchief, dried his eyes and pinched any dribble from his nose.

And please, Will, call me Israel.

Israel.

Yes. The name I adopted.

I did tap on your door yesterday, but I suppose you didn't hear me. Did you know Mr Goldstein had brought me into the group?

Of course. It was expected.

I had not thought that death could so easily undo someone like Leonard.

As in Eliot?

I suppose so.

I think Eliot meant something a little different.

O. What do you think?

The dead of the First War were so many dead; the undone on Westminster Bridge had had their lives undone by the war, so that they're in a kind of living death. The dead for Leonard was the Holocaust, except it didn't undo him; he developed a hunger for retribution and would exercise his wrath on all those who would perpetrate that killing. He was our inspiration.

Will was surprised that Sternbend could access this Eliotine speculation so easily; he was a little disappointed, he'd hoped to impress the older man with the quote. On the other hand, Sternbend would have had to know what it was referring to for it to carry any weight for Will. Sternbend was a character he just couldn't get. A man with his history, which seemed so illustrious, and now his present petit bourgeois existence.

He said: Carla told me about Chile.

The Right is the enemy of the people. Everywhere. It's too easy to get complacent in Cambridge.

Hmm, yes.

Sternbend wasn't sure why he said that. He'd really wanted to talk about Carla, whom he'd loved since first meeting her in Chile, but like her, was married. He could never have hurt his wife with a romantic affair carried on, perhaps understandably, on the sense-heightened merry-go-round of history. Now Goldstein was gone. And an instinctual, ill-thought-out plan occurred to him: he knew Will had got quite close to Carla and that Carla had a soft spot for Will and that if something grew between Will and Carla, it wasn't beyond reason to imagine that Will might bring Carla to his, Sternbend's home. In the absence of any desire to start something directly with Carla himself, this could almost be a relationship by proxy.

Don't worry. Having this chat won't change our relationship. I am still and only your landlord. And you are my student. And you will carry on sneaking young women into your room against the rules!

Will smiled with an apologetic patina.

Sternbend went on: I think it's the girl from The Eagle, isn't it?

We're very casual.

What does that mean?

We allow each other a lot of leeway.

You seem quite close to Carla.

I feel a bit uncomfortable about that at Leonard's wake.

Of course. I will just say, she's very fond of you.

Will was quite shocked. This was not the Sternbend he knew: the austere headmaster in his study behind the hall door. Nietzsche's mask in practice?

Chapter 73

Return to the wake

(Hail Joyce!)

Back at the wake, Will found Carla.

He said: can I get you a drink?

I was wondering where you were.

Listen, Carla. I know it's not the right time to talk about these things, but if you ever need me, in any way, just let me know. You can always contact me at Israel's.

Suddenly, something broke in Carla. She said:

Come with me, Will.

She led him upstairs to her bedroom. Inside, she locked the door. Will thought: this is unbelievable.

Carla began to undress. And then Will joined her.

Naked, she lay back on the bed and opened her legs almost tentatively at first, breathing deeply and as Will gently pushed her legs apart, she began to pant. Her long black hair lay out on the pillow like a black fabric Chinese fan (just like Rose's!)

Will was sufficiently into his cups to not be overwhelmed by this. He said: what about Leonard? This is his wake!

It's what he would have wanted. He would be overjoyed if he knew we were doing it *now*. He would have hated all the pomp and ceremony. He would have wanted me to break free as soon as possible.

Her body was beautiful. Magnificent. Even her vaginal hair had been trimmed – coiffured — as if by Louis X1V's Mdm. Martin.

Are you sure this is not grief? That you may regret it? Then to himself: For fuck's sake, Will! Just do it before she goes cold!

Will!

He put his head between her legs and his tongue inside her. She smelled like fresh spring dewy earth; she tasted like fresh spring dewy earth; tasted like spring rain on a fresh-sprung crocus.

Her breasts were small and needy. He moved up her body, which smelled of orange and roses, kissing on the way until he came to those breasts which he loved, then he kissed her lips, her mouth thrilled by the orphan taste of her own vaginal juice.

She was enraptured. She'd thought about a moment like this ever since the first time she met Will. Leonard had known and had accepted it and found comfort in the thought that when he died, Will would be there. She would never have done it with Will as long as Leonard was alive: it just wouldn't have been kosher! Will was oasis water in the driest place on earth.

As he positioned himself to enter, she took hold of his erection and held it as he pushed, feeling, as if she were a blind woman, the loving acceptance of his penis by her liaising labia. The thrill of participating in this way in this most sacred of all acts.

Chapter 74
Jamesons

(Hail Behan!)

Will needed to see Rose, to tell her of his success.

He first went to her flat but found she wasn't there.

He began to walk towards Parfitt's place. Dusk was falling: the evening a dozing cat, its flickering eyes of little light. It was quite a trek. He stopped for a drink on the way and spent a quiet moment reflecting on his triumph. And he wondered whether the anal Parfitt had been broken by the multi-talented Rose. He felt incongruously at ease about this possibility, but he had convinced himself that he was beginning something new and exciting and serious and long-term with Carla. The evening was surprisingly sharp and chilled like the chip off an ice block, but charming. He passed gardens still flowered, smiling into the gathering dark and gathered the scents to him. Piano students trilled new exercises that fell like scent from mansard windows. Healthy palms sang of the south, where all ills are warmed away.

Will knocked on Parfitt's door. Waited. Knocked again. Waited.

As he walked back to Rose's, he seemed to have walked smack bang into Eliot's *objective correlative:* the night was now gloomy and threatened anti-climax. Now he was wandering both mentally and geographically. Suddenly, he thought: what if I've lost Rose? What if she opens up Parfitt to all the pleasures of that hinterland he's never known and he becomes obsessed with her? She could do it. What if Carla herself is just a fantasy? What if I got marooned at midnight on Jesus Green, threatened by Buckland's knife? I need a drink. He stopped at The Baron of Beef and had a double Jameson's, which had been Buckland's rarely indulged in tipple. What if he was wrong about all these women? It had happened before:

Chapter 75

Hornet

WILL: An Italian with a black moustache had given me a lift to the French border.

I was lonely now for the first time after leaving in Genoa, the friend I'd been travelling with. And it was cold. November. Who knew where I was? No phone calls or cards. I could be dead. Rolled over the cliff into the Med and maybe never found. The bones of a sad vagrant. I cursed myself. A study in carelessness. Always so wrapped up in my own world. Very short-sighted.

The road hugs the coast. I had to get to Paris. The autoroute was no good. You can't hitch on it. The sun was out. I felt cold and rejected.

An old VW camper van pulled up. A lone woman. I suppose I looked unthreatening. Only 19, slight, poor. Her name was Inga. She was going to Nice. Ya. She was lean. Northern European. All you'd expect. She had a wildness about her. Her eyes. And her hands had a robustness. A masculinity. Her voice was alluring:

What is your name?

Will.

You are British.

Yes.

How old?

Nineteen.

Get in.

I got in.

I am Inga. I am German, though I hate Germans. You want fuck?

I thought I'd misheard her.

Can you say that again?

Fuck. You know. You have no disease? No illness? Ok. I understand. You are hungry. We will stop for food.

I've got no money.

No, it is ok. I know. I will pay.

We stopped in a small town before Monaco, just across the border. I was still a bit in shock. Might she want to kill me? Does that happen? She may be a hater of men. Is there a word for that? Homothrope? I never knew in those days whether I was wise or just uneducated.

Nequidquam sapit qui sibi non-sapit.

That's a bit I memorised from Casanova's autobiography. It means "his wisdom's vain who for himself is not wise." I was always unsure about the world. She walked ahead of me. The town was full of the smells of cooking. Fabulous smells. Basil and garlic. Even now! In this month. And meat. And tomatoes! She was about five seven eight. Her shape was sensational. But could such a thing happen? If you filled your hands with seeds, would the birds come and eat them?

She said: we will have one drink in this bar to give an appetite.

We sat at a small table. I had a glass of beer and we each had a brandy. The place reminded me of an impressionist piece. The interior of a Parisian restaurant. There was even a record of Edith Piaf playing. Behind the bar was an enormous mirror like the one in that painting by Manet: *A Bar at the Folies-Bergere,* with its apparently flawed perspective, except it wasn't. Manet, as ever, is making you, the viewer, responsible for the work. Or at least for looking at it. Which is how I felt now, our puppet heads rising above the bar top like Pierrot and Columbine. The mundane world had fled. Everything seemed painterly and musical.

Her eyes were green.

Are you an artist? A writer?

I said: well, I do write. Yes. And I miss it when travelling. I found it difficult to engage with her intellectually as I was still thinking of that other thing.

O, but you must still do it. She pointed to her head.

I drank the brandy quickly. Suddenly, her lips were thrilling.

What about you, I said. Do you live in Nice?

Yes, she said in a little room. I will take you there and you can sleep with me before our onward journey. If you like, we could eat here. You may be a little too excited to walk much.

She knew all about me! It was as if I'd been shipwrecked and she'd found me and brought me bananas and coconut milk and her sweet breath to nourish me, as if she was softening me up for the big sex.

We ordered oysters and steak and a bottle of Provencal rosé.

She ate with an elegance inherited from an aristocratic past. When you read about those defunct royal houses and wonder what happened to all the princesses, this is it. They drive the Riviera roads looking for excitement. After the Piaf, Ravel's Pavane for a Dead Princess played.

Just then, a hornet entered the café. I knew about hornets. I'd studied them for an exercise. A poem I was writing. They make up the genus *Vespa* and can grow up to two inches in length. This wasn't so big but brutish. Hornet stings are more severe than wasp stings because they contain acetylcholine. As the insect flew close to us, Inge suddenly jumped up and cried out.

I cannot…I am allergy!….

And she ran out of the café. And down the road. And she was gone.

I sat in silence for a moment. This was crazy. I kept up a vigil – eyes on the street - with the air of someone simply waiting for a returning partner. After a few minutes, the *maitre'd* came to the table with his pad. I indicated with a waving gesture of my hand that I didn't want anything more. As he began to walk away, I said: Monsieur.

Oui?

I said: I have no…um money. I rubbed my fingers together to suggest this. He looked perplexed.

Comment?

Argent?

I made a cut-throat gesture.

It was clear he understood the unequivocal nature of my position because he started doing a kind of dance replete, I was pretty sure, with curses and insults directed at me and then he took my arm roughly and pulled back the sleeve to reveal my watch and said: Ça.

He wanted my Mondaine Evo Chronograph watch! Worth a few hundred pounds, which Kenny Jones gave me as a gift after knocking off one of those palaces in Cyncoed in Cardiff. I had no choice but to let him take it.

Later, I sat by the roadside. I felt useless. A fool who could write the book on being duped. The night was falling. Before me in the air was a Rimbaud poem. At twilight. Rimbaud. Jesus. She'd taken my rucksack and sleeping bag. They were in her van. And it was getting cold! I thought it would be good to get into the goal. I could steal something from one of those fruit and veg displays outside a roadside shop, then give myself in at the first gendarmerie. They would have to lock me up because I was a thief and had no money. Nowhere to stay to await trial.

Inga, who offered me the world, took everything I had!

Would this happen with Carla?

Chapter 76

Moles

(Hail Le Carré)

He recalled Inga when thinking about Carla. Even though he and Carla *had* done it, he was nevertheless dupable. What about the onward journey with her?

In The Baron, he'd seen Quaid Laurel. Laurel was clearly in his cups.

Will sat at a table and Quaid joined him. Will's downhearted mood took a deeper dive.

Quaid said: given up on The Eagle?

No, I've been over to Parfitt's.

That boy just should not drink.

I was looking for Rose.

Rose? Rose and Parfitt?

We've been to Goldstein's funeral. Thought you might have been there.

I'm *persona non grata*. They think I'm a fifth columnist. I've retreated into my graphene shell.

I think they just couldn't understand your connection with Farquhar-Groyne.

Some intimacies are too perplexing to breathe. Ghosts. I've retreated into my shell of graphene. I know about you. The Swede told me.

What about?

You and him. Sex in Stockholm. When you were a kid.

He's confused me with someone else.

I don't think so. Hey, don't be coy with me. I've got a mind as broad as Norfolk waterways. And I've had experience.

Experience?

The drink was getting the better of Laurel.

Ok. Let me tell you. Farquhar Groyne.

You and Farquhar Groyne?

You're not a natural Cambridge boy. And not a public-school boy. Roy Jenkins legalised homosexuality because he'd been at him himself. For our people, it's the equivalent of the Grand Tour. Incomplete without visiting Venice. Growing up. Incomplete without visiting your fellow enthusiasts. There's one way to sort this fucker out. Sten said you've got a mole at the top of your back, about the centre. Let me have a look.

Fuck you.

Listen, let me have a look. If it's there, so what? What's the big deal? If it's there, you will have shared it with someone. Think of the relief.

Silence.

Listen. You're in denial. But what fucking good does it do? It's like a splinter that rots in your blood and poisons the fuck out of you.

Quaid leaned over the table and pushed the back collar of Will's white funeral shirt down. Will didn't resist. He found something almost sexy about it and could even feel himself getting hard.

Quaid sat down with a perplexed look.

He said: O dear.

What?

It's there. You need to have it checked out.

Why?

It doesn't look right.

Why? What's wrong with it?

It looks like it's becoming cancerous!

How would you know?

In my research into graphene, I've had to look at everything! The whole experience of matter. There's no problem. Just check it out with the doc. As for the other, we do it with the girls – like Rose; we do it with the boys: Groyne and Sten.

His name is Stig.

Then he'd got up and left.

As he walked back to Rose's, the night was now angry, black-tanned, draped in the devils cloak and windows lit hepatic yellow; he wasn't quite sure whether Quaid was saying that he'd fucked Rose and if he was he wasn't quite sure how he felt about that because uppermost in his mind were thoughts about whatever it was Laurel had seen on his back.

Chapter 77

The Curse of Rome

(Hail Moravia!)

Dewey said: you look down, Will.

He was back at Rose's. She wasn't there. Was she at Parfitt's after all? He felt a panic building. He needed to see her now! Needed her opinion on his back!

He said: It's ok.

Tarita said: how was the funeral?

Very Jewish.

Dewey said: did you get to talk to Carla Goldstein?

Yes. Yes. We talked a lot. Listen, will you two look at my back for me?

We've decided we're getting married, Will.

Shit, Dewey, that's sudden.

Tarita said: not really. Let's have a look.

Will began to take his waistcoat off and then his shirt.

He said: when's it going to happen?

Dewey said: we're not sure yet.

Shirt off, they looked, they paused.

Tarita wasn't sure how she felt with the man she could so easily have loved, half naked, while the man she'd just so completely become a part of sat next to her. Though she did know she felt an extraordinary sense of general belonging here with the two, her memory of Rolcord Wyre fading faster.

She said: It doesn't look right.

Dewey said: you need it checked out. I saw a guy in the hospital with something like that. It looks like something you might get with that new virus. AIDS.

He couldn't believe how quickly he'd sunk from a triumphant circuit of the Colosseum to being ripped apart by lions; from riding the surf a couple of hours earlier to scraping the black sand for mercy here in this suddenly hostile room. He had cancer. Or the murderous AIDS.

Chapter 78

Will in Crepusculum

Mortality. The barbed weeds of defining mortality. Until now, Will had never given any thought to longevity. It's the default among the young. Even when being rational, you look for the infinite in thought. Your thought. This twilight seemed appropriate. The twilight of the gods. *Götterdämmerung.* Should he go to a doctor? Just go to A&E at the hospital? There was now a heavy breeze. On the avenue, some had planted leylandii to keep the outside world from intruding; elsewhere, poplars with lenticels scarring the equivocal light. He had become a poplar bark scarred by impending night and death. The wind blowing through the ghosted cedars. It was nemesis, karma. For a selfish life. A phoney life. He wasn't even the poet he posed as. A quasi-poet who can never be more. Never a complete lover because I've never subordinated myself to the one I'm ostensibly loving. Will I lose my skin? That would be appropriate. Be denuded of what's protected my phoniness. He didn't know where to go. He wanted to go to Carla but knew that would be no good. The mood had gone. And anyway, there were probably many party-goers still there. Without registering it, he'd already begun to walk back to Carla's. He was deeply distracted. A car passed full of students, obviously drunk, shouting merrily out of open windows. He felt nauseous. They have no idea how ugly fate can undermine everything. What do they do if it's gone too far? Peel the infected skin off? Bit by bit? He was at the end of the street. Carla's street.

He didn't see the shape standing in the shadow of a great oak.

He turned around. How could he find the kind of optimism necessary to go back into Carla's shindig? In fact, why did he think he'd want to see anyone at all now? This whole thing could not be waited for to sort out and yet he'd have to wait through an interminable night; a night like the last night of earth when the sane have no alternative but to face insanity.

Through the almost dark streets, the standing man, curiously drawn to him, following him like a lost dog following a scent of hope, Will slouched on to his Gethsemene.

Chapter 79

Qeequeg

Will arrived at his door. As he put the key in his lock, a man appeared beside him.

The man's face was a patchwork of tattoos. Illustrated man. But there was something that Will recognised. Will felt uneasy.

The man said: Let's go in.

Who are you?

More urgently: let's go in!

I don't know who you are.

The man held a large knife up to Will's chin.

Will froze but managed to say: You can kill me. It makes no difference, I'm already dead.

The man withdrew the knife. He said: can we go in?

Leave that outside.

Tattoo threw the knife down and they went in.

In the lit hallway, he turned to Tatoo and put a finger to his mouth to indicate that no noise should be made. Sternbend may still have been at the wake, but he may not and he didn't want to be seen going up to his room with this strange one. In the room, Will got a good look at the fellow. It was Rolcord Wyre.

Will said: how are you here? I thought you were in....

Broadmoor. Yeah.

So....

I got out. Got out in the uniform of a nurse.

With a tattooed face?

They're transfers. They'll wash off. I did it after I got out. Fucking joke, eh?

What do you want?

My wife. I know you've got her.

Will indicated the room. Empty.

Stashed. You've got her stashed.

Where?

I don't fucking know! That's what I gotta find out.

You're not allowed to see her.

Will was wondering where this would go. He felt strangely calm. A distraction from his dread.

Who fucking cares? I'm a double murderer! I bet that fucked you lot up!

What lot?

All you arse fuckers and poncy swots. You fucked my misses?

Probably not.

What kind of fucking answer is that, you lying cunt!

What is it you want?

I want you to take me to her! What fucking else are you good for? You fucked her up the arse? That would be up your street, I suppose. Lovely tight arse. Until you get going, then she relaxes and goes fucking wild. Well fuck, you know that. To be honest, I thought I'd find her here, ready for a poking. Fuck me, I need a wank. Where's the shit house?

Across the landing.

Don't fucking move. This won't take long. Unless you want to come with me. I'll tell you what, you tell me where she is and I'll suck you off.

Will looked at him blankly.

Fuck that. Don't want your cum oiling my tonsils.

Will so hated this kind of talk even in a benign situation. Wyre went out onto the landing. He shut the door behind him. Why didn't Will tackle him? Stand behind the door and jump him as he comes in. The knife! He could go down while Wyre is masturbating and retrieve the knife. He snuck out onto the landing and began to go downstairs, immediately seeing Wyre coming up with the knife.

He'd stay cool; he knew the authorities would already be looking for Wyre, though, of course, they wouldn't know they'd be looking for an illustrated man.

When Wyre almost reached him, he said: come on, get your coat, we're going.

Will suddenly kicked out, pushing Wyre down the stairs he'd just come up. Wyre yelled, got up at the bottom, looking up at Will. At that moment, Sternbend came out of his room and said a little fearfully: What's going on, Will? Will said: it's ok, Israel, my….Wyre jumped up, turned to Israel and put his face right up against the older man and raised the knife. In an instant, Israel Sternbend collapsed and died.

Will flew down the remaining stairs and bent down over Israel.

Will shouted into the Sternbend rooms: Mrs. Sternbend! Come quickly.

Wyre shouted to Will: get your fucking coat! No, fuck that! Get out!

We need an ambulance!

Fuck it! Let *her* do it.

Mrs. Sternbend appeared, saw Wyre's frightful face and the knife and her husband's lifeless and like him, collapsed. In fact, on top of him.

A memory flashed through Will's mind of a friend's parents: the father died at work and when they came to tell his wife, she dropped dead on her doorstep.

Will hurried into the Sternbends' rooms.

Where are you going?

To phone!

No, you're not! Wyre followed him. And put the knife to Will's back.

Will shouted: go on! You'll be doing me a favour!

Then Will picked up the old heavy Bakelite phone, swung round and smashed it into Wyre's head. Wyre fell with a crash. Will took the knife from him. He dialled 999.

Will managed to ask for an ambulance and was about to ask for the police when Wyre, behind him, hit Will with an antique, Kashmiri hand-painted candlestick, took back the knife, thrust it into Will's back, and fled out into the street.

Chapter 80

Communion

(Hail Eliot!)

Back at Rose's Tarita, resting comfortably against Dewey, he, with his arm around her, said to Rose:

How did you get on with Parfitt?

He's not like you'd think! Nothing like how he presents himself.

They all grinned, sharing an act of communion.

Rose said: I think the murder of Neil Buckland released something in him.

Dewey said: Interesting. Will's been here. He was showing us his back.

His back?

Tarita said: he's got a mole on it that's going wrong.

Did he say if he was going home?

Tarita said: I should think he would?

Rose said: do you think it could be cancer?

Dewey said: I told him I think he needed to check it out.

Tender feelings for Will rose in her and a sharp spear point of guilt that she'd abandoned him in his time of need.

Tarita said: did I tell you we're getting married?

Really?

Yes.

That's great. Congratulations! When?

Dewey said: I need to get a proper job first. Casual labour's no good.

Tarita said: and we need to find a place. We can't keep staying here. You've been so kind.

It's fine. And then to Dewey: what do you think you might do?

I might rejoin the fire service.

Rose said to Tarita: would you go back to Cherry Hinton? They'd have you back, wouldn't they?

I thought maybe I'd train to be a nurse.

That's a brilliant idea. Look, I think I need to go to Will's. It's a lot to cope with on his own.

They said, ok and Rose went.

Chapter 81

The Whale

(Hail Melville!)

When the police put out a description of Wyre, there was nothing about an illustrated man. They'd used the description on file. So when PC Grimcock approached the strange man in a hood with a face like a speedway track, he was happy to pass on the other side.

And then he reasoned: it'll be night soon, maybe he needs help. There's that place on Suez Road I could tell him about. Very cheap. Grimcock approached him and said:

Excuse me, friend, are you lost?

Keeping his face covered as far as possible with his hood, Wyre said: No officer, I'm ok. I'm going to the bus station. I'm heading for Lincoln.

Afraid you're going the wrong way. You need to go back, turn left and walk down Parker Street until you come to it.

How do you know which way I'm going?

Position of the body. Body language. We learn about it in the force. Your face is quite a picture. Looks more dramatic at this crepuscular time.

What time is that?

Twilight.

Got it from a film I saw. Rod Steiger.

Don't know. I know, why don't I walk with you to the bus station? I can go that way.

Wyre grunted in the affirmative.

They began walking. As they got to the corner, sirens began to wail somewhere near in the near dark city.

As I came into Will's street, I saw a panic of blue lights spinning and flashing. It looked like Will's. I had a deep feeling of increasing dread which built as I approached the lights.

I said to a policeman: what's happened?

The cop said: cold-blooded death.

I thought, how would he know what's happened is cold-blooded? Copote's novel about the slaying of the Clutter family came to mind. But the writer only understood it was in cold blood after finding out the facts from the killers.

I said: I don't know what you mean.

Two dead, one critical.

My boyfriend lives there. Is he one of them?

Chap in his twenties?

Yes.

My heart was racing. Is he dead? The critical?

I don't know that.

How can I find out? What the hell could have happened? I said: have they taken them out yet?

He looked me up and down with, I thought, a salacious eye and said: wait there. One of those who identifies young women in distress and then, later, visits them.

I saw him walk off into the melee of ambulance crew, police and paramedics as if into a mist. When he returned, he said:

The young man's been stabbed in the back. He's critical.

Thank God!

Parfitt had suddenly faded into a past fantasy.

Where will they take him?

Addenbrookes, I'd say.

I thought: that must surely mean the Sternbends are dead! It's hardly believable – what's happened to this city?

Chapter 82

Withering

(Hail Ellis Bell!)

Rolcord Wyre, after his pleasant walk with the dim Grimcock in which he'd set out the experiences his friend Dewey, who'd spent some time in Broadmoor, had related to him, an education for Grimcock which he was grateful for, he settled on a bench waiting for a bus to take him away from this danger zone. Grimcock wasn't yet aware of Wyre's escape. While Wyre waited, Dan appeared, walking between the various bus stops heading for Wyre's shelter. He looked lost and pretty in his twills and white shirt and Wyre, perhaps the greatest villain of his own day, was immediately spellbound and even felt the years of bitterness and aggression melt away, even though he'd left his medication back at the hospital, a cause of his current intemperance and return to his bad old ways.

There's no doubt he was a beautiful young man. Reminded Wyre of some kind of poet. As he got closer, Wyre called to him.

Hey! Hey!

Dan looked at him. He was a little shocked. Thought with a face like that, he had to be a villain. On the other hand, what villainy would he be likely to get up to here? With insignificant him? And did he care?

Chapter 83

The Mountain

(Hail Modiano!)

When he entered The Eagle the previous evening, it was almost empty; Rose was behind the bar reading Anais Nin. It was a particularly raunchy piece in which a black guy with a statuesque member was also wearing a profoundly studious strap-on dildo. Dan came in as she was about to find out what he was going to do with this setup. She was feeling randy as hell as she closed the book and put it under the counter.

She said: Dan! Wow, you look cool.

Dan nervously said: Hi, Rose. I wasn't sure….

Why? Life's too short for petulance. What you drinking?

I've been sleeping rough.

You don't look it.

I met someone you know. Could I have a glass of red wine?

Verre du vin. She took a glass from a shelf and poured wine into it. Who?

Tony.

O right. Did you do anything with him?

What?

She mouthed: did you fuck.

He was dumbstruck when he heard her say that and could only get out a tentative n…n…no.

Then he told her *sotto voce* that he'd been confused, adding that thinking of her had made him a bit mad.

Thanks.

No, mad with love; with obsession.

She said: stick around.

He handed her the fiver.

A fiver! I thought you were sleeping rough!

Tony gave me this, with the clothes.

Keep it.

Thanks.

He took his drink to a table and sat and watched. Watched as the bar filled. The chinless, the martyrs, the haughty, sometimes robed, the sufferers, the secret and the bold, the dancers and rhythmless, the scented and the odoured, the upright and the stateless, the student and the studied.

Occasionally, watching Rose, he'd begun to feel a little more confident. Once or twice, she'd flashed him a smile. He was hungry. The wine had already made him a little lightheaded. He knew that they sometimes would make a sandwich, though there was no standing menu. And the bar was not too busy. He had no money. Maybe a couple of bob…..He had the fiver! He'd been so obsessed with his new

twilled self discovered in the shop windows of his flanneuring.....He
went to the bar....

Dan smiled. He said: I'm starving.

Would you like me to make you something?

A sandwich? I can pay!

She smiled ambiguously.

He waited at the bar while she made the sandwich.

He stuck around.

Later, as she put on her coat, she said to him: come on.

Where?

To my place!

He could hardly believe she said that.

As they walked, she said: my friends may be there.

O.

It's ok, we can go to my room.

As they got closer to her flat, Dewey and Tarita came towards
them.

Rose said: here they are.

O yes. I've seen them before.

Now the sky seemed bluer than blue; sailing the waves of light;
tracking Neruda's mermaid to bring her into the embrace of love;
castaways in a Defoe metaworld, rugged man and his girl.

They all stopped. Rose said: this is Dan.

Hi Dan.

Hi Dan.

This is Dewey:

Hi Dewey

And Tarita

Hi Tarita.

Dewey said: I'm taking Tarita to show her King's Chapel.

Rose said: O right.

Dan said: It's great.

Tarita said: see you later.

Dan said: well, I…..

Rose said: yeh!

In her room, Rose offered Dan the bed. She helped him down. She took off his shoes and peeled down his twill. No pants. His young cock was crowing, reaching for peaks. She took it in her mouth. It tasted of grass and lonely nights. It tasted of sex: strange and glorious. He came and it hit the back of her throat. Young, slightly salted asparagus.

I'm sorry.

She swallowed: no, no.

The *verres du vin* helped him relax and keep his interest and intent high.

Then she stripped.

He got hard again.

She laid back on the bed, legs apart and he put his mouth over her pussy and stuck his tongue in as far as he could. The taste was heavenly! Cucumber and honey with a hint of fennel. He got up. He turned her over. She lifted her buttocks high. She exposed her anus and put her hands behind her and pulled the opening apart. She invited him to enter there and he did. The tightness soon triggered his orgasm and she pushed him back, saying breathlessly: my cunt! And then he put it in there and completed his coming.

The next morning, she kicked him out.

She said: I'm going to a funeral.

But after.

No.

What do you mean?

My life is too complicated!

But this isn't you!

I know. No, it's not. I'm trying to save you.

Save me? You're killing me!

Better to have loved once than never loved.

What the fuck?!

What would Thomas have done?

I don't know!

He would have used his imagination! Created new worlds!

The rest of the day, he wandered. He found nothing in his imagination; nothing that would encourage him to leave this world for another.

Chapter 84

Sweat

(Hail Flannery O' Connor!)

As Dan approached the villain Wyre that evening, Wyre said:

You look lost.

No. Just haven't decided where to go.

Join the club.

Rolcord Wyre was surprised by the softness of his own voice.

D'you want to sit?

Dan sat.

Wyre just loved looking at the young man's face. Dan, sitting so close to Wyre, was intrigued by his tattooed face. He felt there was something fishy about the tattoos – that they weren't real. But he was friendly enough. In fact, he was quite pleased that he'd met him. He'd been feeling a bit too detached from unreality. He felt he could share his unhappiness over Rose without consequence, as the man was a stranger.

I lost the woman I love.

Aren't they just fuckers? What was she like?

Beautiful. A bit of the Spanish about her.

Yeah? Cambridge girl?

Far as I know. She works in The Eagle. Know it?

Yeah. What's her name?

Rose.

Black hair? Eyes?

Yeah.

Know her. This is unbelievable, mate. I lost my missus, too. I think they got together.

Who did?

Your misses and my misses!

Shit!

Yeah. D'you know where she lives?

Who?

Yours!

Yes.

Where do you think you might want to go?

I just want to get out of Cambridge.

Don't want to go round to her place? I'd come with you. Might find mine too!

A police car drove slowly into the bus station and stopped by the two men. It was PC Grimcock and another. Grimcock gave him a cursory wave. Obviously, news of Wyre's break hadn't been circulated yet. And it suddenly occurred to him that they'd be looking for whoever stabbed Will. Fortunately for him, he'd struck up a friendship with PC Grimcock, which proved the adage: familiarity breeds contempt (for the law!).

Rolcord tugged at Dan's sleeve and said: Come on. Dan felt it gave him a reason to call on Rose – maybe one last time: introduce her to this interesting, peculiar man.

The funeral was surely over.

They moved off into the night. Into the past.

Chapter 85

Rose

(Hail Carver!)

Guilt can scar the heart much more profoundly than hate.

Rose was, she discovered, susceptible to the former while she refused to acknowledge the latter. And as she made her way to Addenbrooke's, she thought: I'm missing something; why am I feeling guilty? *I* couldn't have brought this onto Will. It would have to be to do with Rolcord Wyre. Wouldn't it? But Wyre's in Broadmoor! Isn't he?

Then she thought: some right-wing fanatic come to steal papers from the Sternbends, overheard by Will, who's raised the alarm.

O, I don't know. I can't shift this guilt.

Maybe it was because of the way she'd treated Dan. But that was for his own sake! She knew that this was a condition bred in her by her God crazy family and right now she felt terribly that she'd betrayed Will. That if she hadn't been fucking around with Parfitt, she probably would have been home when he turned up and he wouldn't even have bothered to go back to his place. Then, as she passed a telephone box, she thought: fuck it and stepped into the box which smelled heavily of piss and dialled 999.

Police.

This is a strange request, but I was wondering if you could tell me, do you know if anyone has escaped from Broadmoor?

This is an emergency line.

Sorry. But it is a kind of emergency.

What do you know about the Broadmoor escape?

Nothing. *The* Broadmoor escape?

Yesterday. What's your name?

Rose Angwen.

Then she gave the woman on the other end her address and hung up. Wyre may find her address and head for there. When she got to the hospital, she asked for Will Slade, told them she was his fiancée, and they took her to him, saying that he was still very ill but she would be allowed, at least, to see him.

When she got to his room, he was awake.

Hi Will.

He smiled.

She said: What a mess!

Then she told him about her call to the police. He confirmed that it was Wyre and that his face was heavily tattooed, making him almost unrecognisable.

O my God!

She asked: what happened about your mole? Have they said anything about it? He answered with difficulty that he supposed they must have seen it when dealing with the stabbing but hadn't said anything. Perhaps they were concentrating on one thing at a time. That the stabbing had been very serious: had gone right into him. Said he had another operation coming.

In the lobby of the hospital, she phoned the police again and told them about the tattooed face. This information got to PC Grimcock, who immediately felt his bowels loosen and a sensation of rising sickness in his stomach.

Chapter 86

Journey to the End of History

(Hail Fukuyama!)

As they crossed Jesus Green and then Midsummer Common, Dan was preoccupied with what he would say to Rose when he saw her.

Rolcord Wyre said to Dan: how far is it?

Dan said: if we carry on (Dan made a gesture indicating straight on), we'll come to the road. Turn right and carry on down the right and it's the only house with a yellow door. Then Dan was taken by surprise when Rolcord suddenly stopped, pulled the young man to him and kissed him passionately. As they kissed, Rolcord's illustrated face smudged and as they pulled apart, Dan began to rub at the transfers, revealing in this gesture the tension between appearance and reality. The man who kissed him was much more solid than he'd thought.

And then that tension snapped.

Rose was hugely relieved that Will was so far alright, having feared the worst, though she was a bit disappointed that the depth of her relief didn't seem to match the deep crisis of her fear. Now she was determined to get back to her place as quickly as possible in case Wyre was making his way back there. She ran and then she walked and she ran and then she walked and when she walked across the moonlit haunted Green where the trees were like ancient, severe prophets who would always threaten the security of her libertinage she wondered why she ever thought that the boldness of her project to bring the physicality of sex together with the cerebral world in a kind of double helix would somehow be a guarantor of its own security.

When the tension broke, Wyre suddenly let out a desperate yell, took his knife out, held it chest height, turned and raced towards the exit of the green. Emerging out of the mist of his unsettling infatuation, he suddenly realised that this would be his last opportunity to settle things with Tarita. Dan, figuring something terrible was going to happen immediately, gave chase, hoping to get to Rose's place before Wyre and stop him. Faster than Wyre, he soon caught him and overtook him, getting to the yellow door first, stood with his back to the door – Horatio holding the bridge against Lars Posena - as Wyre arrived, raising his foot against the madman. Wyre pulled at his leg, they toppled over and the police arrived as the knife, targetless, entered Dan's body and finished off his already broken heart.

Part Three
Cambridge Dog Days

Chapter 87

Lockdown

(Hail Defoe!)

Rose, early sixties, spinster, is sitting at her window looking out onto the rain in her desolate yard. Lockdown. From a humble trader's wares in a Chinese market, a virus broke out and with the savagery of Hitler's Wehrmacht, began to kill millions. It came to Europe through Italy and after killing many thousands in the UK the government, against the advice of its own right wing, launched the lockdown. You may creep out at night, pass the blinded inns and anaesthetised restaurants, rest beneath monochromatic trees, walk upon the bled blades of sleeping grass, but risk arrest with nowhere to go but home.

Before me on the windowsill are the instruments of my contemplated death.

In lockdown, you're not allowed to go anywhere. One small trip, a short walk a day. I'm here alone with only the ghosts of my philosophy.

Lockdown provides the opportunity to develop self-hate; locked up with that non-corporeal other: Eliot's other. Yourself. Stinks of gangrenous flesh; corpse flower, Durian fruit.

I try to meditate but keep thinking of cocks; penuses. And then there's the smell of my own desuetude! It's a smell I know exists but is absent; its absence is the proof of its existence.

I've bought a dildo. It vibrates. Got it on Amazon. I can't use it in here. The smell; I go to the bathroom and drop essential oil everywhere to lock out the smell of me. I masturbate daily but always feel so lonely afterwards.

I don't want to think about all the moves of my life that have brought me to this pass, but one of the consequences of my recurring bouts of depression is my inability to have the final say on what I think and I torment myself with this self-hatred. Unless I can forge a clever distraction. Except right now, I have little determination.

At the time of Will's hospitalisation, I regularly visited until the day I went to see him and I wasn't able to. He'd had several operations to deal with the complications resulting from the stabbings and it was cancer that they couldn't treat with chemo because he was too weak from the complications. That was when they tried the experimental stuff. Poor, poor Will. I can't talk about it now. I choke up. Like Joni Mitchell said: *you don't know what you've got till it's gone.* He wasn't gone, but he may as well have been.

A few years ago, a package came through the post. From Sweden. From Sten. Stig. He'd written his name and address on the back.

I lay the package on the table. I unwrapped it. A label on the inner package said: *The Love of my Life.*

Chapter 88

Tors

How the hell did he get my address?

She opened the inner packing. It was the video Will had told her about. The one with him and Sten. The label on the cassette itself said: Me and the boy god Will.

She didn't have a VHS player.

She was now in a place where the only concession to life her depression allowed her was breath. The meat of her being in a tremor of interminable rotting; no light except a dimming candela; no way out through her corrupted eyes. She used Prozac. It was like the masturbating – the illusion of freedom as you rose towards the high tor of orgasm and then the return to the ditch.

She certainly didn't feel like watching the tape. Not yet, anyway. Not on this day.

Almost without thinking, she went out to look for a player. She would watch it when the first light broke.

Chapter 89

The Bad and The Beautiful 1

(Hail Cormac McCarthy!)

Months after the horror, a young man was sticking a welcome sign to the café window. Dewey thought it was like a transfer. The word is stuck onto the back of cellophane and then transferred from there to the window.

Dewey said: *Have not for friends those whose soul is ugly; go not with men who have an evil soul. Have for friends those whose soul is beautiful; go with men whose soul is good.*

Tarita said: what's that?

The Buddha.

Why?......

I'm thinking about Rolcord. Watching that guy putting that transfer on.

You mean his face?

I suppose.

She put a hand on his across the table.

But listen, Dewey, he's gone.

During the time I was in Broadmoor, I learned that the purpose of the place is to make those who are not yet mad, mad.

You weren't mad and you're not mad now.

I found the Buddha. He saved me. But how, in a place where all is ugly, where do you find the good souls?

In the Buddha?

We should visit Rolcord.

What?! But he *is* mad!

An act of mercy. A demonstration of the good and the beautiful.

He may go berserk if he sees you! And me!!

Don't worry, they'll have him under control.

It won't do him any good.

We're not looking for reward.

What do you mean?

Any measure of how much good it'll do him. We can simply give him an aura of what's good and beautiful. A gesture of forgiveness.

I'm divorcing him! I don't really want to talk about this. Can we go home? Let's go back. Let me lay on you. Let me not think of Rolcord for now. We can think about it in the morning.

Alright.

He let her take him home.

What if he was to attack me?

Dewey gave himself to her.

Afterwards, she said: I love you, Dewey and I love your kindness and generosity but don't you think you should be concentrating on your studies?

Dewey had begun a law degree after being accepted at Will's old *alma mater* as a mature student. And his independent student grant had allowed them to get their own place on Mill Street while Tarita returned to work in Cherry Hinton.

Will, of course, had not been able to complete his degree after the stabbing and consequent horror. Dewey said: I'm committed to it. For Will.

Chapter 90

Pornography

(Hail Dic Edwards!)

I managed to hire a video player from a rental place. The picture wasn't great because the video had been recorded from a projection on a screen.

As I put the cassette in the machine, I felt a rush of prurience soon subsumed in a wave of sadness.

The first thing: I was surprised at how young Will looked. Yes, he always looked younger than his years, but here he looked like a young teen. And all the hair around his anus and genitals had been removed – my memory took me back to when I'd first coupled with Stig myself. And subsequently. If I hadn't known how old Will actually was, I don't think I could have watched further.

The second thing: (I'm making a record of this for my own sake; not to purvey pornography). The camera was placed very cleverly and, of course, Stig knew how to make the necessary moves to get the best shots. The first was Stig gently playing with the rim of Will's anus always massaging it to open it up with the help of something like Vaseline and saying you must now think of this as the gentle, inviting love cup that it is and Stig discovering as he ventured further inside Will and Stig saying that he thinks that the pill had worked and that Will was soon ready to be fucked and then Stig fucking him at first gently and then more vigorously as Will responded with his own corresponding vigour to the pounding on his prostate which drove him wild and Stig coming on Will's rim and re-entering on the deposit of cum all while the camera filmed. And all the while I employed my vibratorand, as he laid back and Stig plied him, got an incredible thrill watching Will come and as Stig continued his push, watching Will come again as *I* repeatedly came.

I have to say, once I got used to seeing the young Will in this so unfamiliar role, I watched it repeatedly, which, I suppose, only increased my despair.

Chapter 91

Assassin

(Hail Faulkner)

On the night of 28th February 1986, about half an hour before midnight, Swedish Prime Minister Olof Palme left the Grand Cinema with his wife Lisbeth, his son Mårten and his girlfriend. The two couples talked briefly before parting; Olof and Lisbeth began their walk down the central Stockholm street Sveavägen, making their way to the Northern entrance of the Hötorget metro station. On the corner of Sveavägen and Tunnelgatan, the couple stopped to look into a shop window. At precisely 23.21, someone came up behind the pair and shot Palme at point-blank range in the back, killing him. And then he wounded his wife. The assassin trotted off down Tunnelgatan Street and then up the steps to Malmskillnagatan and continued down David Bagares gata.

At first, Christer Pettersson was identified by Mrs Palme as the perpetrator, charged and convicted of the murder. On appeal, he was acquitted. Later, Stig Engström – known as the Skandia Man – became the prime suspect but was never charged.

In 1998, Stig turned up at my door. I let him in. He seemed somehow deferential, as though humbled by circumstance. Although there had been no forensic evidence against him, the public prosecutor had named him as the man most likely to have committed the crime and for this, the prosecutor was heavily criticised. No charge had been brought against Stig, though the epithet of Skandia Man had stuck and he was endlessly discussed. The interest in him sustained by its mystery. The weight of the support given to him by those who said it was not him finally became too much and he came to me to unburden himself. He told me that it was him. That he'd done it. He said he did it because he'd never got over Will, who wanted nothing to do with him. After a meeting with members of his anti-Palme circle, brought on by some devastating news about Will, he decided to act. He needed to take out his frustration on the liberal bourgeois Palme, who he hated. He said he needed to come and tell me because I had been so close to Will. He regretted what he'd done. The shooting. He said he was dying and needed to make his peace.

He looked different. Very. His face had become heavy even though it hadn't been that many years, his youthful grace and beauty lost beneath the meaty assault of middle-age. And he'd lost that aura of sexual ferocity.

I asked him in.

In the years since I'd last seen him, the wine market had opened up and I'd progressed from the Mateus to Australian chardonnay. I took his heavy northern coat and hung it up and he sat, weirdly, with the prim uncertainty of an ageing lady.

I opened the Chardonnay. He needed the calming buzz of the drink: I could see his eyes soften. And as his eyes softened, so did his face and I began to see something of the old Stig.

As we drank, he did the unburdening. It was fascinating to watch him. He wanted to explore every detail of his feelings and motives and delivered it with a benign urgency. We soon finished the bottle and I went out for another. He said: tell me where the shop is and I'll go and get it. I said, it's ok. He said, let me at least pay. I said, alright. He gave me a ten-pound note and I left him.

When I returned, he asked if he could see Will.

I said: do you know what happened to him?

Where is he?

I could take you there, but he wouldn't recognise you, nor you him.

I opened the wine and poured.

What happened? What happened to him?

He found the world.

I don't understand that.

I thought you knew. I thought that's why you killed the Prime Minister.

I only knew that he'd suffered an attack. It was a long time before I found out. I've come now because I've been told I don't have long. I thought that he would have committed himself to your care and I would have lost him forever.

Are you telling me that you came here hoping to find him?

Yes.

And the video?

I wanted him to see it. A last chance to bring him back.

And if he had been here and refused you, would you have killed him, too?

Chapter 92

The Bad and The Beautiful 2

(Hail Byron!)

Back at the time of the killings, Dewey and Tarita got a train to Reading and a taxi from there. As they approached the building, Dewey began to shake. He held onto the book about the Buddha he'd brought for reassurance. The House of Sorrows, as he called it, began to threaten: strip the trees, stain black the flowers, darken the day sky and all the birds detune and fall silent.

He wondered whether any of the nurses would recognise him. As he re-entered the era of his horror, Dewey became aware of the ghost of William Giles, the youngest person ever sent to Broadmoor, sentenced when he was only 10 in 1885 for an arson attack, kept there for 77 years until his death in 1962 at the age of 87. William became Dewey's Saint of Sorrow to whom he would pray at night, asking for forgiveness for the cruelty of men.

Rolcord knew someone was visiting but didn't know who. He thought maybe it was his arresting officer, come to gloat. Whoever he could handle it. The drugs they gave him calmed him down and allowed him to employ convincingly his facility for turning on the charm. And they took away his boredom and the consequent anger.

But he was not expecting to see Tarita! With Dewey! Cheeky fuckers! Trying to wind me up! Thinking I can't touch them.

He looked different to them. He looked benign!

Inside, he was seething, mostly because of the way Dewey had held his balls and thrown him out of The Eagle. He would love to do to him what they said he did to the other two: a hunting knife to the top of the head.

As they approached him, he got up. Charming man. He held his hand out for Dewey. As he shook the former inmate's hand, he said: Dewey! Good to see you! I was talking about you just yesterday. Some people remember you! The Ripper does. And then to Tarita: how are you, my beautiful child? Her body language made it clear to him that she didn't want him to touch her. He said to her: I didn't mean it, you know.

The three sat down,Wyre at his temporary table.

Mean what?

They give me stuff in here. Helps me see the truth.

Dewey said: what have you seen?

Wyre said: what's going down, man?

Dewey said: I brought you a book. He gave him the Buddha.

What's this?

It helped me when I was in here.

How do you know I can read?

Can you?

Tarita said of course, he can.

Wyre: Here's a truth: it's bad for you.

What?

Reading. Life is what you see. That's it. Reading distracts you from getting on with it.

Dewey: so you've been doing some thinking?

What are you gonna do? You can't delete what you can't touch!

Dewey said: I'm surprised to hear that.

Why?

It's not how we remember you. Thoughtful. Almost philosophical!

See? That's what I'm talking about. You read about me in the papers and you think you know me. What do you know? Stalin had Trotsky killed with an ice pick; within a couple of years, he was the world's hero! Uncle Joe. Let's see what your boy says. I'll open the book to a random page! He opened the book and reads:

Shit! Listen to this! *Better than a thousand useless words is one word that brings peace!* You see? He's talking about reading. People always quote what they read. That's what he's talking about. He's not talking about anyone *speaking* a thousand words.

Dewey said: *Peace.*

Fuck it. You know what I'm talking about.

Tarita said: yes and you just read it!

Hey lover, I miss your voice! Well, compared to the cunt wash you hear in here. But don't be argumentative, it doesn't become you.

There was an awkward silence. Wyre slumped back in his chair. He said: It's time for my medication soon. You came a bit late.

Dewey said: we didn't want to take up too much of your time. Look, you're obviously doing a lot of reading and you know what's becoming clear to me? How intelligent you are. Keep the book, Rolcord. Please. And read it.

Wyre said: one thing. Are you fucking her?

Tarita said to him: I need a divorce.

Good response! Ha, Ha!

He suddenly rose, picked up the small table at which he was sitting and threw it at Tarita, shouting: which means you're still my fucking wife!

Once I heard what had happened, I went to find Dewey. All I knew was that Tarita was in a coma. I found Dewey in King's Chapel. I guessed he'd be in shock and went to comfort him. Praying not to God or Jesus. The Buddha.

Those who in their youth did not live in self-harmony, and who did not gain the true treasures of life are like long-legged old herons standing by a lake without fish.

How can there be laughter, how can there be pleasure, when the whole world is burning? When you are in deep darkness, will you not ask for a lamp?

Chapter 93

Carla's Place

(Hail Goncharov)

I took Stig to Carla's.

I'd only seen her once since she'd come to the pub to tell me about the tragedy.

I could sense Stig's anxiety. I couldn't stop thinking about how he'd changed. This wasn't the lion who took me in that hotel room, who fucked me in every orifice, this is the man who committed murder and developed a conscience about it; this was a man tangled up in the moral ambiguities of Kierkegaard's *Fear and Loathing* not the man who heard the Dane when he said that before God sexuality is irrelevant "not only for men and women but also for homosexuals and heterosexuals". When we first met, he used these words to justify his sexual freedom. This was the man who travelled with Abraham's angel on his shoulders, whispering in his ears that he should not have killed Palme, just as Abraham, under the angel's instruction, had not killed his son.

This was the time when Quaid would turn up for a quick one and lament before he left about his role in the disbanding of Goldstein's conspiracy of leftist Jews and how it had led to his ostracism from circles he craved to belong to. And this was the time of Parfitt's flourishing as the philosopher of sex, developing the area of human behaviour he felt sure Wittgenstein would have developed if he could have been honest about his own homosexuality. Parfitt would come to me whenever his libido needed qualifying for the coming onslaught on the page.

Carla had the aura of a sister of mercy.

She asked us in. There was a quite unpleasant odour, like I would have imagined the odour of corruption coming from the just dead Father Zosima in the Dostoievsky, which Goldstein had so worried about. Carla had vigorously attempted to disguise the odour with a variety of artificial scents.

She said: he won't recognise you.

I said: I know.

Not long after the catastrophe, Carla had come into the pub and told me about it. She had shadows beneath her eyes, which added to her natural beauty.

We arrived at the room. I, of course, had been there before and so knew that what he would see would break Stig's heart. You may wonder why I should care? Well, what anyone does is nothing to do with me – unless they're doing it to me! I've got no time for those useless souls who spend their days filling the boredom with the self-righteous judging of others. And anyway, he confessed to me what he'd done and in that moment, I was his confessor and confessors have no opinion. I care because I am a servant of love. And fucking.

Will was in Carla's study. She had him in a chair slumped before a writing desk. As I said, I'd seen him before and didn't want to see him close up now. Stig went in after me.

He said: may I close the door?

We both said: of course. We understand.

We went into the lounge where Will had once sat in the days of Goldstein and we drank some wine.

Carla said: I just couldn't leave him. He was a great lover.

I know.

They say he probably hasn't got long.

I said: He'll be better off.

It suddenly occurred to me that Carla may have thought I was a bit cold, which would be a bit ironic given what Will said about my mourning.

Carla said: Do you know how it happened?

Not in detail. It's all so sad. I think I cut myself off from wanting to find out.

They were operating on the very serious stab wound that had been inflicted by Tarita's husband and his brain was starved of oxygen.

O my God!

Stig came back. He said: he's sleeping. May we go now? I need air.

Sure.

Rose and Stig left Carla's and walked down the leafy De Freville Avenue. Rose suddenly began thinking about Chatterton, not Dan, but the subject of Will's doctorate. She wished she could see him and that it was tactile. Then she thought about Bubovsky. He'd become a huge celebrity, meeting American Presidents, etc. and the international hero of dissenters. She thought about how they'd fucked; how she'd brought him back to life, from the house of the dead. Above them, a pale green sky hosting clouds like cauliflowers in an allotment. They are the gardeners bent with the realisable fading of fortune. The ineluctable advance to absence.

Soldiers cocks are a black burlesque. Stig is a soldier. Rimbaud knew him. His cock mocks all the power it once had. It rots now on a bed of compost, resting on the lap of Will in his vegetative state. Now he is silent and will never again speak of love and the boy who made longing a sting on the soul. He is deep in the reliving of the boy's smells: his mouth, his anus, his wondrous cock with the taste of asparagus, his breath with which he shared that living.

Chapter 94

The associate deaths of Stig Angström

(Hail Orhan Pamuk!)

I never saw Stig again. He wandered off to the bus station and took a bus, maybe to his hotel, maybe to get a train. Before Stig Angström took his own useless life back in Stockholm, Sten wrote to me telling how he'd killed Will, who we thought had simply stopped breathing. A mercy killing. He also admitted he was not Stig Engström. He said he'd adopted the name of Engström after meeting him at a right-wing meeting in his early twenties. He did kill Palme, but the real Engström became the suspect.

Sten Olson died in 2000 of a brain tumour, not long after the real Stig Engström, who killed himself, unable to bear the weight of the accusations against him.

All the deaths so close to me! I wondered whether, in the end, Nietzsche hadn't been right in his theory of tragedy: the Apollonian and the Dionysian.

Chapter 95

Reflections on a Pin Head

(Hail, Jack London!)

Too many things I didn't see - so many things I couldn't see, because you can't boil down everything to a philosophical equation. *Ignoratio elenchi* is the definition of that experience because life doesn't have a predetermined plan. That's what I totally missed: my idea that my searching for the answers in the double helix of sex and knowledge could actually produce results. What I missed was this not being probable – life won't allow it. And haven't I spent a large part of my life blaming myself for some kind of philosophical myopia? Terrorising myself – scuppering any chance of achieving what I should have: strength in sex and knowledge combined with Rimbaud's *deliberate disorganisation.*

The table Rolcord Wyre threw at his wife hit her on the side of the head and knocked her out. Before Dewey could respond, two enormous nurses had grabbed Wyre and dragged him off. Dewey cradled Tarita, kissed her and called out for help. Another nurse arrived and began CPR. Shortly after, paramedics turned up and she was rushed off to the hospital.

Chapter 96

Oradour

(Hail Malraux!)

My relationship with Parfitt was never one you could hang laurels on; he was always so distracted by this or that philosophy, though sometimes I would share his interests. One day, not that long ago, during an afternoon of sex, he said to me: how would you like to go to France?

I said: I'd love it. Paris?

No. Limoges.

Limoges?

It's a beautiful city in southern France. We could stay there for the night and the next morning hire a car and drive to Oradour-sur-Glane. The site of one of the greatest war crimes of World War II.

There was a short silence in which he stroked my lower body. I think he was trying to rouse himself. I thought: what a change in this man. Proof of the liberating power of sex. We were well into middle age, but often more sexually excitable. Then, after some kisses, he said: I'm researching a paper I'm calling *The Atavism of Rage in The Fascist Warrior*. That's a working title.

So what happened?

At Oradur? Well, just before the end of the war, the village of Oradour-sur-Glane was destroyed by a company of the German Waffen-SS. The whole village – more than 600 men, women and children- was massacred. The village was preserved as the Germans left it - as a permanent museum and memorial.

****

We got there about two o'clock. About the same time as the Germans had. We walked in on the Limoges road beneath the Catholic Church, high on an abutment above the road, which is where the women and children got burned. There was a warm, welcoming breeze. Like on the day it happened. A rustle in the innocent trees. This was the road the Nazis had used. Where Robert Hebras, one of the only ones to get away, saw them.

He'd been lazing in a field on the other side of the river. Thinking. Worried about the future. What would he do? The war would soon be over. The Allies were in Normandy. Wringing his hands over a future that didn't exist. (Because it just doesn't.) Then he became aware of the not-too-distant trundle of many trucks.

He stood up to get a better look. He was surprised to see the convoy of German vehicles. They passed his sight line, passed beneath the Catholic church and as they moved towards the centre of the village, disturbed some barn swallows resting in one of the buildings where some of the men would later be killed. Maybe this was part of a German retreat. Were they going home? Why would they come through Oradur? It's not on the road North.

Robert Hebras had two sisters. Sixteen and seventeen.

All this I googled.

We walked to the village square.

At the square, on the Champs de Foire, the Mayor's Peugeot 202 pulls up. There are the two Hebras sisters – sixteen and seventeen – sitting on a low wall with some boys whispering to each other and giggling. The war would be over, maybe in days and they'd go back to those halcyon times of sun and peace and fruitful days without fear of something unexpected.

I said: Look, they're wearing pretty frocks and white blouses. It was as though the whole afternoon had materialised before us.

I said: The Hebras sisters are the village attraction. One dark, one blond.

They always huddle and giggle before opening up to whoever comes near them. Big smiles.

I said: they're beautiful.

Wide, embracing smiles and greetings. In the arms of their young men, toying with their moustaches and enjoying being young, on the cusp of womanhood.

I said: O, Tony, this is so sad. Makes me think of all the world's sad and abused young women.

He said: have you had enough?

No! Let's go to the church.

Are you sure?

As we walked, we passed the doctor's car, which was burning. Everywhere, the burning. Passed a window in flames with a sewing machine and in a yard a sewing machine on a trestle beside a tin bath red with burning and a child's pedal car – all these things still here sixty years later. And the sounds of fear and kids crying.

Behind us, suddenly, the square is full – the whole village rounded up.

Someone shouts: *Papiers!*

Robert Hebras has followed the trucks and there he is. He says: *Papiers?*

And then the soldiers take the women and children to the church. They're coming down behind us.

I said: Look, they're marching the men off. They were taking them to a barn on the *Rue Emile Desourteaux*. They'd placed machine guns there and were going to shoot the men as they went in. And in the legs! So they would take longer to die.

Robert Hebras hid himself beneath some of the bodies.

We got to the church just after the women and the children. We looked inside. The killing was already happening. We could see that the church was decked out with flowers for a wedding.

Children were being shot, they're heads split apart, grenades thrown, women howling, clutching their babies; everywhere, the old and young cut in half by machine gun fire. And then I saw the Hebras sisters and their friend Camille, burning, running into the sacristy where they died.

After it all, all that was left was the frame of a pushchair in which a little child had sat in the company of its mother and all the women and children of the village, safe for the shortest moment in God's house before the Germans entered and made a living torch of that pushchair child and all the others. My eyes filled with tears.

We walked down to the river. We sat there picking daisies. We didn't have much to say, but I said: that church was ready for a wedding!

He said: I think I know what Robert Hebras felt running for his life across rye fields waiting to get shot in the back.

I said: I can't think of anything else to say!

As he drove back up towards The Somme, we were still pretty quiet. Then I said: it wasn't that long ago! My Mum could have been one of the Hebras sisters.

And then, later, for no particular reason, I said: did you know it was the wrong Oradur?

What?

They got the wrong village. Members of the French Resistance had been hiding in another village nearby, also called Oradour. That's the one the Germans were after. Not this village. They were innocent. I read it.

He said: Rose, they were all innocent! The right ones and the wrong ones!

Chapter 97

A Glass of Champagne, please

(Hail Chekov!)

On the ferry back to Dover, a brisk Westerly chilling the summer air on the obliging deck, Rose said to Parfitt: did you get any enlightenment?

The supremacy of absence: If I can believe it never happened, then I know it did and there's the proof. Another way of saying it is that the past is absent from the present. The absence is not the same as nothing; the absence carries a powerful idea. So many of those soldiers may believe that they weren't there, but they would have been feigning an absence and they could never escape the idea that would feed that absence. That's what I mean. And I think I understand: the anger, the atavistic anger that causes the rage in the fascist lies in the absence and the realisation that the atavism, which is the machine of absence, tells them that they've never achieved their fascist dream.

Didn't those soldiers achieve it?

No. The Nazi dream was of a thousand-year Reich. Those soldiers ensured that it lasted little more than ten years.

And where were we? In Oradour?

We were embedded in absence.

She didn't understand what he said, but she knew enough to reason that philosophy, like poetry, often finds its power in the obscure.

*****

The only way I could understand absence at Oradur was in the sense that we weren't there when it happened. But perhaps this was a physical representation of Tony's theory: because they'd left the ruined village like that, the absence of the people made their deaths so much more heart-wrenching; their absence was supreme testimony to their having been there. What Tony was asserting was that the power of the abstract thought was not diminished by there not being physical examples, like Oradur, to prove it.

QED

Chapter 98

Never-never Land

(Hail! Thomas More)

As he drifted away to wherever he was going, Will couldn't get his conversation with Parfitt out of his head: over and over:

So what do you believe? What's your philosophy? Your own original philosophy?

The supremacy of absence.

What's that?

The absence of proof; certainty; ultimately the world.

That doesn't make sense. We're in it!

In order to believe in anything, you have to believe it's not there.

In order to believe in anything, you have to believe it's not there. That's me!

Most of the soldiers who shot the babies, threw the grenades, shot and burned the Hebras sisters were little more than kids themselves. I had never come so close to seeing the hell of humanity. Sartre said: hell is other people. I'd never remotely had any sympathy for that thought; now I slept with it. And how truly liberating was sex in the face of this rampaging horde who would rape the living and fuck the dead? And what about the love whose roots are buried in the aching genitalia?

It was not long after we returned that lockdown began. Oradur will always be there; after technology has reduced the world to a simple equation: a = -a, and the ages of darkness that will follow, through our continuing refusal to recognise *ignoratio elenchi* and the lightning bolt of first sex and the diminishing thunder that follows. Oradur finished it for me. I've hung on trying to make something of my dying interest until I've come to this.

My depression had returned like an Obersturmführer, bitter and inhuman, thrilled with its power to condemn one to where the spiders of vengeance are the only company, alone in the bowels of the deepest pit.

I cried daily after Oradur and news items like the one about the small boys playing who locked themselves in an abandoned fridge and couldn't get out and died before they were found. They would confirm my feeling of despair. From now until the end, I would ride the waves of my anxiety and dysthymia. For years.

*****

Many years later, I was recalling the time I went to look for Dewey after the catastrophe that overcame Tarita. I found him in King's Chapel. Praying. Not to God or Jesus. Buddah. He'd been crying. I'd never seen him so reduced. She was in a coma in Addenbrookes, just like Will had been! Incongruously, I recalled hearing a Scottish commentator at the 1980 Olympics refer to the phenomenon of Ovett and Coe winning each other's expected race win — Ovett the 800 and Coe the 15 — as the 'whirlygig of time' and I'd thought – maybe that's it, there's no God-plan or orderly fate, just the dyspepsia of time.

I said: How are you, Dewey? Is there any news about Tarita?

He sniffed back his tears. He said: The same. Coma. It was my fault. My arrogance. The Buddha said:

Those who, in their youth, did not live in self-harmony, and who did not gain the true treasures of life, are like long-legged old herons standing by a lake without fish.

I said: don't be so hard on yourself. You couldn't know the table wasn't secured.

But she argued we shouldn't go. In case he attacked her. I overruled her. Typical arrogant man. I'm sick of people being nice to me! I've behaved badly and I need people to tell me that!

I'd never seen him so angry.

He said: do people think the world is full of Abba songs and Billy Connelly tales? *How can there be laughter, how can there be pleasure, when the whole world is burning? When you are in deep darkness, will you not ask for a lamp?* A lamp! Truth! If I don't get her back, I'm going to immure myself within four walls and study and look for the truth and like Siddhartha, the Buddha as a child, I will no longer witness the suffering of the world.

As I recalled these words, the recent horror of Oradur came to mind and my sadness deepened.

I'd asked him if he wanted to come with me. Why don't you come with me, Dewey? I could cook something for you.

Perhaps I'll call around later. First, I'm going to see Tarita. I can talk to her and they say she will hear me.

I think that's true.

I've got my Buddha. I want to say only the best things to her. *If a man speaks or acts with an impure mind, suffering follows him as the wheel of the cart follows the beast that draws it.*

But what can you say to her? She knows how much you love her.

I've learned Mercutio's speech from *Romeo and Juliet*:

I don't know that.

O then, I see Queen Mab hath been with you.

She is the fairy midwife and she comes in shape no bigger

Than an agate stone on the forefinger of an Alderman…

I think she'd love to hear that.

It's quite long.

Chapter 99

The End

(Hail Jim Morrison)

She looks sadly and uselessly at the instruments of her suicide.

Then she says: I need to see Chatterton – the real, long-dead one.

The end of lockdown provided her with the opportunity.

Epilogue

(Hail Orwell!)

As she travelled in the train to London, she thought about Tony's supremacy of absence, *ignroratio elenchi,* her own sibling passions of unbridled sex and universal knowledge. In particular, she thought of Tony's almost axiomatically delivered: *In order to believe in anything, you have to believe it's not there.*

He'd said: both Socrates and Jesus left the world without having written a word. It was as if they'd never existed: absent from history. But the fact of this apparent absence brought the supreme writing of St Paul, St John and Plato.

She knew Chatterton wasn't there but believed she would meet him again. She'd had to wait for the end, which had been a very trying time.

As her train motored through the pretty landscape of Hertfordshire and the enchanting approach to Letchworth station, it was as if Socrates appeared in the sky above the home county, urging her to summarise.

The purpose of her journey was not to prove the one thing of believing in the absent but also believing that the present is not embodied in the living but in the continuum of life and the existence of all the living and the dead: this Dewey had told her. The present is in the *idea* (which proves for her that her philosophy is right, that the significance of sex is found in its support for the intellect, that intelligence and intellect mean nothing without the liberation of and liberating impulse of sex). Her philosophy brings the present into absence and in absence, everything that ever existed *is*. Parfitt's theories allow her to believe in the living corpse of Chatterton and that she'll find him (in absence)!

She couldn't put the horror of Oradur out of her mind. How could a nation behave like that, the systematic killing of children and babies, so many babies and now, irony of ironies, the people who suffered most at that time, the Jews, in the state of Israel, are themselves killing a multitude of babies, children of a nation they have put in bondage and made powerless. Poor Goldstein must be raging in his grave for what people are doing in his name.

By the time they were approaching Watton-at-Stone station, she could feel herself shaking inside. Panic building. Why couldn't I have the stoicism of Zeno? To live the good life, one needed to live by the natural order, which doesn't mean planting seeds in a row; it means, amongst other things, nurturing the fruit and flowers of congress, acknowledging the starry skies of ecstasy and sailing there on pleasant currents. And tying yourself to the mast in a tempest!

She walked to Brook Street, which looked the same as it had! She'd stopped in a hostelry and drank a couple of glasses of what we would call port, which filled her with a freeing warmth which embraced her from her groin to the frontal lobes of her brain and the back story of her mind. The place was just like The Eagle and could have been it! In the street, she felt different. She wanted something else. In the street, the men in their long coats and top hats hurried to workplaces, urchins kicked up the dust in the street, the women, some in pilgrim dress, shopped and the carriages in the street.

As she approached his house, she saw across the road, a young woman in a doorway. Something told her the girl was a whore. She felt her heart quicken. She approached the woman, who looked a little surprised and uncertain. Rose was in twentieth-century dress. Only her long, luxurious hair fit the occasion. The young woman was especially surprised to see Rose's rucksack, in which Rose never failed to take with her her sex toys, which she had been doing for years. Like a good scout. Including her strap-on dildo.

Inside, she walked up the familiar stairs behind the girl till she got to an attic room which was so like Thomas's. The girl tapped and someone said: come in.

Inside, in the quivering light of her memory, dressed entirely in black, shades over eyes, laying along Chatterton's *chaise,* an older man of indeterminate age. She was halted in breath and step: was this the right house? Could this, in fact, be him – older?

He said: Come in. We've been expecting you.

The flap of wings of the birds of ages, stalled and history peeled back.

All the moments outside the norm; all the moments of outrageous fantasy; all the moments of rebellion against the pinch of morality where the sexless and fearful burn the books of freedom, all these moments of yours culminate in this extraordinary literary moment.

Ok. Well, that sounded like a literary moment itself.

No one can come in. We're absent. It's enough for us to believe we're here. He stood up and disrobed, revealing an enormous member. The girl undressed. Without a word spoken, Rose undressed. Despite her advanced years, she was still in good shape; pubic hairs trimmed and downy. She took out her dildo and put it on the table where once the *Philosophy of Medicine* lay.

The others looked at it in awe. She put it on.

The girl lay down on the rudimentary but knowledgeable bed. Rose put the dildo into the girl and the girl went mad, wrapping her legs around Rose and pulling her close. Feverishly. The man came to the bed. He rolled the woman over so that the girl was now on top and pushed his enormous dick into the girl's anus. Remarkably, it went in without resistance. The pressure of the strap-on on her pudendal nerve caused Rose to come like a broken water pipe. The man at her rear and Rose's coming caused the girl to come; then the man thought: fuck it and joined in the cum fest. The girl kissed Rose, took the strap-on from Rose and put it on herself. All this time, Rose was in a panic of delight. She just couldn't believe it was happening.

It's what she might have imagined in one of her more ambitious moments. The three took up new positions: the girl in Rose's vagina, the big cock in her backside.

Something told her that the man was her writer.

With the passion of her creator within her, she continued her journey into the eternal night of orgies and endless absence.

And as the darkness folded over her, these words of Parfitt echoed through her reboant bones, through the miasma of death, through the light where there was no light:

Half of humanity is made of people who build bridges; the other half wants to destroy them. The half who build bridges are the scientists, the half who destroy them exploit the scientists. Where's the poison? You may want to say it's with the scientist who created the means to make weapons. This world, our world, is one of communities too hungry to love, choking on coal dust, lacerated by steel, oppressed by concrete and tyrants, drowning in blood. This is a world that even Christ can't save. And these words that Chatterton left her with:

here are the children growing through cruel times

the faintest echoes of the stuttering passage of

nature beyond my window; the sun

only now unruly in dreams reflecting out there

the unnatural world which rests on a paradox: while justice is who sees it? Who does not miss the point about this knowledge?

She'd found the world. In death.

Coda:

Parfitt found her body after she hadn't been in touch for some time. He didn't have a key: she had always wanted to think that she'd just met him: an unexpected visitor.

He'd looked through her letterbox and smelt that unmistakable odour of heaven: The stink.

9 781918 243376